fallen

LAURY FALTER

First Edition: April 2009

The characters and events portrayed in this book are fictitious. Any
similarity to real persons, living or dead, is coincidental and not
intended by the author.

Falter, Laury, 1972-
Fallen: a novel / by Laury Falter – 1st ed.

Summary: When Maggie Tanner lands in the humid heat of New
Orleans and begins to sell her ability to deliver messages to loved ones
in heaven, her past catches up to her and she must evade the enemies
she didn't know existed while trying to discover why the handsome
young man with unearthly abilities has suddenly appeared to keep her
alive.

ISBN: 978-0-615-29498-8
ISBN-13: 978-0615294988

*For Babs, my twin sister, and her impassioned,
unwavering enthusiasm as each succeeding chapter was
written.*

*And for Joyce Durham, whose passing inspired the writing
of this novel.*

∞

YA
424 -3005

CONTENTS

∞

PREFACE

Abaddon's eyes met mine, and I turned to head down the dark street toward a quieter spot, a less public place. I wasn't sure what Abaddon had in mind, but I knew it wasn't going to be pleasant. I didn't want anyone to accidentally find us or to valiantly step in, trying to be a hero.

As I headed farther away from the commotion of Bourbon Street, into the darkness, I didn't need to turn to make sure they were following me.
I could feel them.

As we got farther from safety, my radar grew more and more intense, as if it was sensing their anticipation of what was to come.

I approached a dark alleyway and figured this would be as good a place as any to do it. Only the hazy illumination of a streetlight reached here, and no doors or windows could be seen, just the back sides of two buildings.

An efficient place to die.

It was here and now. I turned to face Abaddon, startled to find him leaning down, merely an inch away.

1. ENCOUNTER

I was picked up my last day of school, in a U-Haul truck. Aunt Teresa was sitting in the driver's seat with map in hand and piles of boxes stacked, haphazardly, across the back seat. She was smiling and waving at me through the window. I didn't feel much like smiling back.

"Can we have another expression?" she called out.

I shrugged, as I slipped into the passenger's seat. "What would you prefer?"

"Boy, anything at this point. Your face has been frozen in a frown for the last week," she complained, turning the key in the ignition. The truck shuddered violently and then rumbled to life.

I glanced out at the sprawling Las Vegas desert, my face stiff and unaccommodating. No, there was no chance of anything other than a frown.

"Think of this as an adventure," she urged. "New Orleans is a fantastic city with lore, jazz, Creole and Cajun food, alligators, ghosts …."

I rolled my eyes. "Right. I'm sure it'll be great."

"It will be," she insisted.

Aunt Teresa is a traveling photographer who would be spending less than an hour in New Orleans before leaving me and flying to Paris for a year-long, nomadic shoot. Because of Aunt Teresa's opportunity, I was being banished to a city completely unknown to me and without a single familiar face.

Aunt Teresa had pointed out, more times than I cared to count, that I shouldn't be so uncomfortable with the idea, and to be truthful, she was right. She and I had changed addresses every three months since as far back as I could remember, so one more address change really shouldn't make a difference.

What didn't thrill me was the realization that I'd be forced to live under one roof for the next twelve months. I was going to miss my wild, unpredictable, roaming lifestyle.

Living in one place for an extended period of time…I couldn't imagine a more dull existence.

Worse, being eighteen and apparently incapable of taking care of myself, I was being forced to stay with her friend, Ezra Wood.

The fact was, I really enjoyed living with Aunt Teresa. There were no annoying rules, no enforced bedtimes, no lights out and no antiquated…traditional…status quo…culturally-enforced family traditions.

Unfortunately, I had the distinct feeling that Ezra Wood would not be so lenient.

It took us a full day, plus five hours, to reach New Orleans proper. Thirty minutes later, we arrived downtown. Aunt Teresa turned onto Magazine Street and stopped in front of a purple and pink Victorian-style house.

We found the ad together which boasted "charming, quaint, and under-valued." That couldn't have been further from the truth. The house had shingles torn from the roof, a yard full of weeds, and a porch which, judging by the

2

number of broken branches and piles of leaves collected in the corners, hadn't been swept in months, if not years.

"I had a different image of it in my mind," Aunt Teresa spoke my thoughts, as she peered warily at the neglected dwelling from under the truck visor.

"I'll be fine. I'm hardier than this."

Aunt Teresa tapped my knee excitedly. "That's the spirit.

It's an adventure, remember?"

"Right," I mumbled.

A beefy man, wearing a pink shirt and green plaid slacks, stepped out of a beaten up Chevy and shuffled toward us.

"Ezra Wood, I presume?" I said, keeping my voice low since the truck windows were rolled down.

"Not funny." Aunt Teresa glowered back at me as she heaved open the truck door, ignoring its groaning hinges.

I followed, reluctantly.

"Mr. Wilkes, this is Maggie. She'll be one of the tenants," said Aunt Teresa, noticeably yanking me closer.

He started to openly assess me.

I'm what you would call a slim girl, and no more than five feet tall, with wavy chocolate hair dangling to my waist. My face alone, with my tiny, narrow nose and overly wide, brown eyes, which I always thought could rival the size of tea saucers, probably gave the impression I was innocent. I was once told I looked like a pixie only several times larger.

Mr. Wilkes must not have found any glaring concerns, because he turned without any verbal acknowledgment and waddled toward the house. He stepped over a long-dead bush that covered half of the front steps, muttering in a thick, southern accent, "Nah, ya ain't goin' ta find a betta place than this."

"Okay," Aunt Teresa's voice sang out eagerly, and I knew immediately that she was ditching me. "I have to get to the airport," she confirmed, already pulling out her cell phone to call a cab.

"Aunt Teresa…already?" I sighed.

"You'll be fine. You've done this enough times. You don't need my help."

That much was true.

"Yes, I need a cab…" she said, into the phone.

I glanced back at Mr. Wilkes, standing on the porch now, frowning. Apparently, he didn't like to be delayed. I ignored him.

Aunt Teresa closed her phone and loped toward me, beaming. "You'll take care of the truck, right?"

"Yes," I replied, though not at all happy about it. "I always do."

"I know. You're so good about it." She gave me a firm hug and pulled away, still holding my shoulders. "You're going to like it here. I can feel it in my bones."

I felt my face settle back into a frown, which she paid no attention to.

"Now go see your new home." She said this with far more enthusiasm than I felt.

Grudgingly, I went to meet Mr. Wilkes at the front door where he was already slipping the key into the rusted lock. He had to shake the lock, jarringly, and rattle the door, harshly, against its hinges, not seeming to care in the least that his potential client was watching from behind him.

I looked back over my shoulder where Aunt Teresa stood, grinning. She gave me an animated wave. I gave her a lackluster one back.

"Yeah…" Mr. Wilkes mumbled, drawing my attention as he swung open the door. "Best place you kin find."

Inside was dank and musty. Clearly the house hadn't been walked through in a very long time.

"Watch ya step. Floorboards slope."

I nodded, realizing the one I was currently standing on didn't slope but sagged.

4

A small room off to the left, which I guess acted as the parlor, was mostly empty with the exception of a cobweb-encased poker next to the fireplace. The remaining rooms were much the same. No furniture, but lots of remnants of the other animals and insects who will be sharing my new home with me.

Great.

Throughout the tour, while I tested lights and turned on faucets, occasionally finding a short or a bad line that would sputter at me, Mr. Wilkes occasionally repeated the same phrase, nodding to himself, "Yea, best place 'round hea."

Then, we reached the first bedroom, and I was sold. The room was fine enough. It was spacious with a walk-in closet, which I really had no use for, because clothes were the last thing on my mind. What caught my attention was that it boasted a full-sized balcony overlooking Magazine Street. Stepping through the doors, I stared off each side. Aunt Teresa was gone now, but oddly, the disenchanted, lost feeling I thought would wash over me never came. Instead, I stood on the balcony watching the street below, and for the first time in my life, I felt like I was home.

A single plastic chair had been tossed, by a hand or by the wind, up against the railing. Instantly, I wished I could upright the seat, settle in, and wait for the sunset – allowing myself to forget Mr. Wilkes' tour and just handing him the first month's rent right then. Prudence and logic fought my need for spontaneity and eventually won. However, I did linger on the balcony, as Mr. Wilkes disappeared inside.

From somewhere in the distance I could hear Cajun music twanging and then the sudden burst of a foghorn. Across the street was another small house with a building in the back, both appearing vacant. From the remaining houses, down each side of the street, I could see residents sitting on their lawns, returning with groceries, or taking their dog for a walk.

It was perfect.

"Yeah comin?" Mr. Wilkes called out from inside the darkness of the house. "Need ta show ya the back."

It took a lot of self-control, but I finally coaxed my body to move and met Mr. Wilkes downstairs.

I followed him to the kitchen where it was obvious from the number of paint peels that it, too, had been neglected. Yet, someone had taken the time to adhere a single strip of wallpaper as a border to the ceiling. It was yellow with tiny, white flowers, and I thought it looked very appropriate in the small room.

"Appliances are a bit old," admitted Mr. Wilkes. For proof he turned the knob to ignite one of the stove's burners and a flame shot a foot above his head. Shocked, he stepped back, laughed to himself, and turned the knob off without another word about it.

He opened a small door from the kitchen leading to the back where we found the yard overgrown but large, with a small, wooden shed in the corner. I immediately approached it, picking up the lock.

Mr. Wilkes stepped up behind me, grunting, as he dug in his pockets for the key. Finding it, he handed it to me, and I inserted it. Unlike anything else in the house, this lock worked fluidly. I swiftly opened the door and found an empty, good-sized shed inside. Good enough for a motorcycle.

"I'll take it," I said instantly.

Mr. Wilkes nodded once, self-assured. "Knew ya would." He then handed the rest of the house keys to me while quoting a price for the rent.

It was slightly higher than what the ad had listed, but I didn't mention it. Mr. Wilkes didn't strike me as a man who would negotiate. I could walk away from the property, having plenty of money stuffed in the backpack slung over my shoulder, and find a far more luxurious house.

But this place had already settled in me. I was home.

I dug through my backpack and gave Mr. Wilkes the amount he quoted. Taking it, he gave me a serious gaze. "Same amount…every first of the month…no exceptions."

"That won't be a problem."

"Hope not. Kin rent this place any time. Best place 'round hea."

I had trouble keeping myself from laughing. I wasn't sure if he seriously believed what he said or not and didn't want to offend him either way. "I understand, sir."

He gave me one final, long stare, spun on his heel and marched back toward the street. At least he was gracious enough to help me unload the bed frame and move it into the upstairs bedroom…for fifty bucks. It was the only piece of furniture I owned as my frequent moves inhibited me from ever buying more. I had learned to live on very little.

A few minutes later, Mr. Wilkes left. I heard his car engine turn on and saw it pass by a few seconds later from where I stood on the balcony.

I pulled a piece of paper from my back pocket and looked at the directions. There was one stop I needed to make before returning the U-Haul truck.

It took me an hour to get there since the house was on the outskirts of the city. I knew I'd reached it when I saw the broken, wooden sign hanging across the gate entrance that read Hicker Ranch. The property was thick with overgrown trees and boasted several decrepit buildings, but the main house wasn't hard to find. Still, it was a challenge to reach, surrounded by weeds that reached my knees. I learned this after I jumped down from the cab. Watching my step as I walked closer to the house hidden in old oak trees, a frail woman in her seventies crossed the wide, sagging porch and stopped at the steps. In a scratchy voice, tarnished by years of liquor and cigarettes, she greeted me. "It's around back in the barn."

With that, I made a sharp right and walked through the dead weeds of her property to find a dilapidated barn. The barn doors were unlocked but it took me a good amount of muscle to push them open.

There, in the dusty shadows, I could see it.

My Harley Davidson 883 Sportster. It was a beautiful mesh of silver chrome and black metal that could take me just about anywhere I wanted at speeds of up to 120 miles per hour if I chose. It didn't look like much on the eBay ad and I didn't know much about motorcycles to begin with even if it had. But, it took my breath away when I first saw it. Even though it was not the wisest purchase for someone who had never owned any mode of transportation before, that didn't matter. It would be all mine.

"You have the money?" The woman's scraggy voice came up behind me.

I nodded, without looking at her. Instead, I reached down into my backpack and pulled out four bills, one thousand dollars each.

She gawked at me before I had a chance to explained, "You said over the phone you didn't mind large bills."

"Huh," was all she replied, mouth still agape, taking the money. I turned away and swung a leg over the bike, settling into the seat; I felt like a queen on her throne. The woman dangled the keys toward me, though her expression appeared uncertain. "You sure you can handle this thing?"

"My aunt's ex-boyfriend taught me to ride," I asserted. For proof, I took the keys and inserted them into the ignition with great confidence.

"Hmmm." She scratched her nose and leaned her head to one side. Her eyes narrowed at me and she said, "Not that I'm accusin' you of anything but...where'd you get this kind of money?"

I paused and it occurred to me that I would eventually need to have an explanation for how I made my income. It wasn't as if an elderly woman selling me a bike through eBay would be the only one to ever ask the question. I needed to have a story; one simple enough to prevent further questions but that adhered to my belief system of telling the truth. I certainly couldn't tell the whole truth so I settled for telling just half my story.

"I'm a messenger."

The woman snorted and chuckled under her breath. "Well…now ya'll have a faster bike."

I grinned back, even while knowing that no bike could get me where I went to deliver messages.

"Ya wanna take it for a test ride?" she offered.

I turned the key and listened to the engine rumble to life – a heavy thud, thud, thud, thud.

I felt exhilarated, a grin drawing up my cheeks.

She handed me a black, shiny, perfectly new helmet which I strapped securely to my head.

I circled her property a few times, getting a feel for how it handled and stopped outside the barn doors.

Her eyebrows rose, questioning.

Then, with a deep breath, I waved goodbye, shifted the bike into gear and pulled out onto the dirt road, heading back to load it on the U-Haul truck.

The bike was mine.

After returning the truck, I drove my motorcycle until just after sunset, unable to stop smiling for most of that time. I decided to find the house I'd rented, and after storing and locking my bike in the shed, I headed upstairs and swung open the French doors leading to the balcony. I took a seat at the edge in the plastic chair and propped my feet up on the rail, dozing while listening to the Cajun music filtering up from the bars.

I had learned to sleep pretty much anywhere, but it surprised me when I woke up the next morning still in the chair. Lifting my head, I felt the kink in my neck from the night before, but the pain ebbed when I remembered I had a new motorcycle to ride.

I hurried to take a shower, using a towel I carried in my backpack to dry off, and headed downstairs. Standing in the kitchen, the house was empty, silent and still retained that musky scent, but I smiled my way out the door anyways.

I rolled my bike from the shed and started it, enjoying its rumble even more today. After a quick stop at a local coffee shop, for a shot of espresso and a croissant, I took a tour of the French Quarter.

The roads were narrow and most were cobblestoned or had broken pavement that made it challenging to ride, but that didn't bother me much. The city was captivating.

The streets were lined with aged, bowing trees that shaded weathered, brick buildings and intricately designed iron balustrades. Small shops opened to colorful art galleries and restaurants propped doors and window shutters open to allow the teasing aroma of spicy southern food to waft out. There was peacefulness to the city, even between the bursts of thrumming jazz music, with everyone moving slowly about their business. Their leisurely pace may also have been because of the soaring temperatures and ridiculous humidity that fell over the city like a stifling blanket. The air was the only thing I would have trouble adjusting to.

After my brief tour of the French Quarter, I arrived at Jackson Square.

It was a raised park of green grass and shrubbery set in a square shape. There is an enormous iron statue of Andrew Jackson on horseback standing in the center. Jackson Square is historic because slaves were often sold here during the 18th and 19th centuries. Now though, along the outskirts of the park, it clearly had become a place for artists to sell their wares and for tourists to have their palms or tarot cards read. The traditional other name for the park is Place d'Armes, but I naturally decided to call it "The Square".

I parked my bike and walked through the tarot card and palm readers, caricature artists, and local craftsman. Then I stopped a few minutes later at a woman's table, scanning the hemp products crowding her space.

"Looking for anything in particular," she asked, pleasantly.

"No." I shook my head. "Actually, I was wondering something…"

"Uh huh," she encouraged me to go on.

"How do you set up a table here…as a vendor?" I asked, even while still wondering if I was going to pursue it.

She explained the lengthy, bureaucratic process and then wiggled her finger at me, beckoning me closer. When I leaned in, she added, "But don't waste your time. Just grease the security guards with a hundred dollars and they won't say a word."

I was surprised at her frankness but appreciated it. "Okay, I will."

"What is it you sell anyways?" she asked, only seeming remotely intrigued.

I opened my mouth to draw in a breath but stopped. I realized that if I told her, she wouldn't believe me anyways. Instead, I decided to respond cautiously. "I'll show you tomorrow."

The woman smiled, now curious. "I'll be waiting."

I strolled The Square a while longer and was about ready to leave when something happened. The hairs on the back of my neck stood up – and they had no business standing up on such a hot, humid day. Suddenly my hands began to shake and my stomach went queasy.

Something was very wrong.

With all the noise and movement, you'd think I could easily have missed him, but as it turned out, I didn't. In fact, I knew he was there before I saw him.

My eyes scanned the crowd with some faint notion that I was looking for whatever was causing this reaction in me. A large man chewing on a sausage, his chin smothered with grease, passed by. Next was a pair of thin women in business suits leaning together and gossiping. Either of these scenes could have made my stomach slightly queasy, but I instinctively knew they weren't the cause of my sudden inability to control my body's reactions.

All of a sudden, there he was…leaning against the wall of St. Louis's Cathedral, hidden in the shade, hands in his pockets, despite the day's heat, and his eyes positioned directly on me. There was no doubt in my mind that he was staring at me because he didn't bother to look away when our eyes met.

As I stood in the sun a chill ran through me.

My first instinct was to run. This stunned me since I never ran from anything…ever, but I couldn't shake the feeling that I needed to leave immediately, as if something deep in my core were screaming at me to escape. This reaction made no sense to me, so I ignored it completely and turned my attention back to the creepy guy.

He was still staring at me.

I noticed that his mouth was turned down now and his nostrils flared out. Clearly he was furious about something.

I wondered if he was an official thinking I was about to shoplift. Wearing a dress shirt and slacks, his professional appearance definitely sent that message. But in a brief moment when our eyes locked, I noticed something different about him. He wasn't old enough to be in a position of authority – even if he came across as holding it. His outward appearance made him look young enough to be my age, yet something in his demeanor, his stance, told me that he was much older.

No matter what his issue was, I was about to leave anyways. It was getting dark and my balcony was calling to me. So I slid up on my bike and headed back to the house.

I was conscious of him as I left The Square, feeling him following me without having to look to confirm it. As I moved through the intersection, I turned to find him sitting behind the wheel of a blue Ford Mustang. Once more, he was staring at me with that same angry gaze.

In reaction, my skin broke out in a cold sweat and my hands started to shake. I never had this happen before – but then I'd never been afraid before either. It took a moment to realize that this was what I was experiencing…actual fear. It was new to me, completely. But I couldn't deny it. I was trying to gain control of my nerves that were now shooting off panic to every inch of my body.

It took me an entire street block before I started to get my breathing under control and that was only after I glanced over my shoulder at the stop sign to make sure the guy wasn't following me. I didn't see him, but the hair on the back of my neck was still standing up, which didn't calm me at all.

I turned down my street and focused on the third streetlight that was lighting the pavement in a dim orange circle. This was the entrance to my driveway on the side of the house, and I was only a few feet from it when something entirely unexpected and unforeseeable happened.

Just outside the hazy glow of the streetlight stood someone who I was absolutely certain had not been there a moment ago. He appeared without warning and from nowhere, suddenly standing directly in front of me, as if he had intentionally put himself in my path.

This last thought occurred to me as ridiculous, but it was the way it seemed nonetheless.

Despite the swiftness at which the event happened, I saw something with absolute clarity. He was handsome, so much so that he'd looked more appropriate on a runway than standing in my street. I knew instantly that he was around my age. But unlike other teenagers, he stood tall and assured, towering over me, even from my height on the bike. What he wore did not reflect the most recent fashion either. His clothes had an age to them, still clean and well-kept but traditional. His hair was dark brown – as best I judged from the reflection of the streetlight – and cut to be shaggy yet just short enough to keep it tidy.

I instantly felt guilty for being in the motion of running him down – which would certainly result in injury at this speed.

What I also recognized in that brief moment was his expression. It was not filled with terror as would be expected when a five-hundred pound motorcycle is bearing down on you. He was not scattered or looking for a way to escape or frightened at all.

He was frustrated.

I, on the other hand, was frantic. My bike was about to pummel a complete stranger, and I didn't seem to have any way of avoiding it. I had felt in control of my bike from the moment I first took a seat on it. Yet, in that moment, I had as much control over it as I did over directing a planetary alignment.

"Right!" he yelled in an English accent, pointing in that direction with a long, toned arm.

But I was already going left – completely by chance. Realizing that it was now or never, I gained control of myself. At least now, with the ability to function physically, I turned the handlebars to the right, but it was too late.

My front tire was less than a foot from him now. We were going to collide.

Suddenly my bike took on a life of its own. It trembled slightly and the handlebars jerked to the right, nearly throwing me off, and just as abruptly, it righted itself as it turned into my driveway. Again, I was almost launched off when my wheels hit the gutter's dip but it caught me at just the right angle. I only vaguely registered somewhere deep in my subconscious that I was not controlling my bike but it was controlling me. It caught me from falling off with each jarring move and each forceful bump. This made no sense to me, so I quickly disregarded it.

I focused instead on the fact that I should have been sprawled on the pavement with my giant five-hundred pound bike on top of me – I was definitely leaning far enough over that it should have happened. But the bike swerved its way down my neighbor's driveway, plowing me into the hedge that separated our properties. The bike ended up leaning against the hedge and the motor cut off a moment later.

Jostled and completely confused about what had just transpired, I took a moment to inhale deeply. It was alarming to realize how ragged my breathing had become. This was the first time I'd ever felt my breath that way. I instead chose to focus on freeing my leg from the overgrown shrubbery.

I wiggled it up and over my bike, falling to the gravel driveway in my effort. I immediately picked myself up, brushed off tiny stones engrained in my palms, and unfastened my helmet.

Already, the fear I'd felt a few seconds ago was gone. Disappeared, and in its place was fury.

I pulled my helmet off, craning my neck painfully in the process and not caring.

All of a sudden he was right there, standing directly in front of me.

"Are you all right?" he asked, although his mouth was slightly puckered and he sounded more aggravated than concerned.

Despite my anger brewing, it dawned on me that this boy was even more attractive up close. I was angry and wanted to stay that way. I definitely did not want to be intrigued; yet, that was how I felt. In the moment of staring at him, I noticed that he had a certain kind of smoothness to his skin that seemed untouched by time. He carried himself with assurance and grace; if it weren't for his size, I would have thought I was looking at someone several years younger. But, this wasn't what stunned me. His eyes, which locked with mine and refused to free me, were the blue-green color I'd only seen in the waters off the coast of Florida. Translucent, warm, and welcoming. I had leapt off piers into that water uninhibited, free – but I was feeling neither of those emotions in my current state.

No, I felt angry.

"Am I all right?" I scoffed. "I almost ran you over. What were you doing just standing in the street? Did you want to be hit?"

His eyes squinted then, reducing their beautiful blue-green color, and I was thankful. It allowed me to regain a bit of clear thought.

He stared back at me as if he were trying to answer a very challenging question. "You're angry with me?" He sounded confused and a bit appalled.

I threw up my hands. That wasn't clear?

"You were standing in the middle of the street! I had to avoid hitting you! I ended up in a bug-infested hedge!" I crossed my arms, waiting for an apology.

He leaned back and folded his own arms across his chest in a seemingly unspoken challenge. "So I understand that you didn't notice the Ford Mustang barreling down the street behind you? The one that was about to run you over?"

Stumped, I turned back toward the opening of the street. "Mustang? What Ford Mustang?" I asked, thinking in the back of my mind. Wasn't the creepy guy from earlier today driving a Ford Mustang?

"It's gone now," he replied, frowning. "You didn't think it was going to stick around after nearly running you down, did you?"

He was mocking me, which infuriated me even more.

"You realize I could have easily killed you?" I demanded.

"I doubt that," he replied. A hint of a smile rested just beneath the surface.

I couldn't comprehend why he thought this was funny. Did he have no sense of self-preservation?

"My bike is a heavy piece of machinery," I stated for emphasis to my point.

He nodded casually, still retaining that subtle grin. He had no rational fear about what had just happened. That much was clear to me.

I laughed at the idiocy of the situation, which made one of his eyebrows lift skeptically.

Finally, he responded. "That doesn't apply to me."

"What doesn't?" I asked, now thoroughly confused.

"Your bike and its dangers."

"How is that? Are you a stunt person?" I asked, coming up with the only logical explanation I could think of on the spot.

He seemed to appreciate that assumption with humor, tilting his chin up and releasing a deep chuckle. When he was through, he brought his head back down and looked me deep in the eyes.

"You really have no idea, do you?"

"About what?" I nearly screamed, thoroughly perturbed at this point.

Then his expression changed from smug humor to stunned surprise. He stood this way for some time, staring at me, with his mouth slightly ajar and his eyebrows creased. "No idea at all…" he muttered then.

"I don't understand what you're talking about," I replied.

"No, you wouldn't," he said, with sincerity, apparently now having overcome his shock at whatever unknown realization he'd arrived at a moment ago.

"Where did you come from anyways? One second you were not there and the next…" I recognized my voice was calming now along with my emotional state.

He seemed to have difficulty answering, opening and closing his mouth several times. Finally, he responded, his voice almost teasing and that slim smirk returning to lurk beneath the surface. "It looked like you needed my help."

"I didn't," I replied, putting my hands on my hips in visible protest.

"How did I know you were going to say that?" he teased, allowing that smile to breach the surface, lighting his face with such beauty it caught my breath.

Something happened in him then. It was subtle but I noticed it anyways. He relaxed. His muscles eased up, his expression loosened. It was as if he'd just now encountered a very old friend and fell into the same welcomed, tolerant pace at which that friendship had existed.

"You didn't answer my question. Where did you come from?"

He considered how to answer for a moment and then replied coyly, "That doesn't matter. What does, is that you are safe…Right?"

I rolled my eyes. "Look," I said clenching my teeth against my irritation. "I don't need your help. Okay?"

His eyebrow went up further with a disagreeing stare. "Well…I would say that everything points to the contrary."

In reaction to that bold understatement, I felt my lips purse in aggravation. To avoid showing that he'd made an observation far too close to the truth, I turned my attention to my bike. It was still leaning against the hedge, making a clear indentation in the once solid wall of green foliage. I reached down and took hold of the handlebars and then leaned back so that my body weight could be used as a pivot to lift the enormous machine back up. It was heavy, despite the adrenaline still pumping through me, and after several struggling heaves it hadn't moved at all. I could sense he was still behind me, watching.

Catching my breath, I warned, "If you laugh, I am going to…" He cleared his throat and I stopped myself. I couldn't be sure but I think he was trying to cover his chuckle.

I could feel him beside me then. The skin on my arm closest to him tingled – not like with creepy guy earlier today – but in a nice way. I had to fight the unexplainable force inside me that wanted to lean toward him, and knowing it just made me angrier. Never in my life had I felt this way about anyone – much less a stranger. Typically, I tried to avoid boys, always knowing that I would be moving on soon, and starting anything would be ridiculous and futile. But, here I was drawn to this stranger. It made no sense.

"Still don't need my help, eh?" he muttered, glancing at me with a playful grin.

"No, I do not," I replied resolutely, despite the obvious contradiction of that statement, as he moved my bike to stand right-side up for me.

Then, it occurred to me that he was not drawing in any heavy breaths at the exertion of what he had just done. Not a single grunt, or even a minor muscle tremor, was released. His body didn't seem opposed to lifting a weight far more than his own. In fact, he did it effortlessly, as if he were pulling out a chair.

When he turned to face me, he must have caught sight of my shock. "Something on your mind?" he asked casually, smirking once again.

"That bike is over five hundred pounds," I pointed out, insinuating.

"And?"

"And you had no trouble moving it."

He chuckled lightly, still easily holding my bike upright for me by the handlebars. "Just be thankful you have me here to help you."

I laughed sarcastically. "I wouldn't be in this situation if it weren't for you."

This time it was his lips that pinched in protest, and for a moment, I wondered what response he was holding back.

I slid into the seat and refocused my glare on my bike, thankful there was no body damage. Then I turned the key. It spurted, hiccupped, and, after a few seconds of honest effort, died.

I looked up at him in frustration and motioned toward it. "Great…"

He then had the audacity to sneer at me as he reached across, grazing my arm - simultaneously sending a shock wave through my body - and swiftly turned the key. The engine rumbled to life.

I glanced up at him, appreciative and amazed. Those feelings were immediately subdued when I heard his English accent shout over the rumble.

"Maybe it was reacting to your attitude."

Appalled at his nerve, I felt my jaw hit the inside of my helmet as it fell open. Before I could even draw a breath, he spoke again. "Looks like my work here is done. Good night and be safe." He then added an afterthought – something I am sure was meant to irk me. "I don't want to have to save you again before daybreak."

With that, he turned and strolled casually toward the street, rounding the hedge's corner and disappearing from sight.

I frowned at him even though I knew he couldn't see it. I rode down to the edge of the property and paused, glancing in the direction he'd gone.

I expected to see him sauntering in all his conceit toward the street corner, but I was stumped.

There was no sign of him.

I stared blankly at the empty sidewalk, a single thought frozen in my mind.

The irritating, attractive boy who had saved my life had just completely vanished.

2. SNAKE

I woke up the next morning to the sound of clanging in the kitchen. Not bothering to move, I laid in bed wondering if the noise might be coming from my next door neighbor. Then something ceramic, or maybe glass, broke and I knew the reverberation was much too close to be mistaken for any place other than my house.

Ezra had arrived.

I slipped out of bed and went in search of my boots, the sturdy ones with metal tips in the toes. I had them both on and was finishing lacing the second one when another loud crash came from the kitchen.

"Yu'll be the one cleanin' that up. Not me," said a rumbling Irishman's voice.

I froze. The voice was male, which Ezra was not. A strange man was in my home…and apparently he wasn't alone.

While fear would have been an appropriate reaction that emotion was virtually unknown to me – I'd only sensed it for the very first time in my life with the creepy guy in The Square the day before. I was more intrigued than anything.

A few thoughts hit me at once then, in a swarm, but I was able to distinguish them. First, why would anyone break into a dilapidated house that clearly would not hold any valuable possessions? Second, why would they be so loud about it? And third, why would they start in the kitchen and care about cleaning up the mess they left there?

Another higher pitched male voice followed mimicking the Irishman but in a mumble.

I grabbed a broomstick left from the previous inhabitants in the upstairs hallway and slipped down the stairs, careful to avoid the steps that creaked. At the end, I peaked around the corner and down the hallway where I could see two men moving swiftly passed the doorway carrying cartons of eggs and milk.

Not something one would find a trespasser doing, I figured, so I rounded the corner and headed down the hall.

A scream made me come to a complete stop as I passed through the kitchen door.

"She's up!" said the owner of the scream, a man with bright orange hair, square-rimmed glasses perched on a long and narrow nose, and wearing a tie-dyed tank top. His bones popped out in places where I didn't even know people had bones, and patches of tendons were the closest thing he had to muscle.

One glimpse at him told me I didn't have much to worry about in defending myself.

Of course, his broad, toothy smile might have been a hint too.

He moved across the kitchen with a feminine swagger, wrenched the broom from my hands, and ushered me to a seat at the table.

If I'd ever experienced a dream before, I would have surely thought this was one and I was sleepwalking. Did a complete stranger just sit me down at a breakfast table that had not been there the night before when I'd gone to sleep?

He did, and shortly after, he shoved a plate full of stark white pancakes at me.

"I made these especially for you," he said, smiling proudly. "Cottage cheese flapjacks. Healthy, tasty, bone-building!" He thumped his chest mightily and then rubbed where he'd made contact.

A meaty man three times the size of the little one stomped across the kitchen and slid fried eggs and bacon toward me. My stomach grumbled as the mouth-watering aroma of the second plate reached me. But the skinny man instantly protested. "She is not going to eat that bacteria-infested carcass."

I glanced down at the plate, noting that it too was new. In fact, quite a few things were new. The stainless steel pans on the stove which the large man was using had not been in the house before this morning. I was certain of it, having done a thorough inventory of the previous owner's possessions left behind. Appliances were now arranged along the counters and small, flowering plants lined the windowsill. There were paintings, drawings, and artful photography thoughtfully mounted to nearly every wall within sight. Even rugs had been placed at the door to the backyard and beneath the kitchen sink.

I stood up, watching them. They didn't notice. It seemed they were too busy bickering while continuing to make breakfast. The beefy man added more bacon to the frying pan and the thin one returned to flipping his pancakes, each insulting the other under their breath. I backed out of the kitchen and headed down the hall, feeling very much like I was the butt of some surprise joke.

I passed the small room off to the right of the kitchen first and noticed it now had a desk, lamp, and mismatched office chairs. Several boxes, with what looked like framed diplomas sticking out, were strewn across the floor and on top of anything with a horizontal surface.

The parlor had now been decorated too. Cushy, forest green couches lined each side of a thick, wooden coffee table. A plant stood in the corner, looking like it had always been there. The mantel over the fireplace was cluttered with candles and vases. Even the poker that I'd left covered in cobwebs stood like a new, shining, gold rod propped next to the fireplace screen.

I did recognize that their additions made the house more like an actual home, but I'd seen enough by then. Heading back to the kitchen, I stopped at the doorway and demanded, "WHO are you people?"

"Now that should have been the first order of business, shouldn't it have been?" said someone from behind me.

I spun around to find a stout, swarthy woman with a mug of coffee and a broad smile. Dreadlocks hung down over her shoulders, lying against a dress swirling with colors and intertwined with the wooden bracelets stacked up both of her thick arms. Incidentally, she only added to the surreal situation.

She held out her hand, and as I shook it, she explained. "I'm Ezra Wood. Cottage cheese flapjacks, here, can be called Felix Pluck. And there," she nodded toward the giant man who'd returned to the stove, "is Rufus O'Malley...We're your new roommates."

I glanced between the three of them realizing they couldn't possibly be from the same family. Ezra was dark-skinned, rotund, with prominent, full facial features. Felix could have passed for a scarecrow and was far shorter than the other two. Rufus stood like a tree trunk: tall, thick, and carved with tattoos and scars. Yet, he had a depth to him. The manner in which he carried himself and his facial expressions told me that although he could certainly do a lot of damage it was not in his nature.

All this sunk in while her final word registered with me.

"Roommates?" I said, snapping my head back in her direction. "Aunt Teresa only mentioned you."

"She has a tendency to ignore details," Ezra replied nonchalantly, standing to pour herself another cup of coffee. She was unapologetic, but it didn't bother me. She clearly knew my aunt well. "We moved in early this morning."

"I've noticed," I replied, my voice sounding defensive though I didn't mean for it to. It was a reaction to my mood.

"Thought we'd wake ya with all the racket," said Rufus over his shoulder. "Felix dropped his side o' the couch three times."

"I told you and you already know it anyways..." Felix whined. "I have bad knees." He then turned to address me. "I am sorry if I woke you."

"I'm a deep sleeper."

I watched Ezra return to the table and then muttered "roommates" to myself, allowing the idea to settle.

I'd never had roommates before. And I preferred it that way. My lifestyle seemed to open up doors, dangerous ones, for others around me. It hadn't taken long for me to recognize that it was safest – for them, for Aunt Teresa, and for me - to keep everyone at a distance and so I had for a very long time.

Felix must have sensed the direction my thoughts were taking because he swayed across the kitchen toward me and patted my shoulder. "Don't you worry," he said, in an attempt to be comforting, as he guided me back to the kitchen table, pulling out the chair and pushing me down into it. "We have fabulous furniture...and with the exception of Rufus's odd feet stench and Ezra's predilection for coffee all day long, we're a good lot to live with."

I caught a glance at Rufus, who flicked a piece of bacon at Felix which hit him square in the nose and caused an offended gasp in return.

I could just barely see the side of Rufus's cheek turn up, and I figured he was satisfied with the reaction he'd gotten.

"Well, I've asked you to take care of it in the past and you refuse," Felix replied, his pride wounded more than his nose.

Rufus picked up another piece of bacon, threatening, and Felix immediately turned away, busying himself. He placed a container of organic soy butter and bottle of sugar-free organic syrup next to my plate. I had to fight not to make a face at them. "Eat up now. It's getting cold."

Rufus looked over his shoulder with a cautionary expression, shaking his head in warning.

"You know, Felix, I'd guess that Maggie is more of a coffee drinker too," said Ezra, pulling a mug from the now fully stocked cabinet. She poured the steaming coffee and slid it in front of me with a wink; I gave her a thankful smile for the excuse. "When it comes to food, Felix likes to suggest-"

"Monitor," muttered Rufus at the stove.

"Suggest we eat in a healthy way. You'll get used to it."

"We must treat our vessels like a temple," said Felix between chews of his own cottage cheese pancakes. By his imperial tone, I guessed that he'd recited this phrase many times before.

Unable to determine an appropriate response, I took a sip of coffee and changed the subject. "I didn't know you all knew each other."

The three of them looked at me with surprise so I explained. "Aunt Teresa did a photography book on mystics a while back so we traveled the psychic circuit for a while. I saw Ezra reading tarot cards in Phoenix, Felix

27

doing palm reading in San Francisco, and Rufus...I saw you in Austin doing caricatures."

Felix placed a hand to his chest and sighed, his teeth biting his lower lip as if he were about to cry. "She remembers..."

"'Course she does," replied Rufus. "'S not like we're easily forgotten."

His statement and the uniqueness of each of them, in physical appearance and in mannerisms, were ironic. On the psychic rounds, you meet all kinds of people with oddities, which they use to make a quick buck. It's so prominent that once you've been to enough of the tourist spots that allow them to congregate you are no longer amazed at what you see.

Still, the three currently in the kitchen with me – my new roommates – had definitely stood out. They were undeniably their own persons, unimpressed and untainted by other's opinions of them.

Ezra turned to address me. "I'm no longer a tarot card reader. I've changed careers and now work with under-privileged children. And there is one requirement I have of all those I watch over."

"Okay..." I replied, hesitant. There was an insinuating tone to her words. She was leading up to something.

"It's one request. Just one," she added cautiously, apparently already knowing I wouldn't like it.

"Uh huh..." I muttered, coolly.

"Aunt Teresa and I selected a private school for you."

She was right. I didn't like it.

"No...Absolutely not." I shook my head.

She was again looking at me with an empathetic but resolute stare. "It's the only request I'll make, Maggie. We both felt this was a school you would enjoy and it'll secure you a spot at any college you pursue."

"Ezra, I endured a private school once. It was full of snobs and authoritarian dictators. No..." I added determinedly. "I won't go."

"Teresa warned me that you would disagree." She paused, assessing my expression, which I was certain reflected disgruntled agreement. "You might be surprised. Indulge me, Maggie. It's only one more year until you graduate."

I looked at Rufus, standing still at the stove with his curious focus on me, and to Felix, where he anxiously tapped his right foot against the ground at a surprisingly rapid pace, and then back to Ezra, waiting patiently for my answer.

When I made a promise, I kept it. So, I took a few minutes to answer. I was already agreeing to live in one place for an exhaustingly full year. To do it surrounded by snobs was downright intolerable. Still, I realized that – in her mind - what Ezra was asking was in my best interest. I appreciated it, but there was one thing I needed to make very clear to her...

"Any other demands and you'll find me gone."

She nodded, understanding the insinuation I made, without any noticeable flinch. "Let's work at avoiding that," she replied, not appearing to be the least bit concerned.

Realizing I'd had enough of this conversation, I stood and left the kitchen without bothering with another word.

"We're glad you agreed, Mags," Felix called out gleefully.

That last word made me stumble and for a second the kitchen doorframe came threateningly close to my forehead.

He'd used a shortened version of my name – a nickname. I'd never had a nickname before. Although my full name was Magdalene no one ever called me by it. In fact, no one called me anything but Maggie and that was just fine with me. Nicknames meant people were getting close to you, becoming friends. I'd avoided friends for the same reason I'd avoided roommates. The closer they came to me, the more potential there was for them to be dragged into the problems I caused.

I went upstairs to shower as the name he'd used swam through my head. In about fifteen minutes I'd decided that I liked it and that I would even respond if he used it again. This was a big breakthrough for me – the one who kept everyone at arm's length.

When I stuck my head through the kitchen's back door to say goodbye, Felix beamed at me and said it again. "See you there, Mags."

I flinched at the name, still unfamiliar with it, but quickly recovered. "Where?" I asked.

"Jackson Square," he replied, chuckling at me.

I blinked, stunned. "How did you know where I was going?"

"We know what you do for a living. We saw you on the psychic circuit, remember?" He winked at me.

"Oh…" Noticing Ezra was no longer in the kitchen, I added, "Will Ezra be there?"

Felix rolled his eyes, threw the dish towel he'd been using over his shoulder, and leaned down to me, whispering, "She won't. And you'll learn pretty quickly that she's not here to imprison you. She's here to protect you."

"Hmmm. Sounds like a fine line to me…," I mumbled.

Felix found that humorous and squealed as he playfully snapped his dish towel at me. "Get going! And save us a spot!"

I quickly ducked out the door before the towel could reach me and went to unlock the shed. As I pulled out my bike, I was amazed at how the morning had turned out so different than expected. New roommates. New school. My mind drifted to the night before. New handsome stranger…

I dwelled on the memory of the stranger's bottomless, sultry, blue-green eyes, as I rode to work. I was in such deep thought that I didn't recognize right away that I was stopped at the same intersection where I'd seen the blue Ford Mustang the evening before. Then I recalled how the guy in the driver's seat had stared at me. I shuddered slightly. In fury, was the only way I could describe it. I'd have bet that it took everything in him not to step on the gas pedal and plow me down right there. My mind was so saturated with the image of that irate stare, the person behind me honked loud and long before I kicked my bike into first gear and moved on.

I reached The Square without any sight of the blue Ford Mustang or any sign of the guy who'd been driving it. Maybe it was a fluke and the guy was just a crazy tourist now on his way home. I considered this, but something inside told me that wasn't the case. I then shoved the thought aside and hurried to set up.

I parked my bike against the fence and set up two chairs bought at the local drugstore. Then, I hung up the sign I carried in my backpack advertising: "Send a Message to Departed Loved Ones," and in smaller letters below, "Proof will be provided or free of charge." I had just paid the guards their money when Felix and Rufus arrived.

Felix drove a lime green Camero with a pink, furry steering wheel and giant dice hanging from the rear view mirror. When it stopped, it made a loud bang which drew the attention of the security guards. I walked over to the car and quietly suggested to Rufus that he slip the guards each a twenty dollar bill to avoid any trouble. Felix and Rufus then set up their tables and chairs a few spots from mine, and I handed over another hundred to secure each of their spots. I could have suggested to either Rufus or Felix

31

that they make the payoff to the guards but their bickering drew enough attention that I thought any interaction with a guard was a potential for disaster.

Throughout the day, passerby's and the other mystics and peddlers chuckled at my service as they walked by or muttered, "That's a new one." But then I secured a customer, followed by another and another. By late morning, I had encountered a surprisingly steady flow of business – more than in any other city I'd worked. There were a few slow times when I simply picked up a book I'd bought on the city's history, and conversely, during rushes I focused on efficiency in my "order-taking".

Everything seemed to be going fine until about midday; that was when the strange feeling returned.

A petite, giggling college student had just sat down when I sensed it. The hairs on the back of my neck sprang to life, pulling and twisting in an erratic pattern.

"Hi," said the girl in a squeaky voice. She tossed her blonde hair back over her shoulder and gave me a toothy smile.

"Hi," I replied absentmindedly, focused on my neck.

"So, can you really deliver messages to the dead?" asked the girl, skeptically.

"Yes, yes I can," I said, drawing up a hand and rubbing at the skin below my hairline. It helped calm the reaction I was having but I still felt the goose bumps below my fingertips.

I saw her friends roll their eyes and sneer at me as they stood a few feet away, watching.

Just as I was turning my attention back to their friend in my customer's chair, I caught sight of him.

A motorcycle had stopped and the driver had twisted his head over his shoulder, staring back in my direction. But this time it wasn't the creepy guy who had watched me from the shadows yesterday and assumedly attempted to run me over. This one looked like someone out of a spy movie. He was hunched over a sport bike, dressed in all black leather with yellow stripes, a shiny black and yellow matching helmet, and a necklace dangling from around his neck. It was gold and a name had been soldered into the end but he was too far away for me to read it.

Through the clear visor I could easily see his face and it had the same intense, heated expression as the creepy guy from the day before.

My hands clasped in my lap began to sweat and I could feel my heart beginning to beat quicker.

"Excuse me…Excuse me!" The college girl leaned into my view. "Are you going to take my money or what?"

I paused to catch my breath, which seemed to have left me, before answering. "No…no. I don't take the money until you receive proof that your message has been delivered."

She blinked uncertainly at me and then leaned back to shove her money back in her pocket, clearing my view. "Why not?"

He was still there. Still staring.

"Um…because others in my line of work have given us a bad reputation. So I don't ask for payment until I provide proof the job is done."

She paused for a moment. "Oh."

I could sense she was getting irritated by my lack of attention to her. Realizing I was being rude and only slightly caring, I decided that I couldn't stop him from staring, so I would just let him.

"So, what would you like to say and to whom would you like to send it?" I asked, making my mind up to ignore him. This was especially challenging considering he made me feel panicked in the same way I had with the guy from yesterday.

The girl beamed at me and then wiggled in her seat as if she were getting herself ready for a big surprise. "I want to send a message to my grandmother. I'd like to say that I miss her and that we're all doing well down here on earth and that I crave her sticky rolls."

"Okay." Easy enough.

Her face twisted in confusion. "Aren't you going to write it down?" she asked, annoyed. Then she glanced over her shoulder to see what I was still focusing on instead of her.

"No, I can't take the pad with me so it isn't much good, but I've done this long enough that I have a very good memory. Don't worry. Your message will be delivered verbatim."

She didn't believe me and made me recite the message back.

"That's fine," she assessed. "So…what now?"

"Give me her name, when and where she passed, and I'll deliver the message tonight. If you come back tomorrow, or any other day thereafter, I'll have her response for you."

The girl's mouth fell open. "Really? I mean you'll really be able to tell me what she says?"

"If she has anything to say, I'll tell you." I shrugged, familiar with the shocked response.

The girl's face lit up with a smile. "My friends told me not to waste my beer money, but I am SO glad I did!"

"Thanks…" I replied, hesitantly. I didn't think she intended to be offensive.

"Now…" She reached forward and patted my hands that were folded in my lap. "You go over to that boyfriend of yours and make up. He looks pretty upset with you!"

"What boyfriend?" I asked, bewildered. I didn't have a boyfriend. I didn't even have a single friend in the city.

"That one on the bike," she said, surprised, pivoting in her seat to find him.

We both looked toward his direction at the same time, realizing that he was no longer there.

34

"Oh, well…when he comes back…" she said with a smile and one final pat on my hands.

I was so focused on searching for him in the crowd that I didn't even notice she had stood up and joined her friends.

As it turned out, I didn't need to search too hard to find him. Around late afternoon, I asked Sylvia, the hemp jeweler, to watch my spot and my bike while I went for a muffaletta, a delicious olive sandwich that I'd eaten for lunch the day before, and was instantly addicted to on my first bite. I'd almost reached the deli shop when I felt my hair stand on end again and I instinctively looked behind me. He was quick, but I still saw him before he slipped inside a souvenir shop that sat behind a stand of masquerade masks and Mardi Gras beads. I hesitated but decided to confront him. I walked briskly to where I'd watched him disappear. As I entered the shop, I quickly searched the colorful aisles that were full of voodoo dolls in all shapes and sizes, dried mixes of Cajun and Creole spices, and shirts printed with catchy phrases. Nevertheless, after a thorough search, I found that he was no longer there. Figuring he'd slipped by me, I chose to forget it, quell my frustration, and go pick up my sandwich.

When I reached The Square again, I went back to taking customer's orders. It wasn't until the sun touched the cathedral's rooftop and the last of the tourists began filtering away did he appear again.

Felix pranced up to me just as I was considering packing up my chairs for the day and stated excitedly, "Tofu." He reminded me of a dog anticipating the taste of a bone.

"What?" I spun in my seat to face him, keeping an eye on a twenty-something guy who was deciding whether to be my next customer.

35

"Tofu. Also known as soybean curd. Do you like it?" he asked, his eyebrows rose in expectation.

"I-I've never really had it," I replied, nervous as to where this conversation was headed after remembering his choice of breakfast foods.

It turned out, my concern was legitimate.

"Excellent! Get your chops ready 'cause I'm making my special dish tonight...Tofu Turkey Tacos!"

"Mmmm," I said, trying not to show my disgust.

"Not to be confused with tofurky, which is tofu made to look like turkey. I use a mixture of tofu and turkey so you get a variety of proteins and tastes!"

He beamed back at me.

"Wonderful..."

"We're taking off now. See you back home!"

"Okay..." I nodded in response, ignoring how the way he said "home" made a nervous jolt run through me. Instead, my mind raced through all the fast food places available from here to the house.

Felix gleefully spun on his heels but quickly stopped, adding from over his shoulder, "Oh yes...Godzilla over there..." He nodded toward Rufus. "He asked me to mention he's making hamburgers, if you want any of those too." He rolled his eyes and shrugged, as if he couldn't understand why.

I heard his car's engine thunder to life a few minutes later, just as the twenty-something guy had moved back into the crowd. I sat patiently watching the last of the bustling tourists pass by, in no hurry whatsoever to rush home and smell tofu and turkey sizzling in the same pan.

By the time the din in The Square had quieted and the last of the tourists disappeared down a side street, I began to feel it.

The hair rose up on the back of my neck – just as it had the day before, just as it had at lunch today. I drew in a frustrated breath and scanned the crowd, looking for the reason.

Slowly, the sensation grew more intense causing goose bumps to rise on my arms, peaking when my eyes landed on him.

The one dressed in the yellow and black leather rider suit was on his bike again watching me. A security guard approached him, but before they could interact, the guy took off down the street with dirt and exhaust kicking up behind him.

He was back a few minutes later and the hair on my neck began to steadily rise again, growing higher with each step he took as he arrogantly strolled toward me. He removed his helmet, and I could see he had dark brown hair that hung to his shoulders and the type of chiseled good looks I'd seen only on GQ models. He had striking clear blue eyes which bore into me as he stopped just behind my customer chair.

His stare especially unnerved me. It was unavoidable and contradicted his cheerful demeanor. While his jovial expression told me to relax, his feverishly concentrated eyes sent a silent alarm through me.

"Ello," he said with an Australian accent. The goose bumps rose higher. His broad smile told me that he had no idea how his presence made me react. "Will ya take one mo' customer today?"

I assessed him for a moment longer than I would others because of the affect his presence had on me and his oddly intent gaze. Despite my best efforts, I couldn't rationally find anything wrong with him. It was easy to believe that he was just another tourist with a quirky manner.

Besides, there were still a few straggling vendors left in case something did happen.

"Come on…" he said with a beguiling tone. "I promise not to be a problem customer."

I gave in, lifting a shoulder in a half shrug. "Sure."

He eagerly took a seat in the chair opposite me, throwing his green canvas bag down with amazing precision right next to mine.

Later, I wished I would have paid more attention to its position.

"My name's Sharar."

"I figured."

His eyes widened in surprise at my response.

I glanced toward the necklace lying against his chest. I could see the name clearly now and pointed to it.

"That's good. You're good. I just returned from Taipei. Ever been there? Taipei?" He kept talking without waiting for an answer. "Bloody hot down thea. Got used to it though."

"I guess that would explain why you're not affected by the heat here," I said when he paused. He gawked back at me in surprise. "Your jacket...and leather...neither is conducive to today's temperature, yet you're not even breaking a sweat."

Sharar's face lit up and he tossed his head back to release a long, loud laugh. "You're observant. More than I gave you credit for."

I didn't respond immediately because my mind had caught his words clearly and I was a little taken aback by them. That was a statement someone made when they'd known you long enough to make that kind of conclusion. If what he said was true, he'd met me less than a minute ago and already he'd judged me to be observant. Unless I had met him before...which was a possibility considering how many people I'd met on the road.

"Do I know you?" I asked, instantly thinking back to all the places I'd been; clearly realizing that not one face in my memory resembled this man's.

He gave me a peculiar stare. It looked as if he were trying to determine whether I was joking with him. "No, but we do run in similar circles."

The hair on the back of my neck reacted to what he said. "Really? What circles?"

His broad smile wavered and I got the impression he wasn't being entirely honest with me. "Eh...Enough about me." He waved me off. "Tell me how this works," he said, leaning toward me with resolute interest.

In reaction I leaned away, not wanting him that close. He noticed – I could tell by the disruption to his frozen grin – but he didn't adjust his posture. Uncomfortable with our interaction, I launched into my typical spiel. "Well, I take your message, deliver it, you return for proof-"

"No...no," he stopped me abruptly, his smile remaining stationary, unnerving me further. "How do you actually...do it?"

I took a moment to clear my throat, reminding myself that this was a fairly common question asked by my customers. However, this one appeared to take the question more seriously than usual. I began to feel as if he was researching me, and I considered ending his session.

As if he read my thoughts, he said suddenly, "I don't mean to scare ya." He allowed his artificial smile to fall. "I'm not so good with...humans."

The fact he called people "humans" made his admission that much more exaggerated, and despite my reaction to him, I actually felt sorry for him.

"Me neither," I said suddenly and then became embarrassed to have divulged that discomfort to a complete stranger, even if he had done it first.

"You too?" He seemed to feel slightly more relaxed at my acknowledgement and by affect more...human.

"Ever since I was younger and found my...gift. It set me apart from everyone else."

He nodded sincerely. "You are definitely unique."

I felt there was a hidden meaning behind his comment, but I wanted to veer away from me as the topic of conversation. "So, back to the business of delivering your message…"

"Ah, yes, that…"

"Yes…that," I replied a little too abruptly.

He didn't seem to notice. "Where were we? I believe you were about to tell me the ways you use to find the dead."

"Right," I agreed, a little uncomfortable with his stark choice of words. "There are ways to find your loved ones who have passed-"

"What ways?" he demanded, his smile returning to soften his assertiveness.

"Um…why is it you ask?"

"Curious," he replied and when he saw that wasn't a good enough reason, he added, "I'd like to make sure you're not a phony, that my money will be well spent."

His focus on our conversation still unnerved me, but I had to admit his rationale seemed consistent with other customers' needs for confirmation, so I gave him the benefit of the doubt.

"Well, while I'm sure there is more than one way, I only use one in particular method. In the afterlife, with your loved one's name and their place of death I'm able to easily locate them."

He sat silent for a moment, staring. "Name…place of death, eh?"

"That's right," I said, not sure whether he believed me. "And if your loved one had a common name, such as John Smith, I ask for the date too…to help identify them."

He leaned back in the chair, quietly assessing me. I noticed that his behavior had changed almost instantly. His grin was gone completely now, replaced with a tight, thin line. The kindle in his eyes had changed too, becoming muted. They looked vacant, dead. Now he didn't look friendly at all, and I felt that I was finally seeing the true Sharar.

"Well, was bloody good to meet ya," he said flatly, standing to leave.

"Did you want me to deliver a message?" I asked, confused.

His response was cold, distant. "Nah...Just wanted me confirmation."

"Confirmation about what?"

He didn't bother to answer. Instead, he strapped on his helmet and picked up his canvas bag. As he sauntered away, he called over his shoulder with an offhand comment. "You're an interesting one, Messenger. I'll give ya that."

I couldn't be sure because his voice was muffled, but he almost sounded wistful to me.

I watched him walk away, toward his bike parked not far from us at the curb.

That was when I noticed The Square was completely empty and the gas lamps lining the streets of the French Quarter were now lit and flickering hazy shadows against the old buildings. I tensed, and my body reacted, as I heard Sharar's bike start with a rumble. I glanced in his direction to find him taking off down the street.

He was gone, I told myself. Gone. Yet, the odd sensation I was having in response to him hadn't ebbed at all.

Wavering between whether I should begin to figure out why I was having these sensations or if I should simply ignore them altogether, I took my chair and folded it. Shoving it between the slits in the fence panels that encircle The Square, I hid it behind a shrub; this will be my free storage space during my stay in New Orleans.

The last bit of light from dusk slipped away then. I was completely alone in the dark. The storefronts surrounding The Square were now closed. Even Café Du Monde, a coffee shop that stayed open year round, was vacant, sending an eerie reminder that even when it seemed that others were nearby…they really weren't.

As I bent down to pick up my other chair – this one for the customers – I heard a slow, quiet whistle begin a few feet behind me.

I was instantly on guard.

This hadn't been the first time someone – even someone with ill intent – had walked up behind me in the dark. Only this time I wasn't perfectly calm like I normally would be, as ludicrous as that seems. Yet, the hair was still standing on the back of my neck and I was dwelling on the odd meeting with Sharar. I wasn't sure if either one of those was the reason but…I was shaken.

In one smooth motion, I turned around, lifted the chair, collapsing it with a slam, and held it up defensively. The weight of it in competition with my slim frame almost took me down with it. I stumbled; realizing I must look like a bungling defender and wanting to kick myself. Steadying my balance, I looked up and planted my feet in preparation, only to find out it wasn't Sharar at all.

Beneath the halo of the street lamps, I found that it was someone far more annoying - the lofty guy I had nearly ran over the night before.

My breath caught in my throat as I recognized him. I couldn't mistake the elegant contours of his facial features or the way he stood straight, being so comfortable in his own skin. He swaggered toward me, thumbs tucked into the pockets of his dark jeans – jeans that fit him perfectly in all the right places. His blue shirt was pulled out to cool him off because he wore a buttoned up black vest. The clothes he wore fit the mold of his muscles and defined his body, which beneath them was clearly perfect. I watched him approach, my breath still caught, knowing that only he could pull off that type of style on a summer evening in New Orleans.

He was smirking at me. "What are you planning on doing with that?" he asked in his thick English accent. I could feel my heart quicken.

"Defend myself," I retorted, stowing the chair next to the other one. I found myself trying to avoid staring at him and hoping he wasn't realizing it. "What are you doing here?" I demanded, while standing up to face him.

He freed one hand to tip the rim of his cap toward me, which must have been his version of a greeting. I thought it was a haughty gesture…yet charming at the same time.

He was a foot away now, and I could feel myself being drawn toward him, enticed by him.

"I've actually been here for a while," he said, casually, as he leaned back against the gate.

I felt his eyes on me even as I looked for something else to do, trying to keep him from seeing what he was doing to me. In the end, he was unavoidable.

"But why? What are you doing here?" I persisted.

"Well," he said, struggling not to grin at my obvious irritation. "Despite your sentiment last time we saw each other, I came by to see if you needed help."

I sighed, loudly. "You were checking up on me?"

He shrugged, a guilty expression marring his handsome face, although I knew he didn't feel an ounce of remorse.

"Didn't I tell you I could take care of myself?"

"Yes, yes, you did…" He nodded in agreement. "I still came."

Neither of us moved, allowing silence to surround us. It was as if we were staring each other down, willing the other to speak first.

His sultry eyes watched me, curious and teasing. How could anyone be this beautiful and aggravating at the same time? I was sure he missed nothing…my now rapidly beating heart, my visible shortness of breath, and my busy eyes flickering away from his.

In the end, I decided it would be me to break the silence, or I was going to pass out right there.

"I've been in dangerous situations before, you know."

He seemed unimpressed. He nodded his head downward once, submissively, and uttered, "I'm sure you have."

Apparently he wasn't getting my implied point. He wasn't moving; instead, he remained poised against the fence. Maybe he needed further clarification.

"I can take care of myself," I insisted. It was something I meant and intended to prove, if I ever got the chance.

"You've made that clear," he replied, flatly.

I wasn't sure if he was being facetious or sincere, but I decided either way, it didn't matter. The message I wanted to get across was that I emphatically did not want him to think I was so weak that I needed someone watching over me, trying to be a savior.

"Well, you can stick around if you want…waiting for a building to collapse on me…but you're going to be sorely disappointed." I said this even as I realized my body was still feeling the effects of Sharar, and I noticed that the goose bumps hadn't disappeared from my arms yet.

"Are you in that much of a hurry to get rid of me?" he asked, disrupting my thoughts and drawing my attention back to him. It seemed like he was a bit appalled, possibly even hurt at the idea.

"Get rid of…no…I just don't want you to waste your time."

I certainly didn't want him to leave, even if I was a bit conflicted by his presence. I liked him being here…anywhere really so long as I was there too. I felt comfortable in his presence as if I had known him my entire life and could say nearly anything that was on my mind.

I simply wanted him to be here for a different reason, a reason that didn't include me being a damsel in distress.

He obviously saw himself as a hero, but a hero was only a hero if the person being saved wasn't strong enough to save themselves. I was certainly capable of saving myself.

He folded his arms across his solid chest and settled back against the rails - into what I was finding to be his natural, smug demeanor. "Well...I don't believe I'm wasting my time. Eventually you'll need saving."

My mouth fell open at his audacity. "See that...that belief is truly wrong. You do understand that I've survived eighteen years without your assistance. Right?"

"I do," he agreed readily, and to my relief it seemed that he finally understood my point. Then he went a step further, eradicating any good will. "I just don't know how."

I clenched my jaw in response, and seeing this, he bowed his head to chuckle.

I knew I had three options. I could release the torrent of words and curses that were racing through my mind and make it unmistakably clear that I did not need a savior. I could silently suppress the emotions brewing inside me, pick up my backpack, and head home, although this wasn't really an option for me, or I could change the subject to avoid further aggravating myself. I chose the final alternative.

"So are you going to tell me your name?" I shrugged, trying to break his stare. I began to realize that, whenever he was near, I was so conscious of him I forgot to breathe; as a result, I took a deep breath for good measure.

A wide smirk contorted his face; that, I was learning, must be his trademark expression. "I was wondering when you were going to ask. I'm Eran."

"Maggie," I said. It could have been the fact that he simply stared back, showing no sign that he was storing my name in the back of his mind, but I got the distinct, albeit irrational, feeling that he somehow already knew my name.

My instinct was to extend my hand in greeting, even though I knew this was not typical behavior for someone my age. Nevertheless, living on the road you grow up quickly.

He seemed to have the same inhibition because he didn't immediately take my hand. Instead, he stared at it as if he was torn between being cordial and being rude.

Clearly feeling his discomfort, I began to withdraw the invitation and pulled my hand back. Upon realizing what I was doing, he had second thoughts and quickly reached to grasp it.

As his hand came around mine, the rush of his words registered with me. "I run hot."

His long fingers encircled my own as his palm - twice the size of mine - pressed down, engulfing my hand.

He wasn't kidding about the heat.

From the second we made contact, I felt as if my skin was shrinking, its moisture evaporating, and a thin layer peeling back…shriveling like a grape that withers in the scorching afternoon sun.

The heat from his skin created an invisible fireball, burning into my flesh. I felt like I reacted instantaneously, but it was still too long. I wrenched my hand free even as he pulled away.

"I'm sorry," he whispered. "I shouldn't have allowed that."

I didn't bother to respond. My attention was on my hand and the fact that even as the piercing pain subsided I noted that no damage had been. If it weren't for the throbbing, I wouldn't even have known we had touched.

"Are you hurt?" Eran asked with sincere interest.

"No," I shook my head, more in astonishment than to enforce my answer. "No, there…there are no marks."

Eran was leaning in for confirmation, so I showed him. "See? Nothing."

Only after I had turned my hand over – twice – did he believe me. He straightened up, clearly remorseful, though I couldn't understand why. It wasn't his fault. He didn't know I would hold him for as long as I did. It must have been a deep, unavoidable desire causing me to seize the opportunity and hold on despite the pain.

Eran tucked his thumbs back in his pockets, as if it would prevent them from doing any further harm.

Deciding the best course of action to help him overcome his evident guilt was to change the subject, I did just that – trying not to wring the pain from my hand as I spoke.

"So, Eran, how is it that I've crossed paths with you more often than anyone else in this city? Are you stalking me?" I said this in jest, and thankfully my tone conveyed it, despite the persistent ache in my hand.

"You're sure you're all right?" he asked again as if my answer might change. I wondered if he could somehow see that the pain lingered.

"Perfectly fine, really."

He stared at me, disbelieving. After a brief pause, he must have realized I wasn't going to confess, so he decided to refute my accusation instead. "I have far better things to do with my time than to be a stalker."

He was still glancing at my hand so I pressed the conversation further, hoping to divert his attention. There was no sense in dragging out our discomfort. "So how is it then?" I persisted.

"How is what?" He brought his eyes back to mine. This was good. Progress.

"That I keep running into you?"

The side of his mouth turned up in a confident grin. "I suppose you're just lucky."

That response triggered anger, so fluid it quickly flooded my veins. Here I was trying to make the fact that he'd burned me a passing thought for him, and he used the opportunity to mock me.

In return, I laughed sarcastically. "Well…Eran…It's getting late, and I should be going." I hoped he saw through the fake cliché of those words. Let him be offended.

The stinging throb in my hand had disappeared now, so without waiting for him to reply, I reached down to grab my backpack. In truth, I was torn between wanting to stay here and banter, though I certainly did not want to give him any reason to believe that his cockiness was welcomed, or to leave and head home for a hamburger and tofu turkey tacos.

Fate made up my mind for me. As I took hold of the thick green strap, something twitched inside.

I paused, wondering if I'd really just felt something move.

Then a head peered out. It was black and triangular and its flickering tongue tested the air toward me.

I yanked my hand back.

The head darted forward, and the ten-foot long body of a shiny black snake slithered out.

The next moments were a blur, running together like ink bleeding on a page.

I vaguely sensed that the snake came straight at me, even as I ran backwards to avoid it. It was fast and within seconds had reached my toes, even though by then, I was more than ten feet from my backpack.

Out of the corner of my eye I saw Eran move toward it. I tried to warn him against it, but my throat had gone dry and the sound came out a whimper.

By then, he'd reached down and seized the snake by its head. Even in my panic I realized how fast Eran had moved – far too fast. He appeared distorted, as if he were nothing more than colorful images blending together. On a subconscious level, something registered in my mind. His speed was not normal, but that thought didn't linger once I saw the snake's head lean back. It opened its jaw and snapped down toward Eran's hand. Offering little resistance, its fangs easily punctured Eran's flawless skin. The fangs went so deep, I watched its gums disappear into Eran's heated flesh.

I heard a scream but didn't immediately recognize that it came from me. The snake released its iron grip. Yet, Eran didn't move. His hand remained still. Instead, his head jerked up searching, bewildered, for the reason that caused my reaction.

"Your—your hand," I mumbled, pointing to where the snake had bitten him.

He glanced down at where its fangs had made contact. "Oh, that. Didn't even break the skin."

I felt my mouth fall open in shock at his nonchalance.

"No...I saw it. I saw its fangs out. They sunk in...they went deep into your skin. I saw it, Eran."

"I'm fine," he replied calmly. "See for yourself."

With the snake firmly in his grasp, Eran's thumb had been caressing the top of its head, and its body – all ten feet of it – had begun to stop writhing. After a few seconds, the snake was limp.

I took a step forward, my eyes locked on the snake's head, in case it should move again, and Eran held his hand out for me to take a closer look.

"See? No harm done."

I leaned even further forward. I knew what I'd seen. There must be puncture marks. Nearly two inches of fangs had disappeared into his hand, but Eran was right. His skin was smooth, without even a red blotch visible.

"Careful," he said, moving his hand away from me, the snake's tail twisting in reaction and hitting the ground with a thump. "He might wake back up."

"It's asleep?" I asked in disbelief. "That thing's asleep?"

"It's not a thing, Magdalene," he chastised. "It's a serpent."

"Well excuse me …," I said, abruptly pausing. The name he'd used was like a trigger to my mind. "What did you just call me?"

He glanced up from the snake to casually reply, "Your name."

"No, you said Magdalene."

"Isn't that your name?" He looked confused.

"Yes…but no…"

"Well, which is it?"

"Everyone calls me Maggie, so how did you know to call me by my full name?"

"Call it a good guess," he replied, his head bowed toward the snake. Yet, I still caught a glimpse of the knowing smile to some private joke he harbored. He began to talk again and didn't bother to fill me in. "Even if you won't admit to it, you're fortunate I was here after all. This particular serpent is a dangerous one. It's called a Fierce Snake. The venom from a single bite can kill a hundred men."

I glanced back at its now lethargic body and shuddered.

He seemed not to notice and continued explaining, "Thankfully, it is especially rare. In fact, it's a long way from home. You'd more commonly find him in Taipei."

"Taipei?" I repeated, awestruck by my sudden realization.

Hadn't Sharar said he'd just returned from Taipei? I tried to remember back to our conversation, but it had been so wrought with emotion I couldn't be sure if he'd said Taipei or somewhere else in Asia Pacific. At the realization that there was no way to be sure, I decided to disregard the thought entirely.

I watched Eran for a moment and couldn't help but declare, "I saw that snake bite you."

"And yet there is no evidence of it. Is there?" he asked. When I didn't answer he persisted. "Magdalene? Is there?"

I ignored him and his effort to get me to concede, by changing the subject. "You don't seem afraid."

Eran looked up at me, amused. "No," he replied, and left it simply at that.

"Do you...do you know much about snakes?"

He balked at me in mocking shock. "Are you starting a friendly conversation? I didn't think you had it in you."

I sighed. "Do you?"

After a light chuckle, he decided to answer. "I've certainly had my fair share of them. Serpents have been used for centuries to attack enemies. I've also seen them used in medicine, ceremonies...they're an interesting species. Though, I would have to say, I've never had the pleasure of running across this particular one before."

"Pleasure?" I scoffed.

"Let's just say this serpent is more dangerous to you than it is to me." He saw me open my mouth to argue and cut me off. "Before you contest, note that I am the one holding it."

"Regardless-," I started my rebuttal, to which he responded with an annoyed sigh; however, I never got the chance to finish.

Someone was calling my name.

"Mags! Over here!"

I followed Felix's voice to where he sat in his unavoidable, lime green car.

"Do you need a ride? We were worried. It's getting late...," he called out the passenger window. With a pout, he added, "And I'm hungry!"

"Just a sec!" I called back.

"Besides, what are you doing out here all alone?" he asked, shrugging.

I turned back toward Eran, and sure enough, he was gone. There was nothing. Not even the snake was left behind.

"Come on, Mags!" Felix called out again, eagerly shaking.

I scanned the area, doing a full sweep, and I made note of something that would stay with me for several days afterwards. There was no humanly way for someone to disappear that quickly from where I stood.

"COME ON!" shouted Felix.

I shook my head, perplexed. To Felix's relief, I didn't protest. I got on my bike, secured my helmet, started the engine, and followed him back to the house. After today's unusual events, I decided I could use a good old-fashioned hamburger.

3. FIRST DAY

With just two weeks to go before the first day of school –
which I'd dubbed The Penitentiary, to Felix and Rufus's
enjoyment – I spent the remaining days of my parole at
The Square. There, I was kept busy with customers, but
my thoughts could not be quelled and were, more often
than not, focused on Eran.

I hadn't seen him since the night he'd saved me from
the snake, but I remembered him clearly in my mind –
more specifically his hand, where the snake had bitten him
and where there had been no resulting wound. That image
kept creeping back to me because it was unthinkable that
he had remained unharmed.

Then, there was the fact that he could move at lightning
speed. Here one second, gone the next. He left no trail, no
residual breeze, and no sound.

I had met more than my share of people with oddities
on the road, but no one had been as inimitable as Eran. No
one came close. His abilities were beyond anything I'd
ever encountered before and – if I allowed my mind to
register the thought that kept pestering me – they were not

human traits. There was no one on earth who had impenetrable skin and moved as fast as he could.

I couldn't make sense of him; maybe that is why he captivated me. He harbored a secret, something that gave him these abilities; a secret he evidently did not want to share with me. But, his secret wasn't the only thing that kept me spellbound. The memory of him...the sound of his alluring accent...the image of his muscular, statuesque frame...the way he peered into my eyes...the engaging confidence in him, all of these attributes both thrilled me and irritated me at the same time. He was too perfect, and as much as I didn't want to admit, I knew I could never match him.

The unrelenting images and stream of thoughts about him dominated my mind for the next two weeks. In fact, the only time I was able to avoid them was when I listened to Felix and Rufus bicker about Felix's fondness for tasteless, foul, healthy food and when Ezra broached the school subject. I was actually thankful when she announced where I'd be attending.

Because she knew how I felt about the issue, Ezra postponed any conversation about school until it was absolutely necessary. That meant it was the day before classes began when she handed me a map, a set of school books, and a letter to hand-deliver to the principal.

"Academy of the Immaculate Heart?" I didn't bother to stop the groan that naturally followed.

"At least you won't need to wear a uniform," Ezra said, trying to soften the blow. We were in the kitchen, where she filled up her coffee mug even though it was nine o'clock at night. "It's the only private high school nearby that didn't require a uniform. I thought you'd appreciate that."

"I do. You saved me from having to find a place to burn it."

Rufus snickered from behind a forkful of mashed potatoes until he noticed Ezra's glare. He then quickly dished out another serving of Shepherd's Pie, attempting to avoid her.

"Besides, considering the affectionate nickname you've given your new school, I think you'll find the principal's name fits right in with your line of thought."

I scanned the principal's note she'd handed me.

"Mr. Warden?" Despite myself, I laughed.

"He requires a meeting with all new students. Yours is set for seven o'clock tomorrow morning. Think you'll be able to make it?"

"Do I have a choice?" I retorted, but she didn't bother to answer. "I have a challenge understanding why anyone would ever demand this of someone who obviously cannot stand structure and authority."

"Ah, a self-aware young lady," said Felix, as he happily trotted into the kitchen and took a seat at the table. He'd already eaten earlier, refusing Rufus's menu choice. "Such a rare thing these days," he added.

"Indeed," replied Ezra. She winked and turned her attention back to me. When she spoke again, her voice was soft and patient. "I have something to…to mention that may make going to school a bit easier for you."

"Okay…"

"When I was a child…," she paused, sighing deeply and refocusing on me. She was struggling to tell me something profound. That much was clear. "I lost my parents in a plane accident."

"You did?" I asked. Suddenly realizing how meek and faint my voice sounded.

"We had a skilled crew. It was the weather that took down the plane."

"You had a skilled crew?" I repeated. My question emphasized that her choice of words sounded odd to me.

"We owned the plane. My parents were wealthy," she stated simply. "When the police arrived at the house, I was told to pack a bag, and I left the only home I had ever known."

Stunned, I forgot about the plate of food in front of me and the books stacked beside me. "Where did you go?"

"From one relative to another, but it wasn't me they squabbled over…it was the inheritance. I was just added baggage."

I drew in a sharp breath, shocked.

"By my junior year in high school, I had no interest in family, far less interest in studying, and I fell in with…well, with the wrong kind of crowd. And then, I met your mother!"

"She was in the wrong crowd?"

Ezra laughed lightly. "No, not exactly. She was my tutor; and trust me, I would never have met her if I hadn't been forced into taking her studying lessons. It was either meet her twice a week or take summer school."

"Not much of a choice there," I pointed out.

"And that was a good thing. If it wasn't for her, I'm not sure where I'd be now. As it turned out, your mother and I became good friends. I taught her about boys and she taught me Algebra. She was the only reason I went to college and why I value education so much. I believe your mother would value your education, too."

I thought about Ezra's office next to the kitchen. It was fully moved in now with books double-stacked along the newly installed bookshelves and countless diplomas lining the wall.

Looking across the table at her, now, I had a new found respect for her. She was no longer the guard; she had become an inmate, one who had risen above her lot. That, I could relate to.

I made the decision right then to stop complaining about school.

"So…what classes am I taking?" I asked, sliding the paperwork on the table in front of Ezra toward me.

She smiled, satisfied that I was showing a little interest.

"One's I think you'll enjoy." She took a sip of coffee and proceeded to fill me in. "English Interpretive Literature, European History, Biochemistry, Calculus, and Fencing."

"Fencing?" I asked. "That's a class?"

Ezra nodded. "This is a school for advanced students. I didn't think public school would be challenging enough to hold your interest."

I groaned and returned to my dinner.

"Actually, I saw your transcripts, Maggie. You are a very good student."

I swallowed a mouthful of mashed potatoes and shrugged. "Yeah…well…studying always comes easy. It's hiding the fact that I deliver messages to the dead, that's difficult."

The moment the words left my mouth everyone at the table shifted in their seat uncomfortably. I glanced around and found they were avoiding eye contact with me.

"What?" I demanded.

I had the distinct feeling a discussion about me had taken place.

Ezra cleared her throat and laid her fork down in order to free her hands. She wrapped them around the coffee mug in front of her, though I noticed she didn't bother to take a drink. "Maggie, do you plan to offer your services to the students?"

Ah, that was their concern. I hadn't actually given it any thought. In fact, over the past few weeks, just thinking about school made my brain short-circuit, forcing me to switch topics immediately. It would certainly make for interesting gossip. It could possibly get me kicked out – an appealing thought until I remembered that I'd made a commitment to Ezra. No, this time I was going to be a good little girl, despite my incredibly strong reservations, and I was just going to attend classes like everyone else.

"Don't worry, I'm not planning on it," I responded and everyone visibly relaxed.

"That'd be good," said Rufus as he picked up his fork and scooped up a mountain of meat and carrots, "'cause we wantchya to be happy here." He swallowed the forkful in one gulp.

Felix rolled his eyes at Rufus before he tentatively added, "And delivering messages...well, it might cause some...friction."

"Well...we wouldn't want that," I replied teasingly, though no one else saw the humor.

"Who knows, Maggie, you may end up liking school," said Ezra, as she smiled from behind her coffee mug before taking a sip.

I snickered. "Don't count on it."

A private exchange of glances between Felix and Ezra took place before anyone spoke again.

"What?" I asked again.

This time, Ezra could barely contain her enthusiasm; suddenly smiling wide and exclaiming, "Now that you're done with dinner, I suppose we can let you in on the real reason why Felix chose to eat earlier. He was putting the finishing touches on a present we bought for your first day of school!"

I was stunned. "Really?"

They nodded in unison. "It's in your bedroom," Felix said; as he giggled and his shoulders rolled upward, displaying his giddiness.

I stood and nearly ran from the kitchen, up the stairs, and through the door to my room.

Inside was a queen-sized bed, its posts so high they nearly scraped the ceiling. It was draped in a thick, down comforter and so many pillows only half the bed showed.

It was more fitting in a castle bedchamber than in my tiny, old bedroom. It was beautiful.

I choked back a sob just as they came up behind me, each, grinning from ear to ear.

Spinning to meet them, I stuttered, "I-I don't know...I-I can't believe..."

"We couldn't have you sleeping on that old mattress the night before your exams," said Ezra.

"Thank you so much!" I leaned in and hugged them all at once.

"Rufus put the wooden parts together and I decorated the bed," Felix proudly explained.

"You did a great job ... both of you."

They seemed to be pleased with that acknowledgment.

"Get some good rest," Ezra said. She closed my bedroom door as they all turned to head downstairs, leaving me in the privacy of my newly transformed room. "School starts tomorrow."

Oddly, even those words couldn't stifle my contentment, and that night I fell asleep more easily than I ever had before.

I woke up the next morning a bit less enthusiastic, with not a single nerve of excitement going off. It didn't matter that I was about to meet new people I'd be forced to spend time with for the next ten months. Slowly, and with a great deal of effort, I left the comfort of my bed and gave very little thought to what I would wear. I opted for blue jeans, a black t-shirt, and a grey ivy cap. I was so disappointed because I would be stuck inside classrooms all day as opposed to the sunlit, bustling Jackson Square, that I chewed and swallowed the egg white, veggie omelet Felix gave me without even noticing how it tasted. At least he was pleased when I left.

The academy was less than five miles from the house so it took very little time to get there. When I pulled into the parking lot, there were several things I noticed immediately. It was a far cry from the public schools I'd attended. There were no security gates, bars on the windows, or trash piled up in the corners. In fact, it looked more like a mansion than a place of learning. It was a lone, three-story, brick and ivy, U-shaped building with an enormous park in the center of the U. Trees and benches dotted the park where I could envision students hanging out and studying hard, as I'm sure would be the case.

I knew that driving up on my loud, rumbling Harley Davidson motorcycle was not going to leave a good, first impression with anyone who saw me.

I didn't care.

Even the astonished looks from the teachers who'd arrived early, as they stared at me from across the parking lot, didn't bother me.

What did bother me was the blue Ford Mustang parked in the student lot. It looked like the one that had followed me a few weeks ago, the one that possibly tried to run me down – if I chose to believe that Eran had been right about the driver's intentions. There was no one in the car, but if the owner was around, I knew I would recognize him instantly.

I walked toward what looked like the main entrance, set in the center of the middle building, where a sign read Main Hall. Arrows pointed to either side reading East Hall and West Hall.

I found Mr. Warden's office in the far left corner of the West Hall and was just about to open the door when my hand paused on the knob. It started to rattle and I registered that it was a result of my hand - still holding it - now shaking. I felt sweat begin to bead up on my forehead just as the hair on the back of my neck began to rise.

This feeling was, by now, all too familiar to me.

I peered down both halls, searching for the creepy owner of the blue Ford Mustang or for Sharar, but I found I was completely alone. Not even a teacher was in sight.

Get a grip, I told myself; I felt foolish. I chalked up the feeling of fear to the fact that this was my first day of school, but since I'd had so many first days at new schools, my rationalization was weak and laughable.

I shrugged off that thought and opened the door; I found a heavyset secretary sitting behind a cluttered desk. She frowned at me, and I recognized her as one of the ladies in the parking lot that gaped at me as I rode up. She stopped typing long enough to point a thick, sagging arm toward a separate room.

"Thanks," I replied, but she ignored me and directed her attention back to the computer that was precariously perched on top of the messy desk in front of her.

My voice must have alerted Mr. Warden that I had arrived, because he was standing by the time I entered his office.

"Ms. Tanner …,"

"Maggie … actually," I said, extending my hand to meet his abrupt handshake.

Mr. Warden was stoic; he showed no hint of a smile and offered no reply.

Immediately, I noticed that he didn't look much like a warden at all. I'd pictured tall, meaty, and stress wrinkles. I got the stress wrinkles right, but he was shorter than me, looked very frail, and had a receding hairline. Glasses were hanging from a chain around his neck, like you'd see on secretaries in the late 1960s, and that made him all the more disarming. Still, I'd already decided that he would be The Warden from now on.

As he closed the door behind me, my attention was drawn to the diplomas and the pictures of him, posed with people who appeared to be prominent and wealthy, that crowded the wall behind his desk … an ego-wall. So The Warden had a prideful side, I contemplated, as he ushered me to a seat facing his desk.

I sat, still fighting the shaking and the sweating, trying desperately to appear normal despite the physical reactions my body was suffering.

I guess that was why I didn't see the creepy owner of the blue Ford Mustang seated in the chair next to mine.

I discovered he was there, watching me, when I glanced in his direction while The Warden took his seat.

I froze when I saw that the guy had the same intense, angry gaze focused on me that he had last time I saw him. I gripped my backpack, full of books, as that awful, sick feeling of fear overwhelmed me. If The Warden noticed any of this, he gave no sign.

"Ms. Tanner, this is Achan," said The Warden; I made a mental note of how Achan ignored me in favor of turning to address The Warden with a friendly, relaxed smile.

I also made note of Achan's outfit. His brown, creased, tweed slacks, his white, collared, cotton shirt, and his shined, leather, dress shoes made it easy to see how much older he dressed than people my age.

He didn't appear to survey me at all. In fact, for the remainder of the meeting, Achan didn't look my way once.

However, I learned that Achan had recently arrived from a private school in New York City. His parents were not planning on relocating, so they had bought Achan a house in the famous Garden District. Joy, I thought after hearing this information. Maybe his sour expression was the result of him being a snob. The Warden went on to explain that Achan's transcripts had revealed his status as an expert archer, and that made The Warden eager to see Achan on the school's archery team. He was confident that Achan's skill would make his new school proud. After that announcement, The Warden escorted Achan out of the office but not before a jovial pat on his back and the reiteration – for the third time – that he was so happy to have a student of his stature join the academy.

Curiously, when Achan left the room, the fear that plagued me began to slowly subside. This caught me off guard so I didn't immediately notice that The Warden had closed the door behind Achan and returned to his desk.

He didn't have my full attention again until he lifted a foot-high stack of files from the floor and allowed them to crash loudly onto his desk.

He was watching me, his face now far more displeased. "Your files, Ms. Tanner."

"Maggie," I corrected.

"I heard you the first time," he said, indignantly. "Sixteen schools in your short eighteen years of life. I'll have you know, Ms. Tanner, that is a record."

He glowered at me until I realized he didn't plan to stop. Someone was going to have to break our deadlock stare. Realizing there was no point in antagonizing him further, I dropped my eyes to the floor. Only then, he spoke.

"Sixteen previous schools. A Harley Davidson for transportation. Performing psychic readings for money in the French Quarter. Do you know what these are, Ms. Tanner?"

"The result of good research on a new student?"

"Now we can add impudence to the list ...," He frowned, before continuing. "These are red flags, Ms. Tanner. I wish you to know that I've met with each of your teachers prior to your arrival, and they will be reporting back to me about your behavior ... consistently. So it would be in your best interest not to act up." He paused, contempt radiated from his glare, as he lifted his chin toward the door. "Go."

I guessed that was my cue to leave. It was just a bit different than Achan's exit, so it took a moment before I reacted.

"Go!"

I hauled my backpack up over my shoulder and left the office, though not as quickly as The Warden would have liked. I knew this because I noticed that he rolled his eyes as I closed his office door behind me.

Then, it dawned on me that I forgot to hand Ezra's letter to The Warden, so instead, I left it with Ms. Saggy–Arm on my way back out to the hallway.

Instinctively, I looked around for Achan; thankfully, I could not locate him. However, there were plenty of other students now roaming the halls and each one seemed to get in my way as I struggled to find my first class.

Like I was being punished further for some unknown crime, I found the room … on the top floor, in the far right corner, of the East Hall. It couldn't have been farther from The Warden's office, or any more difficult to find, so I was five minutes late.

A very tall, thin, German woman approached me when I entered, which I knew must be my new English teacher. Ms. Gleichner introduced me to the class, while the students silently scrutinized me, before directing me to a corner seat in the last row.

This quickly proved to be the end of my lucky streak for the day, when the hair on my neck began to tickle and reach outward, as I walked farther and farther down the aisle. By the time I was at my seat, the hair felt like it was being pulled by a strong magnetic force. Thankfully, I didn't have the shakes or sweats that accompanied this reaction earlier, and I was able to pass myself off as being somewhat normal.

I was almost certain the effect I was feeling was caused by the guy in the seat next to mine, even if he did look harmless enough. His hair was dark brown and unkempt; he wore simple, wire rimmed glasses and a short-sleeved shirt with a collar. His shirt looked like it had been stolen from a 1980's sitcom so, clearly, he didn't run with the same crowd as Achan. When I finally arrived at my seat, he didn't bother to look up at me.

Others, however, peeked in my direction all throughout class, but after the bell rang, someone actually spoke to me.

"Excuse me," said a girl with straight blonde hair pulled back into a ponytail, exposing diamond drop earrings.

My first reaction was to act like I hadn't heard her. The tone of her voice wouldn't be considered friendly by anyone's standards. Unfortunately, she was sitting directly in front of me and had turned nearly all the way around in her seat.

"Excuse me," she repeated, more insistent.

I finished shoving my book back into my backpack and zipped it up, before responding.

"Yes?"

"Are you the girl who sits in Jackson Square and takes money for delivering messages to the dead?"

By now, everyone who hadn't left the room was watching me.

"Why? Do you have a message to deliver?"

The girl snickered. "No."

Then she stood and muttered to a mousy, dark-haired girl across the aisle, "Yes, it's confirmed. She's a freak."

The two of them left the room whispering together – which I was certain was about me.

The boy who sat next to me, the only one not to sneak a quick glance in my direction during class, leaned toward me.

"That's Bridgette Madison. Her friend, who sits in front of me, is Ashley Georgian. Best to stay away from them."

"I'll try if they let me," I said, happy to find someone who seemed decent at my new school. "Thank you. It's always helpful to know someone who's been around the school longer."

"Actually, I'm new too," he said, as he forced his own books back in his bag.

"Really? How do you know the two girls then?"

"They were my tour guides, after my introductory meeting with Mr. Warden, last week."

"Lucky you."

He rolled his eyes. "Right … but it does help to know who not to know though."

"True. So where are you from?" I asked, starting to feel a kinship with him already, despite the warning my neck hair was giving me.

He dipped his head and appeared to be embarrassed, though I didn't understand why. "All over. I don't have family. I've been living off my inheritance, making my way from place to place."

"I move around a lot too." That connection made me like him even more.

He smiled sheepishly back at me; I wondered if he felt guilty for mentioning he had money, because I didn't. I couldn't have cared less, so I changed the subject, hoping it would help him forget about it.

"Why New Orleans?"

"Huh?" he asked over his shoulder, as he stood.

I picked up my backpack and followed. "Why did you end up in New Orleans?"

He started to walk down the aisle but stopped suddenly and stared at the floor, as if he were deciding how to answer. "I came here looking for someone," he finally said.

"Did you find him?"

At that point, he glanced up and smiled broadly at me. "Her. And, yes, I found her."

As the words left his mouth, the strangest thing happened. The hair on the back of my neck went haywire. It felt like the ends were dancing … crisscrossing …

twisting together, as if I had just been electrocuted, but only the back of my neck was affected.

I absentmindedly slapped a hand there to still them.

Then, to avoid answering any question he may throw at me about why I slapped my neck for no reason, I reached out my free hand. "What's your name?"

"Gershom," he replied, not moving.

I reminded myself that my actions were not typical of people my age and let my arm drop to my side.

"Sweaty palms," he explained with an awkward glance; he then brushed them on the side of his slacks for emphasis.

"It's alright," I shrugged. "My name is-"

"Maggie," he finished. "Yes, I know."

"Curse of being a new student, right?"

Gershom laughed to himself and muttered, "Something like that ..."

As he finished talking, my neck hair ignited. Gershom was already heading down the aisle, so he didn't notice that I had to abruptly slap my neck to impede this reaction again. I was beginning to wonder if I might have an issue with my electrical impulses. No one else I've known has had this problem. How could I be the only one?

As I pondered my newly found oddity, I also noticed the room was empty which meant I was going to be late for my next class ... again. I caught Gershom in the hall just in time to say goodbye, to which he responded with a weak smile and quickly headed in the opposite direction. I thought maybe I offended him somehow, but without any way to tell, I decided not to dwell on it.

My second class wasn't as far away, thankfully, but it was a repeat of the first. In fact, all my remaining classes were almost a step-by-step replay of first period: awkward introduction to the entire class, students sneaking peeks at me until the next bell rang, and the inevitable question of whether I was 'that girl' who delivered messages to heaven; although, none of the other inquisitors were nearly as rude as Ashley and Bridgette.

At lunch, I found Gershom sitting alone underneath a tree outside the cafeteria. He was pulling his lunch out of a bag and spreading it out on the grass. Before crossing his legs, he glanced around, as if he was looking for someone but trying to be inconspicuous about it. When I approached him, my neck hair lit up again, so I stopped.

There had to be a reason for this happening. Then, I realized this boy could help me understand exactly why my body reacted this way.

I moved forward and stopped right behind him, about to ask if I could sit beside him, when he spoke.

"Watch out. The grass is wet in some places."

I wasn't sure if he was talking to me or not. But he was no longer glancing around, agitated, and instead was turning to look at me.

"Yes, I was talking to you."

"How did you know who I was without seeing me?" I wondered if I had one of those, strange squeaky or loud heavy, walks that can identify someone before they enter a room.

"Lucky guess," he replied casually, turning back around.

"Huh," I muttered and took a seat next to him, cautious to avoid any damp spots.

After a few minutes of quietly laying out our lunches, – mine being a muffuletta and his being a traditional turkey sandwich – I broke the silence.

"So where did you come from?"

"All over. I think I mentioned that." He was busy pulling open his bag of chips, but I got the distinct impression he was using it as an excuse to avoid looking directly at me.

"Right, but … where were you last?"

All of a sudden he appeared uncomfortable and fidgeted with his sandwich. Finally, he answered, though it was in a low voice that I had to strain to hear. "Las Vegas."

"Me too," I said, interested.

He kept his eyes downcast, slowly, methodically eating his chips. The only sign that he was listening to me was his nod and an uncomfortable "Uh huh…"

"My aunt is a traveling photographer who left me here while she spends the year in Paris on a shoot. So, I'm staying with a friend of hers. What were you doing in Las Vegas?"

"Oh … research …,"

"Really? On what?"

He drew in a breath and held it. He looked like he didn't want to answer. I was about to tell him to forget it – knowing how much I didn't like it when others pried – but then he spoke.

"On the person I was trying to find."

"The one who is here?"

He nodded, still looking down and away.

"Huh, guess you did a good job with your research," I commented, smiling.

He stifled a laugh. "It was more blind luck than anything." Then, he was looking at me, suddenly having overcome his shyness. "What about you? Tell me where you've been. I know you have better stories to tell than I do."

"Oh, I don't know about that," I replied. I would have persisted in trying to dissuade him, but I saw his honest curiosity. Ultimately, I conceded.

After we changed the subject, away from questions about him and I began to tell him about my past, Gershom then became noticeably more relaxed. Eventually, we moved on to talk about school and who we'd each met so far. Then he filled me in on school gossip.

As it turned out, Ashley and Bridgette were great gossipers, because they filled Gershom in on nearly everyone at school during his orientation tour which he promptly relayed to me. But there was only one person who truly interested me, Achan. Unlike the girls who now swarmed him and fawned over him, I wanted to do my best to avoid him. I had never truly been afraid of anyone before crossing paths with him. I deciphered that blindly hating him was a natural response to the fear that consumed me when he was close by. Gershom didn't know much about him other than to say, "Looks like another one to avoid."

I agreed, completely.

Unfortunately, after lunch, when I walked into European History, it became clear that avoiding him would be a problem.

Knowing he was in the room without having to look was easy. The moment I walked through the door, the electrical sensation jolted back to life, but only affected the back of my neck. I did look, though, unable to control myself, I found him sitting in the last row of the class. Even though his eyes weren't the only ones focused on me, while Mr. Morow hastily introduced me, his were the only ones narrowed with unashamed animosity. A quick scan told me there was only one desk open, and it happened to be two seats in front of Achan.

I sighed, thinking about how I would spend the entire class wondering if Achan's glare was focused on the back of my head.

Mr. Morow shooed me down the aisle before returning to the white board and launching into an overview of the syllabus. Before I turned to take my seat, my eyes connected with Achan's. Acting on instinct, I narrowed my own to slits and tried hard to direct every bit of anger I could muster into the glare I returned.

What happened next surprised me. It was so brief I nearly missed it.

Achan flinched.

His glare loosened and his eyes widened before returning to their former position. When he clenched his jaw, clearly enraged by my blatant, unspoken reprisal, the hair on the back of my neck went wild again. My body responded with a shudder, which I easily hid by settling into my seat.

For the next hour, I shuddered uncontrollably every few minutes. I believed this was also every time Achan directed his fury at me and I tried to ignore the protest being launched on the back of my neck. It was a real struggle. In fact, sometime toward the end of class, when Mr. Morow called on me to answer whether I'd covered the same points of his lecture at my previous school, I replied as earnestly as I could.

"I'm very familiar with European history, sir."

"Is that so? And don't call me 'sir'. I'm not a police officer."

"Sorry."

"So, Ms. Tanner … is that why you're paying so little attention in my class."

"I didn't realize I was."

"No, you didn't realize much at all, did you?" Mr. Morow said, taking a seat at the edge of his desk. He faced me with a scowl. "If you're so familiar with European history, Ms. Tanner, why don't you answer this for us … in 410 A.D., a Germanic tribe sacked Rome. It was the first time Rome had fallen to an enemy in 800 years. What was the name of that tribe?"

As if on cue, everyone in the class shifted in their seats to get a better view of my response. A few students even shook their heads in pity, and I wondered if Mr. Morow's tactic to get students to listen better had been used before.

I realized that I should have simply told him I didn't know and allowed him to ridicule me. He would have done so with pleasure, and the lecture would have continued peaceably; but I'd already had enough of the teachers, The Warden, and the students mocking me.

"They were called the Visigoths."

I glanced around the room and noticed every student was facing me, their expressions all the same – each one in total shock. Mr. Morow released a harrumph, and everyone's attention turned to him, waiting for confirmation about my answer.

He held in his anger fairly well. I only saw a slight quiver run up the side of one cheek before he said, "Where did you learn that?"

"I told you. I'm well versed-"

"Where?" he demanded, a little too forcefully, which caused other students to turn their heads.

"I read a lot."

He laughed through his nose. "We'll see about that."

"I'm sure we will," I replied, under my breath, as he turned to face the whiteboard. "Mr. Moron."

Students close enough heard me clearly and did their best to muffle their laughter. Still, Mr. Morow spun around and marched to my desk.

He towered over me, with his hands on his hips.

"Would you like to repeat what you just said?"

"I said … I'm sure we will," I countered, intentionally excluding my new term of endearment for him.

He didn't move for an exaggerated minute. Other students in the class became uncomfortable during this pause, even though they weren't the ones being pinned by Mr. Morow's unrelenting stare. Finally, he turned to march back up the aisle.

"Didn't you also call him Mr. Moron?" someone jeered from behind me.

Granted, I'd only heard the voice a few times, but still, I instantly knew who it belonged to.

Achan was calling me out.

I turned to face him. A smile was threatening to invade his face, hiding beneath his smug expression.

"I think you heard wrong," I challenged.

He lifted one eyebrow. "No, I don't believe I did," he replied, coolly.

It was the first time we spoke to each other, and based on this initial conversation, it was evident that we both harbored an unwavering disdain for one another. When our eyes locked, sparks of distrust and loathing surged along an invisible conduit that somehow connected us.

This was also the first time I was given a direct view of Achan. Being this close to him, it occurred to me that hidden beneath his boyish face and good looks, if you chose to look close enough, his age could truly be seen. I couldn't put my finger on it, but I was certain that he was far older than the average teenager.

The bell rang, interrupting my realization, but no one moved.

"Well," Achan finally said. "I have another class to get to."

When he stood, the rest of the students mimicked him and walked out of class, like mindless followers, to fervently discuss what had just happened.

Mr. Morow, the only one left besides me, suddenly appeared uncomfortable in my presence. I collected my books, zipped up my bag, and headed for the door.

"Ms. Tanner?" he called out.

"Yes, Mr. Morow," I replied only slightly turning to look at him.

His face was grave. "Behave in my classroom. You were already on thin ice before the day even started."

I wanted to ask him exactly what I had done to get there but realized no good would come of that. So I simply nodded and left. I managed to avoid the cluster of students gathered around Achan in the hall, but they stopped gossiping long enough to stare at me as I passed.

I headed for Fencing, glad it was my last class for the day. It was held in a musty, archaic gym the size of a single tennis court. I was accompanied by twenty other students who all seemed to know each other and showed no interest in meeting me. Still, it was better than a classroom with Achan in it. The class seemed long, went by slow, and was generally dull.

After class, I cut across the back lawn in order to reach the parking lot. I was so eager to get to my bike that I had to fight the urge to strap on the helmet that I'd been carrying around all day.

If it wasn't for the hair suddenly standing up on my neck again, I may have done just that. In hindsight, it was probably a good idea.

The next few moments happened very slowly for me; though I'm sure in reality, everything else was moving at lightning fast speed.

I heard a commotion that I only vaguely registered as screaming in the distance. I didn't pay much attention, because something else had already caught my interest.

Someone was now right beside me.

I had walked across the field on my own, after letting the rest of the class go ahead, so I couldn't figure out how anyone could get close enough to me without my noticing. Yet, without a doubt, I knew someone was near me. I could feel them, even if I didn't immediately see anyone.

I spun around, searching for the person, but found myself standing squarely in the middle of the field; a staggering distance, no less than two-hundred yards, separating me from any structure.

In a split-second, my body tensed, bracing for an impact, but there was no logical reason for this reaction. Maybe only a millisecond had passed when I felt a force hit me; firm, but not hard. Simultaneously, a feverish voice boomed around me.

"Watch out!"

The playing field's cold, hard ground met my spine with a smack, but the contact had far less impact than I would have expected. Something broke my fall.

My eyes fluttered open as I tried to comprehend what had just taken place. I was trying to understand how I could be standing one moment and end up lying on the hard earth in the blink of an eye. I spent the next few minutes focusing, trying to stop my head from perpetually spinning. It took me a considerable amount of time – I'm not sure how long but a good amount – before I realized someone was on top of me.

I blinked, adjusting my eyesight, and found Eran staring down within inches of me. The entire length of his body pinned me to the ground, his arms propping him up slightly to avoid crushing the air from my lungs. I appreciated that.

"Are you hurt?" he asked, his usual irritated tone had been replaced with genuine concern.

"I-I don't think so … No," I said, mentally checking random parts of my body for pain.

"Are you sure?" he insisted. "Shock sometimes masks the symptoms of an injury."

"Yes, I'm pretty sure," I said.

"Good." He seemed to breathe a sigh of relief. "That was a close one."

"What was?" I asked, not realizing my gaze was intently focused on him.

He stared back, seeming to suppress a smile. "You didn't notice a thing, did you?" Without waiting for an answer, he said, "Is this going to be a regular occurrence? Keeping you alive?"

I noticed his body was still covering mine, his heat intense yet comfortable at the same time. Worried that he could see the excitement swelling in me, I frowned at him. "You may have more luck if you avoided shoving me to the ground again," I replied, wryly.

He released a soft chuckle, and I could feel his ribs move with his laugh. Then, to my disappointment, he rolled off of me and chivalrously offered me a hand up.

"So ...," I said, brushing the grass off my clothes. "Are you going to explain why you tackled me?"

"You won't like what I have to say," he warned.

"Do I ever?"

"Good point ...," he conceded. "I was saving your life ...yet again." There it was ... his grandiose arrogance was back.

I shook my head in disbelief. It wasn't possible. "From what? I'm on the grounds of a private school with security guards at nearly every corner. I couldn't be safer ...," I paused to watch his handsome mouth pinch in disapproval of my defense. "Do you have a Hero Complex?" I asked, annoyed.

He laughed whole heartedly at that question, not offended in the least. "I have a feeling you'll regret saying that." He glanced over my shoulder, and I turned to find a group of guys running toward us. "Just be more alert, will you?"

"Of what? You still haven't told me why-"

"I think I'll let your friends here explain," he said, looking over my shoulder again.

When I followed his gaze, I saw that the group of guys sprinting in our direction had nearly reached us. Each of them was carrying a bow in one hand and an expression of fear frozen on their faces.

"Are you alright?" One of them asked.

"At least he has ...," I said, turning back to Eran. My voice trailed off once I realized he was no longer there.

Eran disappeared again ... in the middle of an open field ... within seconds of me looking away.

Embarrassed, I slowly turned back to face the group, noting that many of them exchanged apprehensive looks. Someone from the front of the pack cleared his throat before speaking what was probably on everyone's mind, "I'm not so sure ...."

"I think ... maybe ... she should go the hospital. Have her head checked," said a short guy with dark hair – I thought I remembered him from my first class.

"Actually, I'm fine ...," I confirmed, to the sea of disbelieving faces.

However, given that this kept happening between Eran and me, I began to wonder if the hospital wasn't such a bad idea. "Really, I'm not hurt. No need to go to the hospital," I repeated, exasperated.

An older man ran up behind the group; he was a bit more overweight and clearly out of breath. He wore a jersey with his name, Coach Acer, embroidered on his chest, and I recognized him as one of the coaches I'd seen talking to the school's athletes at lunch.

"Young lady ... are you injured?" he asked between gasps. Bending down, he grabbed his knees to support his body weight.

I was going to get very annoyed if that question kept coming up. My response was resolute, just to set the record straight. "Absolutely not."

Still heaving for air, he said, "That ... that's good. Where's the ... arrow?"

The group of guys began to spread out, their focus on the ground, scanning the area surrounding us.

"Arrow?" I said, though the words barely escaped my mouth. Is that what all the ruckus about? "What arrow?"

"The one that almost hit you," muttered one of the guys, milling around.

"Oh," I faintly replied.

One of them bent down and stood up triumphantly. "Got it!"

He brought it back to the group, inspecting it along the way. "No blood …."

"I told you … I'm fine." I laughed, uncomfortably. "You really thought that hit me?"

"No, we saw it hit you," corrected the guy that was holding the arrow. "You fell to the ground."

"I was actually push …." I stopped, allowing my words to trail off. I knew they would never believe that Eran had just been here a few minutes ago or that he caused my sudden plummet into the dirt.

It dawned on me, Eran had been right. He once again saved me. I didn't want to admit it, but if he hadn't been here, and the arrow hit just the right spot, I could have easily been critically injured.

I laughed, apprehensively. "You know … whoever shot that arrow should know he's not all that great with his aim."

The guys began to chuckle, and someone mumbled, "Expert archer … yeah, right …."

"Expert archer?" I repeated, curiously. I'd heard that same term earlier today. My mind filtered back through the day's events, but someone else in the group was faster.

"Achan … he's definitely no expert."

Hearing his name made my body stiffen and my breath stop. Achan, the one who stared at me, with brazen hatred, in The Warden's office and called me out, with obvious delight, in Mr. Morow's class (both for no apparent reason) had shot that arrow at me?

My guess was, Achan actually was an expert and if Eran hadn't been here to divert my body, Achan's aim would have easily hit its intended target.

"Where is Achan?" Coach Acer furiously called out.

"Probably ran off … embarrassed," someone heckled from the crowd.

Coach Acer grumbled something and then he addressed the rest of the team, "Okay, show's over. Back to practice!"

The group turned and began to head in the same direction they came from, but the guy who'd found the arrow stopped beside me and held it up for me to see. The razor-sharp edges of its blade winked eerily at me in the sun.

"You're lucky, you know. These were just sharpened today, for the first practice." He shook his head, stunned. "Probably would have killed you, if it had hit you."

I nodded, but truthfully, I was more focused on calming the fear, still trembling inside me, than on formulating a response.

Whether intentional or not, Achan's action had certainly threatened my life, and I couldn't help the nervousness I felt at the prospect that there was more to Achan than I knew.

"Thank you, Eran," I whispered. Even if he couldn't hear me, just saying the words pacified the regret swelling up inside me; the lament that Eran had warned me about. I took a deep breath, trying to steady my hammering heart. I knew I would never confess my feelings to him directly, but I was still glad he had been there.

On my way home, I kept myself alert; relaxing only as I pulled into my driveway. Ezra was the only one home when I walked inside.

"Maggie?" she called out.

I walked down the hall and stopped at her office door, wondering if Coach Acer had called her about the incident.

"Yeah?"

She was sitting behind her desk, centered between a stack of papers and a steaming mug of coffee. She was also smiling, so I guessed no call had been made. Relief washed over me, because recounting what happened at school was not a welcomed idea.

"How was your first day?" she asked, attentive yet untroubled.

No phone call had been made. I was now certain.

"Fine," I said, repeating the same word I'd used on the field because it was the only one that came to mind.

"Good. Did you like your teachers?"

I could see she was hopeful, so to tell her the cold, hard truth would only be cruel. I opted for honest, yet vague. "I'm still getting to know them."

"Hmm." She nodded, thoughtfully. "Did they give you homework?"

"Lots …," I sighed. "Already …,"

"Then I won't keep you. I'll call you down for dinner."

"Okay, thanks."

That meant no prep work for me tonight. In light of my discernable lack of culinary skills, I traditionally performed all cutting and measuring in addition to dish washing. I decided to still pitch in on the dishes after dinner, but it was nice not to have the other responsibilities tonight.

I headed upstairs to begin my homework feeling a dark cloud settle over me. I knew it wasn't from the disappointment of having an immense amount of work awaiting me for the first time in months. What had me concerned was the feeling that all was not right. After today's events, I felt on edge.

I threw my backpack on the bed and slid down beside it, staring through the French doors, across the balcony, at nothing in particular.

With thoughts swimming through my mind, I didn't move for a very long time. While both curious and terrifying, they all revolved around one single notion. I was incapable of comprehending how Achan - a person I had just met and barely spoken to - wanted me dead.

4. ANSWERS

The field incident was the third time that Eran had intervened to save my life, and there were similarities between each event that I could not deny. He had appeared instantly and disappeared just as fast, without making a single sound; no one acknowledged his presence or gave the impression of being able to see him; and he was always left unmarked and unharmed by the assailing weapon.

It didn't take me long to determine what I needed to do. But first, I had to manage through unavoidable formalities. At dinner, my rush did not go unnoticed. I shoveled the food from my plate to my mouth at such speed it made Felix proud – and I wasn't even sure what it was Felix had prepared. Before anyone else was finished, I had already started the dishes, scrubbing hard and rapidly, trying to get them done. That, too, was not overlooked.

"Someone has a bit o' the fear in 'em ...," Rufus pointed out, coming up behind me and taking the sponge from my hand.

"Are those teachers already loading you down with work?" asked Felix, incredulously.

I sighed, thinking of the Calculus questions that would undoubtedly take me several hours alone to finish. Rufus, who must have seen my reaction, stepped between me and the sink, slowly pushing me out of the way. "Git on with it then."

"Are you sure?"

"Git," he repeated, more firmly, already dipping his hands in the wash basin's soapy water.

I breathed a sigh of relief. "You are wonderful."

"I know it," he replied, simply.

I was still chuckling at him, as I closed the door to my bedroom and sat down on my bed. It was enormous and amazingly soft, so I laid back, sinking down until the covers encased me.

My Calculus homework lay directly next to me; the edges of the paper tickling my forearm, teasing me. I was torn. Homework should have been my first priority, especially since what I was about to do would very likely be a complete waste of time, anyways.

There was no possible way I could conjure someone to my bedroom. It was an irrational expectation. Eran was human, flesh and blood, incapable of knowing my unspoken desires. I was going to end up exhausted from my attempt, embarrassed at myself for trying, and feeling rejected by Eran – all this and he wouldn't even know I was attempting to reach him! The idea was so ludicrous; I almost gave up before I started. Despite how crazy it seemed, I still laid there debating whether to take the sane approach and delve into the mountain of homework that awaited me or choose the alternative and follow my curious desire.

I groaned, knowing that eventually my desire to see Eran would win; so I finally gave in.

Five minutes, no longer.

I wiggled deeper into the fluff of covers and got comfortable. I was going to need uninterrupted concentration to pull this off, the kind that's very difficult to achieve after a long, trying, tiring day. Still, the thought of seeing Eran again helped me overcome my anxiety.

Memories of him flashed through my subconscious. His beautiful, scintillating face was so clearly defined in my mind, I felt like I could easily sketch him. The presence of his conceit was undeniable, always there, barely submerged beneath the surface…annoying me. As these memories broke apart and dissipated, I wanted to reach out and keep him with me.

I could not understand why he had such a strong pull, so much command, over my emotions. It wasn't fair, even if it kept me intrigued. There was something about Eran that I could not figure out. Eran…who did not live in my neighborhood or attend my school…had the uncanny ability to suddenly appear whenever I needed him.

As ridiculous as it made me feel to admit, none of this made any sense. This is precisely why I was calling him here.

The real question, however, was…how? How did one summon somebody to their bedroom?

Think, I told myself.

Eran appeared only when I was in trouble, or more precisely, when I was about to be in trouble. What plagued my mind was how he knew. There was the possibility that he followed me, but I discarded that thought almost immediately. I was observant enough that I would have seen him. It could have been dumb luck, but that seemed out of the question. Too improbable. Regardless, being in trouble seemed to be the key. So I concentrated on how best to create trouble for myself. This would be difficult, especially in the comfort and safety of my own bedroom.

Think…think….

I laid like that for several minutes, trying desperately to come up with something, anything, that would put me in danger, but short of burning the house down, I came up blank.

I was sure my five-minute time limit had passed long ago, so despite my disappointment, I resigned myself to the failure, opened my eyes, and sat up in a huff.

And there he was.

Eran stood directly in front of me - at the foot of my bed - smirking.

"I was beginning to think you weren't going to sit up again," he stated in his captivating accent.

We were inches away without a single part of our bodies touching, invisible currents of excitement charged between us. If he was breathing, I didn't notice, but my breath was trapped in my lungs for a punctuated minute, as we continued staring, at each other, silently, hesitantly.

I recognized that my head was beginning to swim from lack of oxygen, which he must have noticed too.

"Inhale, Magdalene," he coaxed, softly.

I finally allowed my lungs to open, enjoying the cool, refreshing feeling as they filled up. Still, our eyes were locked, and I nearly shook with the thrill of having him so close. Surprisingly, I was able to contain it.

He watched me curiously, unmoving, as I collected myself.

"How-how did you get in here?" I asked, finally able to formulate words.

"Weren't you interested in seeing me?" he responded, being only slightly troubled.

I was uncomfortable with the fact that he called me out, but denying it would do no good. It was obvious to me now – though I had no idea how I achieved it – that he had come because of me.

"How did you get in here?" I repeated, feeling stupid.

"You have a trellis up the side of your house."

"I do?"

He nodded.

"Oh."

"You don't look like you're in mortal danger so did you need something else specifically?" He lifted his eyebrows, insinuating.

I hesitated, uncertain of wanting to go through with the line of questioning I brainstormed. But I knew, now was the time to ask them, or I may never have another chance. Given Eran's unpredictability, there was no telling when he would show back up.

"How did you know I wanted to speak with you?" I demanded, quietly.

"Ah, that …," He took a step back, leaning against the dresser Rufus gave me so I'd stop hogging the bathroom. His hands curled around its edges, allowing his muscles to expand across his shoulders and chest, straining against the thin, black sweater he was wearing. I was momentarily distracted.

Regaining my composure, I asked, "Are you going to answer me?"

"I wasn't sure how."

"The truth always helps," I suggested.

"No…that's not what I mean…" He seemed to struggle for the words to explain. "I'm…I'm not sure how I do it."

It was clear he was as frustrated as me. I gave him time, glancing around my room and noting that I hadn't picked up a single stitch of clothing in what looked to be a week. I made a movement to begin straightening up, and make my room presentable, when he began to speak.

"Typically, I don't feel you. Most of the time there is…nothing. Then, something happens. It's either a slow build up or…or an intensely quick response, but suddenly I'm overwhelmed with a feeling that I can only attribute to the sensation of panic."

Oddly, I was able to discern that he just uncannily described every instance of fear that I was beginning to sense these last few days. I nodded, asking him to go on, and waited.

His eyes dropped to the floor, flitting back and forth, as if they would reveal some understanding of what he experienced.

"Then I have an uncontrollable need to find you, to protect you." His eyes were usually so certain, but now, so confused, rising back up to meet mine. In a rush of words, making me think he was slightly embarrassed to announce them, he declared, "I can think of nothing else then until I see that you are safe."

"But you came tonight...even though I wasn't fearful, or in any danger."

"Right, I did," he said, still perplexed. "Tonight was different. I...I felt a...yearning. From you."

The realization of those words spread through me like hot liquid, and now, it was my eyes that dropped to the floor, avoiding his. I could feel the heat creep up over my cheeks and across my forehead. I had never been more mortified in all my life.

"It's nothing to be ashamed of," he assured me, though I detected humor beneath his words.

Yet, it was something to be ashamed of. He had no control over the feelings that pestered him when it pertained to dealing with me – he'd just made that clear - whereas I did have control. I had no excuse.

I realized he was waiting patiently for my reply, watching me with his intense blue-green eyes.

"I have more questions," I whispered, my head still down, wishing the flush would fade faster.

He stepped forward, tucking his finger under my chin and gently lifting it so I was forced to look up. A shock ran through my body when he touched me and intensified when our eyes met. "I don't think any less of you for asking me to come here." He exuded a tenderness that made his words unquestionably sincere.

I gave him an awkward smile, intended to be an unspoken thanks for pacifying my ego. He really could be chivalrous, when he put forth the effort.

But then, he dropped his hand and stepped back against the dresser again, adding playfully, "It's really not your fault. You can't help yourself when it comes to me."

I sneered at him, but still laughed. "Funny …."

"Not really. I rather enjoy it."

I couldn't be certain, whether he meant what he said or he was still teasing, but I decided it was safer to change the subject anyways.

"I did call you here for a reason …."

"Yes, you said you have questions." A smile played on his lips. "Shoot."

I sat up on the foot of the bed before beginning. I needed to see his reactions, and that position gave me a better vantage point. My flushing was finally starting to diminish, thankfully.

"You're not from around here, are you?" I asked, starting with an easy one.

"I'm close enough."

"Where?"

"Close enough." There was no arrogant grin accompanying what appeared to be teasing banter. Instead, his face was firmly set, undeterred.

I sighed. "You agreed to answer my questions."

"I did and I will. But you'll need to allow me to do it on my own terms."

"Is that the new agreement?"

"It is."

I rolled my eyes. "Alright then … under the new agreement, will you explain to me why you only appear when I'm in danger?"

"Well …," He chuckled to himself. "The simplest answer is, you need saving."

I sighed in frustration at his perception, muttering, "What I mean is, why don't I ever see you any other time? You don't live in this neighborhood, I've checked."

His eyebrows rose. "You have?"

I ignored him. "I also noticed you don't go to my school. So where are you when you're not … here?"

"Busy, very busy."

"Saving others?"

"Nope …," He shook his head back and forth slowly. "You demand too much of my time to allow for that."

I groaned. "Thanks for the reminder."

He moved, startling me; but seeing my reaction he stopped halfway to the bed. "May I?"

"Yes …," My heart began to pound harder, knowing his intention was to sit beside me, narrowing the space between us.

When I felt the weight of his body dip down, causing its own indention in the mattress, I thought my heart was going to explode through my ribcage.

I was almost certain its heavy pounding was audible, when he asked, "You're sure?"

"Of course…"

The nearest parts of our bodies were inches away again, and I could feel the heat radiating from him. Although, when I glanced up, he didn't appear flushed at all. He was calm and collected. "Look, I'm not certain how to explain this but…I will do anything…anything to keep you safe. It's not a burden. You're not taking anything away from me. This is my willful choosing."

"But why? I don't understand. You barely know me," I asked, bewildered by his declaration. "We just met a few days ago, and I've only seen you three times before tonight."

He dipped his head, displaying a bemused, secretive grin. There was something he wanted to explain, something to confess, but he held back. Instead, he seemed to choose a different response. "You are more important than you give yourself credit for, Magdalene."

"How could you possibly believe that? There's no reason to...."

"You're important to me."

Hearing those words made my heart flutter and my head snap up, facing him for the first time since he'd sat down. He was already staring down at me. "I am?" I whispered.

He smiled softly. "More than you know."

I felt a grin slowly invade my face.

The tension was quickly growing between us. We were captured in each other's eyes, unable and unwilling to break away. I clasped my hands in my lap, steadily working them, trying to expel the strain of having him so close and yet so untouchable. He, too, seemed to be struggling. His jaw was clenched tight, and his breathing was short and shallow.

Suddenly, his body stiffened and he blurted out, "Your questions...Do you have more?"

I was startled by the blunt ending to our intense moment. Feeling the flush return to my cheeks, I wondered if I had just imagined it all. No...I decided...I saw the unmistakable craving in his eyes.

I was confused; why did he abruptly end our moment? Stumbling over my response, I answered "I...yes...I do...actually."

He seemed to breathe a sigh of relief, but I couldn't be sure. "How did you move so fast when the snake came out of my bag?"

"Would you rather I let the snake attack you?"

"That's not what I mean...."

After quietly pausing, he admitted, "I know what you mean."

"Then will you answer me?"

"Yes, but before I do, I'd like you to answer one question for me."

"Sure," I replied, hesitantly. Now I felt the scrutiny that Eran must be feeling.

"What else have you noticed about me?"

I shrugged. "You're impenetrable, you move extremely fast, and..." I let my voice trail off, surveying everything I had noticed.

"Yes," he pressed.

"No one else seems to see you but me."

He allowed his gaze to drop, but he didn't answer. So I went on.

"You appear and then vanish like a ghost. You aren't injured from venomous snake bites. You aren't killed by wayward, incredibly sharp arrows." Then, I reiterated, "I am the only one who can see you...how is any of this possible?"

"You do pay attention," he said, sounding almost regretful, though I didn't understand why.

"Yes, now will you tell me how you are capable of all that?"

He paused, still looking at me, as he collected his thoughts. The muscles throughout his body visibly flexed, tensing as he prepared his answer. "I have certain...gifts...that not many others can claim...gifts of speed, healing, and regeneration, to name a few."

He paused, waiting for my reaction.

"Don't worry so much," I said, teasingly. "I'm not going to run screaming for the door."

We quietly laughed together for a brief moment. When I felt like he was comfortable again, I asked my next question.

"So, where did you get these gifts? Did your parents take some sort of special drug?"

"Not exactly. I can't answer that, as much as I know you'd like me to. Just suffice, Magdalene, to know that without these gifts, you wouldn't be here right now."

"I realize that."

"That's good. It'll make my job easier the next time."

I rolled my eyes. His assumption that there would be a next time was arguable, but I knew bringing up that point would be futile. "So what are your other gifts? You hinted that there are more."

"Oh...I can control mechanical things. Your motorcycle...for instance...the first time you saw me. Remember, you were about to collide with me in the middle of the street and thought you were losing control, but really, I took over...turning it for you before the Mustang could make contact."

"Really?" I was intrigued. "So why did I end up in the hedge? Hmm?"

He grinned at me. "Now that wouldn't have happened if you hadn't been counter-steering."

"How was I supposed to know you were trying to handle the bike for me? I just wanted to avoid crashing."

He threw back his head and laughed, quietly but full of passion. Finally subsiding, he spoke again in a hushed tone. "It's also how I got through your balcony doors tonight. I can pick locks, without even having to touch them."

"Really? That must come in handy..." I mused.

"It does." He beamed mischievously at me. "But I don't want to startle you. I wouldn't have done it if I hadn't sensed that you wanted to speak to me."

"Thanks, but it really doesn't bother me. I have nothing to hide."

"I see," he mumbled thoughtfully. "I wish I could say the same."

The severity of his tone made me fall still, a reaction he must have sensed. Tension surged between us again; although, this time it was uncomfortable.

"If you have nothing further...," he said, standing suddenly. He was tight-lipped, not bothering to wait on a reply from me before heading toward the balcony.

"Wait!" Not wanting him to leave, I reached out and grabbed his arm. I was instantly reminded how hot he was to the touch when our skin made contact. It almost felt like a flame had solidified, and I was holding it. Without thinking, I jerked my hand back.

"Are you hurt?" he urgently asked. I detected softness in his voice.

"No, I...I just don't want you to leave." I couldn't believe my ego just allowed me to speak those words.

"I think it is best," he said, turning to face the door. "I've told you all I can."

"But...I still don't understand who you are...," I whispered. My voice sounded as if I was pleading.

He didn't answer immediately. Instead, he turned back toward me, his expression slowly changing into longing. The look on his face made me feel ashamed to have asked and desperation came over me, reflecting my own needs. I wanted to help him answer, but I knew any sound I made would threaten the delicate balance he was clearly now fighting. In the end, he erred on the side of caution and chose not to tell me the truth. "You know my name...," he stated finally.

"There's more to you than a name," I replied, almost sounding bitter. "Even if you won't tell me, I see it. Whatever you are holding back...whatever your secrets are...you can share them with me; I won't judge you."

I saw a flicker of unease cross his face, I assumed in reaction to my insight.

I heard footsteps outside my door and realized someone was approaching. Despite Eran's searing heat, I instantly grabbed his arm again; wanting to make sure he didn't get away.

Sure enough, after a quick knock, Felix's head popped through the narrowly opened door.

"Ready for dessert?" he asked, gleaming like a kid who'd just been given a cookie.

He looked directly at me...not beyond, where I was still holding Eran's arm.

I yawned as convincingly as possible – which proved to be a challenge since my heart was racing from the excitement of Eran being here and the trepidation surrounding our conversation. "I'm more tired than hungry, but thanks Felix."

"Are you certain? Its rhubarb pie made with gluten-free, corn crust!"

"I'm sure. Thanks," I said, waiting for Felix to close the door before turning back to Eran.

I released Eran's arm, snapping my hand away and shaking it vigorously; as if that would stop the pain tingling through my fingers, reaching up my palm.

"How is it you are so hot all the time?" I asked, staring at my hand, amazed that once again no damage had been done.

"Sorry about that," he said, although he was grinning. "Sort of goes with the territory."

I shook my head in exasperation. "Do you know how hard it is for me to have you stand here and still not be able to figure you out?"

He scoffed. "Do you have any idea how difficult you make this for me?"

"Make what difficult exactly?"

"Being around you. You're impossible to please, you know. You think I'm puzzling...you're the enigma, Magdalene...you don't want to be rescued even when it is painfully obvious you need it. You keep me busier than I've ever been...and that's saying something! You have a desperate desire to help others, yet you never let anyone else close enough to help you."

I was disturbed by his rant...especially because he seemed to know me so well in such a short amount of time.

Silence filled the room as we stared at each other, his intense eyes boring into me.

When I spoke my voice was no higher than a whisper. "You know, even if I'm important to you, as you say...it still doesn't seem as if you like me. I don't understand why you're trying to help me at all."

He moved a step closer, his body heat hitting me like a tidal wave so forcefully that I had to steady myself against the bed. He must have thought this meant I was taking a step back because he froze in reaction, but when he spoke his voice was tender.

"It will be much easier on you if you simply let me do what I need to do."

"Well, it doesn't look like I have much choice in the matter, does it?" I spoke lightly.

He laughed. "No, you don't."

I shook my head, truly mystified. Why wouldn't he just tell me what he was holding back? Then I looked up and saw his smile and it became more difficult to breath. How could he be so handsome when I was so angry at him?

He headed for the balcony again, but just before he stepped out the door, he turned back.

"You're wrong about me not liking you," he said earnestly, and I felt my heart skip a beat.

As if he heard it, he flashed a smug grin and disappeared over the railing.

I stood there anticipating the impact of his landing, but there was only dead air...no crash...no commotion. I darted for the balcony to lean over and examine the trellis he used.

My mouth dropped open.

There was a trellis, but it was leaning against the back of the house...twenty feet away. I walked the perimeter of my balcony, searching for any possible way up.

There was none.

A curious smile rose up as I shook my head in amazement.

Once again, he'd disappeared - quickly and quietly – without any trace.

Staring out from the balcony at the vacant street below, I realized that a big part of me – far bigger than I wanted to acknowledge – was hoping and waiting for his return.

Groaning in frustration, I decided I was too exhilarated to sleep. Before I was even downstairs, I heard Ezra, Rufus, and Felix passionately debating the value of oil versus butter.

Stepping into the kitchen, Felix let out a hoot.

"You came!" he squealed, jumping up to hastily prepare a plate of pie.

"Think you'll be regrettin' it..." said Rufus.

"Hey...you're eating it!" Felix retorted.

Rufus winked at me – signaling that the pie was edible.

After setting a slice in front of me, Felix sat and continued devouring his own.

"So Felix..." I said, picking up the fork he gave me. "Where did you ever learn to cook so well?"

Rufus broke into a fit of laughter. In reaction, Ezra elbowed him in the shoulder.

Felix scowled at him before answering. "I studied under the top chef in Paris," Felix announced. "I'll have you know."

He gave me a firm, proud nod.

"I didn't know that. Very impressive."

Felix went on to explain how he'd branched off and began learning to appreciate creative expression using various foods that most would consider too healthy to incorporate into their dishes.

Much later that night, long after we'd all reinforced Felix's belief that he was an excellent cook, I laid awake listening to the jazz music coming from bars down the street. As I analyzed my conversation with Eran from earlier, I paid close attention to how I felt at each moment.

I rolled over to look out the French doors I'd left open a crack. My mind was focusing on Eran's sudden appearance through those same doors only a few hours ago and I had to fight the wishful feeling that it would happen again…right now.

I swung my legs over the tall bed and slid down to the floor. I then quietly tiptoed out onto the balcony so as not to wake my roommates.

I glanced down and recalled how Eran had managed to land soundlessly. Considering the distance to the ground, it was nearly impossible.

Not being the least bit tired, I sat down in the chair and propped my feet up on the railing to think back over tonight's passionate interaction with Eran and, in particular, his last statement to me.

He admitted to liking me. Not in those words exactly, but it still lingered in my mind like a pleasant daydream. He also called me an enigma, but he was the epitome of an enigma, something I'd have to express to him when I saw him next…which I found myself hoping to be very soon.

5. MESSAGE

By the end of the first week in school, the arrow incident had become nearly legendary...thanks to Ashley and Bridgette, who both enjoyed flaming the story. Teachers even knew of it, and I got special glares from The Warden between classes, so I was certain he'd heard about it too. I really didn't feel it was all that noteworthy and just wished people would drop it. Although, I did notice it seemed to help everyone overcome their fear of talking to me. Even if Achan's intent was to harm me, he'd only succeeded in escalating my popularity.

The one question everyone kept asking was how the arrow didn't leave a wound. A few people even asked me to lift my arms, proving I wasn't hiding an injury to my torso.

Truthfully, I couldn't explain it either, and this seemed to frustrate everyone else as much as it did me. Of course, I never mentioned the fact that Eran had interceded and suffered the brunt of the arrow...not me.

Most of the time I tried to listen more intently to the teacher's lectures, trying to ignore the fuss over the incident and take my mind off the seemingly impossible task of steering my attention away from thoughts of Eran.

Friday, I met Gershom under the tree we ate lunch at and saw he already had his sandwich and chips spread out in front of him. I also noticed the annoying electrical sensation was once again building inside me. With each step I took toward him, this reaction intensified.

"So you stick with the same sandwich too?" I noted, ignoring the pulling at the back of my neck.

He was in the middle of chewing, so he responded with a nod. After swallowing, he informed me, "You are at the top of everyone's mind."

"Oh…so you've heard."

"Achan was given a lot of razzing for it in first period," Gershom said as he chuckled softly.

Good, I thought…let him squirm.

"He's in my class along with a couple of the guys on the team and they made it pretty clear they don't believe he's at the skill level he boasted."

I intentionally continued chewing my sandwich so Gershom would keep talking. This was the first I was learning of Achan's reaction to the incident and the curiosity of it had been crowding my thoughts lately. As if on cue, Gershom was answering my unspoken questions.

"He sat there without saying a word. Apparently he's not too happy about the situation."

I laughed through my nose at the irony, knowing that was an understatement.

"Did he make any effort to apologize?" Gershom asked, taking a bite of his sandwich while watching me out of the corner of his eyes.

"No, but I don't expect one."

"Really?" His eyebrows lifted, and when I didn't explain further, he asked, "Why?"

I honestly did not want to go into my reasons, knowing that Gershom might think I was being paranoid to believe he was actually aiming for me all along. Instead, I offered a more politically-correct answer. "He doesn't strike me as to the type."

We both glanced over our shoulders at Achan, surrounded by his group of friends. He was sitting on the table with his feet on the seat, and despite his friends conversing around him, he didn't bother to engage. His attention was on me, directing a hateful glare at the back of my head. If he had a bow and arrow right then, I'm pretty sure he would have taken aim and used it.

"I think you're right," Gershom speculated, turning back around.

"I really don't care."

Gershom snickered. "No, you don't strike me as the kind of person that would."

He fell silent for a moment, looking out over the field at the distinct line marking the woodlands beyond. This time when he spoke, he was more serious. "Maggie...that arrow...did it come close like everyone says it did? I...I heard it came pretty close."

I shrugged. "That's what they said. I never saw it...never felt it." I summed up my escape for him the same as I'd done for everyone else. "I think it fell short..." suddenly an afterthought escaped my lips. Although my intention was never to vocalize it, I thoughtlessly added, "...much to Achan's disappointment."

Gershom's head abruptly swung around to face me. "You think he was aiming for you?"

I laughed uncomfortably because I really didn't know for sure, and I didn't mean to allude to it. "I was just saying that he's gotten a lot of harassment for his aim since then."

"Hmmm," he replied, turning his focus back to the lawn. "Can I ask you something?"

"Anything."

He was focusing on the field again but in a pensive state. "You don't seem to ever talk about your…ability," he ventured.

"No. Unless people inquire and want me to use it, I think it makes them uncomfortable."

"Yeah, I can see that happening."

I had a feeling Gershom wanted to ask me more questions, but he fell silent for a few minutes. In fact, he waited until his sandwich was gone entirely before speaking again.

Glancing at me hesitantly, he asked, "So…can I ask how you… finally knew?"

"You mean that I could talk to the dead?"

"Right. But it's more than that, isn't it? I thought…I thought you visit the afterlife…or at least the place people consider is the afterlife."

I let my sandwich fall to my lap because I knew my explanation would take some time.

"I do…but I didn't know for a long time actually. Since it happens in my sleep, I thought I was dreaming like everyone else does. You can't really jump into other people's dreams and compare them to your own, so I didn't know that people talking to you in your dreams regularly was…uncommon." I paused to laugh at myself, but Gershom didn't join in. He waited patiently for me to continue, his grave expression never wavering. "But then one day my next door neighbor passed on and that night he came to me, asking if I'd deliver a message to his wife. He wanted to tell her that there was cash stored in a coffee container in the back of the pantry. So that next morning, I went over and told her. I was young enough then, or stupid enough, to do it without understanding the consequences."

"Not stupid," Gershom corrected. "Brave."

I snickered. His perception was not quite accurate. "Bravery implies knowing the cost of opening the door…letting others know what I could do…and then

100

doing it anyways. No, I'd have to say I was not prepared for the penalty."

Gershom emphatically disagreed. "Even at a young age we know if we are different. We understand common behavior and know when we are deviating from it. I'm sure you did too. I think you're being modest."

I watched him closely for a moment. "You have a lot of wisdom for an eighteen-year-old."

Suddenly uncomfortable, he dropped his stare. "Being on the road…and alone…you learn a lot."

I knew the truth to that statement.

"So, I'm assuming you went ahead and told your neighbor's wife about the money," he persisted.

"Oh, yeah, I did. She slammed the door in my face, probably thinking I was playing some kind of mean joke on her. But later…while I was sitting on my doorstep questioning my sanity…deciding if I should get help…she walked across the lawn toward me, shaking, with a coffee can in one hand and a wad of cash in the other."

"Wow," Gershom said under his breath.

"And so…that's when I knew."

He nodded again, understanding. "Have you learned why you have the ability and others don't?"

"You know, that's something that I've always wanted to understand but have never been able to. I mean, look at me. I don't have any special markings or distinguishing characteristics. I don't surround myself with religious leaders or attend church regularly. I can't even recite a single scripture. As far as I know, I don't come from any holy gurus or spiritual leaders. I have no exceptional skill set that would explain me having this ability. There's really only one distinctive quality that I can think of that sets me apart."

"What's that?"

"I died just after I was born."

I expected Gershom to turn and gawk at me…lift his eyebrows…show some sign of surprise. But he didn't. Instead, he remained stoic, nodding slowly.

"My Aunt Teresa told me. It was in the same accident that took my parent's lives. I…I was the only one able to be revived."

My throat closed, chocking off any other words. Though, I had no intention of going on anyways.

I was sure Gershom noticed because he casually brushed crumbs from his jeans and changed the subject. "Do you enjoy doing it? Delivering messages? Or is it just something you feel you should be doing?"

"I visit each night whether I have messages or not. It's not by choice that I go there. But when I don't have anything to deliver, I get bored. I wait in the same place that I'm pulled to until I fall asleep again, then I'm brought back here. Sometimes it can be a very long night. So delivering messages keeps me busy…and it makes others happy."

"Why don't you just go visit people, the dead I mean?" he asked, seeming puzzled.

"Well, I don't really know anyone there. I've moved – either houses or cities - nearly every three months since…well, since I can remember. It's hard to keep friends when you change addresses that often. So, I don't know anyone really well, not anyone who has passed on anyways."

He thought about this for a moment and asked, "Why don't you just make friends with other people while you're there?"

"I have thought about it. I think about walking right up to someone and starting a conversation. But I feel…I feel like I'm overstepping a boundary, like I'm trespassing."

"You do? Don't people who have passed on exude an overwhelming feeling of acceptance?"

I drew in a deep breath, taking a moment to think about how best to answer, "They do," I confirmed, but I continued, offering more insight. "When I visit there, I don't know that I've actually crossed over. I've never been strapped to a machine while I sleep to record my heart beat or brain activity…And when I get there, I don't have the ability of flight or speed or telekinesis. I don't have any of those…proficiencies, for lack of a better word."

"You don't?" he asked, sounding baffled. "I wonder why that is."

"You got me."

He watched me observantly. "I don't think I've ever known how little you fit in…here or there…and how that must be challenging for you."

"It's tough, sure. But then you decide you don't really care if you fit in or not."

Gershom lit up with a comforting smile. "That's a healthy perspective."

"It's the only one, in my opinion. You can't live by others' expectations of you."

"That sounds like a belief developed over time, helping you deliver messages regardless of the naysayers…"

"It is."

"Maybe the reason you were given this ability then…is because you're the right person to use it," he theorized, sincerely.

"Honestly, Gershom. I'm not sure what to believe. I'll just keep helping others as long as this ability lasts."

"You know," he said, more to himself than to me, "you've done all right on your own."

"I like to think so."

"Can I ask you another question?"

"Gershom, you can ask me anything."

"With your ability to visit the afterlife…have you…" He paused awkwardly, taking a few seconds to overcome whatever was troubling him, and rapidly finished asking, "Have you ever tried to find your parents?"

I frowned and he immediately recanted, "You really don't have to answer that."

"I don't mind. I've wondered – a lot – whether they had the same ability as I do. So, sure…I looked for them. But the only way I know to locate people in the afterlife is by knowing their date and location of death, and I've never been able to find that information here on earth. For some reason, every record in existence that contained that information has disappeared. Isn't that strange?"

Gershom pinched his lips closed, reacting to what I'd just said. When he didn't answer, I went on.

"I mean think about how many documents record a person's death…police reports, death certificates, obituaries, cemetery plot purchases…every one of them is gone."

"Yeah, that's strange," he replied, flatly.

Although he was now looking away, I could see pain on his face and was taken aback by it.

"It was a long time ago, Gershom."

"Not so long ago…" he said under his breath.

"What was that?" I asked, my heart skipping a beat.

But he was already starting to stand up, his expression blank. "Huh? Oh…I said I gotta go."

"You did?" I swear I'd heard him clearly, even if he was mumbling.

"Yeah. Look, do me a favor, okay?" he asked quickly glancing over to where Achan was sitting. This made me curious because I didn't understand what Achan had to do with Gershom's request.

Still, I replied, "Sure. I'll do anything for you." And I meant it.

That proclamation made his painful expression return. "Could you deliver a message for me to someone?"

"In the afterlife?"

"Yeah," he replied, stuffing his trash into his lunch bag.

I paused, watching him and remembered my promise to Ezra that I wouldn't provide services to students at school. Had I really promised though? Wasn't it more of an agreement to an unspoken request? I was rationalizing, and what harm could it do? It was only one measly little delivery. Of course, I knew I was only convincing myself. Still, Gershom was my friend...and I'd already said I would. So I ignored the knot in my stomach, deciding to commit the information he was about to give me to memory.

"Look, I know how this is going to sound but...he died July 3rd, 1863 in Gettysburg, Pennsylvania-"

"At the Battle of Gettysburg?" The surprise made my voice rise and those nearby started glancing in our direction. I lowered my voice, asking, "How do you know someone from back then?"

"I don't," he said, pausing and looking over my shoulder. He was now facing me and I got the distinct feeling that he was seeking out Achan.

As expected, when I turned just enough, I found Achan's spine-chilling gaze fixed on us. The hair on my neck had been antagonizing me the entire lunch hour sitting next to Gershom, but all of a sudden, they went absolutely haywire. I was really getting annoyed with this response.

"Listen," Gershom went on, a little more urgently. "I never actually met the guy but...just humor me, alright?"

"Okay," I shrugged, completely confused. "What's the message you'd like me to bring to someone you never met and who died around a hundred and fifty years ago?" I teased, pointing out the absurdity of his request.

"Tell him that he should consider coming back."

"To earth?" Again, my voice raised and I snapped my mouth shut.

Gershom's shoulders fell in frustration. "Just give him the message."

He turned and headed toward the cafeteria door when I stopped him.

"Gershom? What's the guy's name?"

I thought it was odd that Gershom didn't just shout it out. No one would have understood what we were talking about anyway, but instead, he returned to where I was sitting and crouched down. This time, I was facing Achan's direction and noted that he was still intently watching us.

"His name is Eran. E-R-A-N...Talor...T-A-L-O-R."

"Eran?" I enunciated. The sound of that name caused all the nerves in my body to come alive, and to my embarrassment, it was obvious because Gershom's eyebrows immediately creased, displaying a puzzled expression.

"Yes...why?"

"Oh," I laughed, embarrassingly. It was idiotic that one name had such an impact on me. "I just...I met an Eran recently. So of course he's not the same guy as yours because...well...he's here on earth."

Gershom didn't crack a smile. He just stared at me, unblinking for a moment and simply said, "Of course." He began to stand again but paused. "You'll deliver the message tonight, right?"

"Sure," I nibbled a piece of my sandwich, hiding the fact that the mention of Eran's name still had me tingling. "Tonight."

Gershom then hurried across the lunch area and through the glass doors. I watched him leave, wondering what the probability was that he and I would both know an Eran. It wasn't a very common name, despite its meaning. I remembered it from a book I had read a while ago. The name had its heritage in Hebrew and meant watchful and vigilant. It was definitely an appropriate expression for the

Eran I knew because his intentions are to keep me alive. Gershom hadn't given me any reason to believe the two were the same, but something deep inside, a feeling I couldn't explain, made me think they were one and the same.

If they were, that would mean Eran was...I couldn't bring myself to even think the word. I looked out across the field, tossing around the idea of it, and the word suddenly popped into my mind, as if willed there by someone else.

Supernatural.

That would certainly explain why no one but me could see him and why he was immune to injuries. But it didn't lend reason to why I could speak with him...or touch him...or feel his intense heat.

When the bell rang I stood, headed for my next class, fencing, and continued silently debating the impossibility of Eran being supernatural.

I noticed that rain clouds had moved in when the first sprinkle landed on my nose. Then, by the time I was inside the gym, it started coming down in sheets.

Inside, the gym smelled even mustier with the drops pounding the thin roof overhead. The lamps mounted to the ceiling flickered once, causing a few gasps, but they stayed on. Ms. Valentine, a heavy set woman with a voice deeper than most men's, didn't seem to care. She was going to hold class with or without light and marched to the center of the gym floor.

"Sit," she commanded, like a military officer, and we obeyed, moving like cattle to position ourselves around her in a circle.

Ms. Valentine's class is relatively liberal, allowing us to choose any place on the mat we wanted in the absence of chairs. Of course, I decided earlier I wanted to arrive late, so I would have to sit in the back. So much for that idea.

Lying at Ms. Valentine's feet were three sword-like weapons which she reviewed in great detail with us, pointing out that the foil was the one we would use for this class. She was naming each part of the foil when the hair on the back of my neck stood up again. I almost uttered a curse word under my breath when the gym door opened and The Warden walked in.

"Ms. Valentine….," he interrupted without waiting for her to end her sentence. "I'd like to introduce your newest student."

He snapped shut his umbrella and ushered in a girl so stunning that a few of the guys audibly drew in their breath. She was Indian and had dark brown hair that hung straight down, nearly the entire length of her petite frame. She was wearing a white tank top and a red pagmina wrapped around her shoulders which made her dark skin that much more striking. I would guess that every other girl in the room felt they paled in comparison. This was probably because every guy in the class instantly sat up. Their undivided attention settled on the new student, waiting for her introduction.

"Sarai Patel…this will be your fencing class," The Warden said, his fingertips lingering on her shoulder as he guided her through the door. "Ms. Valentine will ensure you are treated exceptionally well. Won't you, Ms. Valentine?" He turned to our teacher, pursing his lips and flashing a fierce expression.

She must have been just as stunned as I was by his sudden change in behavior because she stuttered over her words. "Of-of course. She'll-she'll be well taken care of."

"Sarai is from Hawaii. She'll be staying in New Orleans for the remainder of the year, while her parents are taking an extended vacation in Bombay."

With The Warden's proximity to Sarai and his stern protection of her, it almost looked like The Warden was under some sort of trance.

The girl, however, didn't seem to notice his overtly personal interest in her. She had her attention directed at the class.

During The Warden and Ms. Valentine's brief discussion, Sarai was busily scanning the room, until her eyes landed on me. They locked with mine and something in them flashed. It seemed to be hatred, but I couldn't be certain.

Ms. Valentine escorted Sarai to a place on the mat. Only then did she break her stare as she was forced to sit in front of me, facing the teacher. Matt and Josh, sitting on each side of her, immediately leaned in with broad, giddy smiles and introduced themselves, fighting for her attention.

The Warden lingered at the door a few minutes, watching the display and appearing disgruntled. As Ms. Valentine continued her lecture, he reluctantly opened his umbrella and stepped out into the rain, watching Sarai until the door clicked.

For the remainder of class I was now the one staring at the new girl – along with most of the guys although not for the same reason.

If I had been given a pop quiz on the rules of engagement using a foil, I would have failed. I missed the entire lecture. Instead, my mind was focused on Sarai and how she made my hair stand on end, just like Achan…just like Sharar…just like Gershom. I was searching for any possible link between the four individuals who were capable of eliciting such a severe reaction from me.

They didn't come from the same place. This I knew because Achan had relocated from New York and Sarai was from Hawaii. None of them seemed to be from the same economic background, or even the same ethnicity, and they weren't the same age.

As far as I could tell, they didn't appear to know each other. Gershom knew of Achan from a distance, but they weren't friendly with each other. It was evident that Gershom held some level of disdain for Achan, though it probably wasn't as high as mine.

By the time I left the gym, there was only one thing I was certain of. They each scared me...beyond understanding; and I had never even been fearful before...of anyone or anything...in my life.

6. THE GIFT

I was shocked when I got home and found Felix in the kitchen. It was Friday, a very good day to make cash on tourists coming in for the weekend. He was puttering across the tile floor with his typical white apron emblazoned with the words, "When all else fails...everyone is gagging...and the stove is on fire...I read the recipe." Those words couldn't be truer, but today, surprisingly, the kitchen actually smelled delicious.

"What are you cooking?" I asked, dropping my backpack on the table. I immediately noticed the ceramic white holder that was absolutely taboo for Felix. "You're using butter? Good for you."

He gave me a wide-toothed grin. "Lard too."

"No!" Bringing my hands up to my hips, I demanded, "What's gotten into you?"

He cocked his head back regally. "I am making everyone a good old-fashioned southern meal!"

"Really?" I was intrigued.

"I am, of course, only using organic ingredients."

"Of course," I said, grinning back. "What's the meal?"

"Blackened catfish, sautéed greens, black-eyed peas, and cornbread muffins!"

"Sounds great!" It really did, so much so my mouth began watering. "Can I help? It's Friday so homework can wait."

"No, it cannot," he insisted.

It always amazed me at how dedicated my roommates were to my education.

"Don't worry, Felix. I can do it at The Square over the weekend." It was hard to resist laughing at his adamancy.

To my relief, that seemed to placate him. It surprised me when he started untying his apron.

"What are you doing? I thought we were cooking."

"There's one last ingredient I have to pick up…and I need your help to get there. Will you drive?"

"For this delicious meal? Anywhere."

"Excellent!" He immediately went to work finishing what he could while I made sure to turn off the stove, the oven, and the broiler. When Felix cooked, no single appliance went unused and every cooking utensil, pot, and pan in the house ended up stacked in the sink. Since it appeared he was only midway through the meal preparation, the dishes were only barely breaching the sink rim, but I mentally prepared myself for more.

"So where are we going?" I asked, arranging the dishes in the sink for easier washing later.

He peered over his shoulder with a mischievous grin. "Well…I had to leave the car for Rufus – knowing his arteries are clogged with animal fat I figured I shouldn't push the subject – but I still need to pick up alligator for my appetizer." He made a tantalizing sound and announced, "Cajun Alligator Sausage."

"Alligator?" I was appalled and didn't mind showing it.

"Darling, you'll love it," he said enticingly. "I need a mode of transport to and from and that, dear Mags, is where you come in."

Brushing the last of the flour from the counter into the sink, I smiled at him even though he had his back to me. I was getting used to him calling me by my nickname. In fact, it was almost endearing now, something I wouldn't have bet my life on a few weeks ago.

"Come, come." He clapped the rest of the flour from his hands noisily. "We mustn't keep our fishermen waiting." He grabbed my hand and dragged me with him out the back door.

"Fishermen? Felix, where exactly are you taking me?"

"Oh, you'll see…," he replied mischievously.

A few minutes later the shed was unlocked and my bike was ready to go. I handed him a spare helmet I happened to pick up recently for just this type of situation and he frowned. "Blue? This color does not go with my outfit."

"Felix," I groaned. "No one will know it's you."

"I will," he grumbled, slipping it over his head anyways.

Once on, I didn't bother to stifle my laughter.

"What? I look ridiculous, don't I? I knew it."

With his orange hair spiking out from underneath the helmet's edges, he almost looked like a cartoon character. "It's fine. It's not high fashion. It's safety equipment, meant to keep you alive so you can look good another day."

"Fine, fine. Let's get on with it." His voice was muddled through the helmet, but I could still hear the dissatisfaction in his tone.

I ignored it. Helmets were one area I did not budge on.

He refused to give me a final destination saying it was too many turns. He was right. He chose instead to direct me with taps to my shoulder when he wanted me to turn right or left, and there were a lot of taps. He led me to the freeway heading out of town, where he tightened his hold on me as I increased the speed.

"Relax! Enjoy the ride!" I yelled back to him.

He screamed something in response but the wind carried his voice away. I was able to catch something about his stomach being left behind.

We drove for a good two hours, exiting close to Lafayette. From there, he took me on a road with more potholes than smooth pavement – which was not easy to maneuver on a motorcycle. The route was chaotic too. We took so many turns that I was surprised Felix remembered them all. Eventually, we ended up on a dirt road running along a wide, muddy river. Green trees ran along the side of us obstructing anything set farther than fifty feet, except for two colossal alligators resting in the shallow marshes. It looked like we were going to meet a dead end in the middle of nowhere and I was getting ready to stop and insist we turn around when a shanty appeared up ahead. Felix began tapping my right shoulder feverishly, so I figured we'd finally reached our destination.

I parked my bike next to a decaying pickup truck - which looked like it'd been cured in swamp water for at least a decade before being hauled up - and an equally rusted bicycle with one flat tire, although it was standing upright as if it had been ridden here.

The shanty sat at the very edge of the swamp. It had been painted red at one time, but the humidity had taken its toll until it became a mixture of rotting grey wood and maroon paint peels. The trees here were covered in moss and so dense you couldn't see farther than twenty feet into the water. A porch wrapped around the shanty, sagging so much on the right side it dipped into a large muddy puddle stretching up from the swamp.

"How do you know this place?" I asked Felix, as we unstrapped our helmets.

"Ah, the culinary world is full of friends who are more than happy to suggest where to find good eatin'."

"So you were referred here?"

"Yep," said Felix, attempting to balance his helmet on the seat and failing; so he placed it on the ground, open side up.

"Ever tried their catch before?" I asked skeptically, noting the dirty moss creeping over the boats anchored to the porch.

Felix grinned back at me. "Have faith. In this part of the world, the older an establishment...the better the food."

He winked at me and sauntered toward the shanty.

In the porch shadows we could see a robust woman wearing a dark purple dress and an overwhelming number of different bracelets on both arms. She sat in a rocking chair, slowly creaking back and forth, smoking a pipe with a single curling wisp of white drifting up, collecting at the top of the porch overhang. Sitting next to her was a man well into his nineties, rocking in sync with her and wearing jean overalls with a white tank top. He, too, held a pipe, although his didn't seem to be lit.

Pulling the pipe from her mouth, she spoke with a thick Cajun accent, "Well podna, whot is it jew need? We gotta lotta caimon but ain't mucha of the crawfish."

"Caimon?" I whispered to Felix.

"That's alligator in Cajun," he leaned, whispering to me, but then yelled out to her, "Well you certainly have enough moustiques!"

She gave one bellowing laugh, "Ha!"

"Mosquitoes?" I asked, inferring.

"Good! You're quick, Mags." He smiled and launched into a Cajun dialect. "You canbe talkin' like one of them soon enough."

I snorted at the impossibility of it.

Even though we were approaching them, the woman didn't get up until we reached the porch. The man never once looked in our direction. He simply continued rocking back and forth with the pipe barely hanging on from the edge of his lips.

"We're looking for some plump, juicy caimon," said Felix, not bothering to hide his excitement.

"We got it," said the woman who'd already walked passed us heading for the screen door.

"I won't be long," said Felix with a quick, reassuring pat on my back before hurrying to follow the woman.

Their voices from inside were muffled, but I figured she was showing their catch of the day judging from the "oohs" and "ahhs" coming from Felix.

Outside, it was instantly noticeable how much more quiet it was here. I could hear a few crickets making chirping noises and the old man's rocking chair groaning in protest to the constant motion, yet these were quiet, slow sounds. Everything else was still.

"Mind if I take a seat?" I asked the old man, leaning in to see the name printed across a coffee mug sitting on the table beside him. "Battersbee…."

He didn't look at me or utter a word. In fact, if I hadn't been watching him, I would have easily missed the slight nod he gave toward the other now-available rocking chair to his left.

I took a seat, appreciating how comfortable it was even though it was made of wood.

"Nice…" I mumbled, as I stared out across the dirt road toward the trees lining the edge of the grassy weeds.

A few seconds passed with the two of us rocking in unison, Felix and the woman's voices reached us muddled from somewhere inside, and then the old man spoke. His voice was gritty and thick with a southern accent that I couldn't place. He wasn't Cajun, but I'd guess somewhere from the woods of Arkansas or Tennessee. That wasn't what left an impression with me, though. It was his words that caught me off guard.

"Brought a spirit wit ya, I see."

"Excuse me?" I didn't think I heard him clearly. "I thought you said we brought a spirit."

"I did," Battersbee replied bluntly.

"We brought a spirit with us?" I asked, wondering if the man was senile. "How do you know that?"

"Oh, I kin see him. Out ova thea." He pointed with a nod of his chin toward my bike. "He's hazy...but he's thea."

I stared in the direction he'd motioned to, but I only saw an overgrown fence ending at the roadside.

"Who? Who's there? I don't see anyone."

"How should I know who he is? I neva met 'im," he replied, indignantly.

Battersbee rocked a bit more and started to describe the figure he saw.

"Tall...dark, wavy hair...limba – or as you Texians say," he drew out and pronounced the last word. "Limber."

I couldn't avoid the fact that his description sounded oddly like Eran, sparking my curiosity more.

"I'm not Texan," I corrected him, still staring in the direction he'd motioned.

The old man laughed to himself, but sounded slightly offended when answering. "It's what we call all you that ain't Cajun."

I chuckled at that, but Battersbee didn't join me. Returning to his original subject, I asked, "Why do you think he's here?"

Battersbee snorted. "How should I know?" He ventured on, guessing, "Sometimes thea tryin' to communicate. Sometimes thea just curious. Sometimes thea lookin' afta someone they know. Neva kin tell..."

A few minutes passed silently. I must have glanced to where Battersbee pointed no less than twenty times. Never seeing anything, yet I couldn't ignore the distinct, strong feeling of being watched.

"I still don't see him," I said, slightly frustrated.

"Maybe he don't want ya to. N' if that's the case, ya won't…that's the way it works. Communin' with the dead ain't done the same by everyone all the time. Different people…different times…different ways…."

"So you can commune with the dead?" I asked, watching his response.

"Used to. No need to now. I'll see 'em all in a short while anyways."

"A short while?"

Keeping his gaze focused straight ahead, he answered, "I'll be dead soon."

I stopped rocking immediately and sat motionless for what seemed to be an eternity, waiting for him to break into a teasing smile. He remained calm and continued rocking, as if he was just commenting on the weather. I had never seen anyone use such blunt words or emotionless acknowledgment when speaking of their alleged, impending death. It jolted me to the core. "I'm…I'm very sorry," I offered, not knowing what else to say.

"I ain't…my time is up n' I'm ready."

The way he said this comforted me in an odd way. Most likely because it never occurred to me that some people I deliver messages to in the afterlife were prepared to leave their loved ones on earth.

I watched him, wondering if I'd be ready when my time came.

"Thank you," I said, quietly.

"Fer what?"

"Informing me that death can be peaceful."

"That ya already knew," he stated simply.

I began to shake my head but he cut it short by reinforcing, "Ya know it 'cause you've got the gift."

I didn't reply immediately, my mind refusing to believe this complete stranger could know such an intimate, personal detail.

"The gift?" I asked, looking for clarification. I needed to make sure that he wasn't talking about something else entirely.

"Ain't many with that gift, though a lotta phonies."

I was still staring at him, but he never once looked my way...he just kept rocking.

"How-how did you know?" I stammered.

"When ya've been around as long as I have, ya get a sense fer things," he said, plainly. "Best take care yerself. Those with our talents don't stick around too long."

"That sounds like a warning," I said, staring at him and finding no comfort in his blank expression.

"It is." His tone was not ominous or dramatic. It was straight forward and unaffected; but I appreciated it.

Still the goose bumps rose up on my arms. "What do you mean?"

"They're out there. Lookin' fer ya. Anyone with our gifts. That's the way it works."

"What exactly...is the way it works?" I demanded, softening my voice, "And who are...they?"

Finally, Battersbee stopped rocking and turned to look at me. His face was impassive, but the way he whispered the answer chilled me.

"The Fallen Ones. You'll know them when they show up." He tapped his head with his finger. "We have built in radar."

My jaw fell open as images flashed through my mind, instantly switching from Achan to Sharar to Sarai to Gershom. I noticed even though none of them were with us, simply as a result of my thoughts, the hair on the back of my neck responded.

The strangest, most unexpected thing happened. I was flooded with relief. It made complete sense. I had known who they were before I understood it. The hair rising on the back of my neck told me so. I wasn't dealing with some odd affliction to my nervous system. I was sensing when they were around. This reaction had mystified me – a feeling that I hadn't been able to shake since the first time I saw Achan – or rather when Achan first saw me. It was as if I'd been walking around with a tack in my shoe, and each time I met any one of them, the annoying tack would land straight up as I stepped down. Battersbee, without even intending to, had just removed the tack.

I gasped in reaction to my realization.

"Hadn't known it, eh?" Battersbee chuckled.

"I didn't," I admitted. "I couldn't figure out why the hair on the back of my neck stands straight up when they're nearby."

Battersbee grunted. "Huh, they make my skin crawl. That's how I know. Everyone's different…."

I drew in a deep breath, feeling as if I had just finished a long, important exam.

A moment later, my relief was swallowed up by alarm. My dilemma had now changed from one of irritation to anxiousness, the kind you feel when you know someone's coming after you.

"They can be stopped though, right?"

Battersbee chuckled again. "You're one of them optimists, ain't ya?"

"Are you saying they cannot by stopped? That once they find you…you're dead?"

"That's about right," said Battersbee, indifferently.

"Are you sure?" I refused to believe there was no way to survive.

Battersbee reached over, lifted the coffee mug to his lips, and drew in a deep swig. A few seconds later, he dropped it to his lap and continued. "Knew a guy in Tulsa who'd been spotted. Thought the same thing. Surrounded himself with weapons, all kinds. In the end, they found him dead, weapons right beside him. Unused. They strike when ya least expect it. Nothin' ya kin do to stop 'em."

I laughed wryly. "I can vouch for that."

"Had some dealings with 'em, eh?"

"In a way."

Battersbee shook his head. "Best thing ya kin do now is run."

"Running isn't in my nature," I said, knowing I was being obstinate.

Battersbee glanced at me pointedly. "Is dyin'?"

I didn't bother to answer. It was a rhetorical question meant to make a point, and he'd made it just fine. But I did want to know more. Battersbee was the first person I could talk to about this situation, and he seemed knowledgeable.

"Where do they come from?"

"Been here long before any of us."

"How many of them are there?"

"Used to be hundreds. Not so many anymore. Died off I suppose," he replied, thoughtfully.

"They can die?"

"Oh, yeah. In their own way."

"How?"

"Depends. They all come with their own defenses. Some kin be burned...some stabbed...some beheaded. None of 'em die the same way. Ya have ta figure it out durin' the fight," said Battersbee, candidly.

"But they have vulnerabilities...," I said, eagerly searching for something positive, something hopeful.

Battersbee took another loud slurp from his coffee mug and said, "They're a lot like us from what I kin gather." Sighing heavily, he added, "N' not so much either."

"So...if they're similar to us there must be some good and some bad, right? Just because we're reacting to them can't mean every one of them is dangerous," I said, though my instinct was telling me that I already knew the answer.

"Radar was given to us fer a reason," Battersbee stated, plainly allowing his answer to be implied.

"So don't ignore it...is what you're saying, right?"

"Do what ya want," Battersbee said, shrugging, "It's yer life…yer death."

Felix emerged from inside the shanty carrying a thick bundle wrapped in white butcher paper.

"Alright, Mags, we got a couple of beauties!" Felix grinned widely, holding up the bundle as if I could somehow see through the wrapping.

I smiled, complimenting his choices, though I wasn't at all interested in the alligator.

"You ready?" Felix called out, already down the steps and heading for my bike.

I wasn't, but it didn't look like I had a choice.

I paused, shifting slightly in my chair to face Battersbee. It was disappointing that this man, who had such a significant impact on my life in the few minutes I had known him, would be passing on. "Could I…visit you again?"

He must have known my ability without having it explained, because he didn't seem the least bit surprised by my request. He simply nodded once and said in his gruff voice, "Any time."

He stuck his pipe back in his mouth and began rocking again, as if this pivotal conversation had never taken place.

I smiled at the woman as I passed her, but she was focused on Battersbee, sending him a questioning stare.

"Come on, Mags!" Felix called out, eager to get home and cook his alligator meat.

By the time we were backing up, the woman had taken a seat next to the old man. Both were watching us. I nodded, and they nodded back. I cautiously turned the bike and started down the dirt road.

Inside my mind, in case he had some extrasensory ability to hear my thoughts, I called out. "You take care, Battersbee…."

I would bet money that I heard his thick southern accent reply in the back of my ears, "You too."

I was thankful our drive home was going to take nearly an hour. It would give me time to think. My mind was busy sorting the information Battersbee had just given me.

I wasn't able to shove aside the realization of how foolish I'd been. All along this internal intuition had been trying to send me a signal, warning me against danger, and I completely ignored it – even tried to prevent it at times. To my defense, it wasn't like I could figure it out by simply studying the faces of those who elicited this response from me. Whenever they looked at other people they were impassive and showed no real joy or disappointment or anxiety, but when they looked at me their expressions grew dark and bitter, instantly reflecting what could only be defined with one word…hatred. Gershom was the only one who remained emotionless when focusing on me. Even if my sensor inside was triggered the same way with him as it was with the others, I never felt fearful of him.

Something didn't set well with me, like a piece missing from an otherwise complete puzzle. If all of the Fallen Ones were bad, that would include Gershom, but I couldn't comprehend how Gershom…who was so timid…so praising of me…and seemed so frightened of everything…could be dangerous.

Even if Gershom had wanted to hurt me, somehow overcoming his evident morality, he hadn't done so yet. There had been plenty of opportunity too, especially during every lunch period we spent together, and yet I remained unharmed. He had never even touched me. In fact, it always seemed like he went out of his way to make sure our fingers didn't connect, either when we both dug into a bag of chips at the same time or when I handed him half of my muffuletta sandwich. I took this as a sign of respect or a hidden message, indicating he was strictly interested in friendship. Still, I knew there must be some reason my signal went off whenever I was near him. Even if he didn't harbor the same ill intent as the others, there was no doubt in my mind that he was a Fallen One.

Knowing what he was, forced me to decide whether we could be friends. The level of danger involved automatically escalated beyond that of traditional friendships. With Gershom, the concern wasn't whether I could trust him to keep a secret but whether I could trust him with my life. Yet, Fallen One or not, Gershom's intentions always seemed to be in support of me. He had done nothing to prove himself to be anything less than a genuine friend. If I rejected him or his friendship, simply because he was a Fallen One, that would be just as prejudice as the other Fallen Ones' disdain for me based solely on my ability? I would be forced to consider myself equally as discriminatory as The Fallen Ones.

By the time we reached the house, I had decided firmly that until Gershom proved himself to be anything less, we would remain friends.

Tonight, I would still deliver Gershom's message. Fallen One or not, Gershom is my friend and he had asked me to do this.

Beyond that, there was one other reason I decided to follow through in delivering the message for Gershom. A reason that made me cognizant of how involved with Eran I was becoming, and I would take any chance I could to see him again. A part of me hoped, pleaded with the cosmic forces that made things fall into place that Gershom's Eran and my Eran would be one in the same.

7. DELIVERY

As I was getting ready for bed, I noticed how nervous I was. I should have been concentrating on how to keep myself alive considering the recent infiltration of the Fallen Ones, but all I could think about was Eran.

It took three tries just to get my toothbrush through the little hole in the stand, and I hit my hand so hard against the wall, trying to hang my towel, I was sure it was going to leave a nasty bruise.

You've done this before, I told myself. Many, many times before.

I knew delivering a message to someone in the afterlife tonight wasn't what had my heart racing. It was the prospect of who that "someone" was.

It made me feel ridiculous, but I kept considering whether the Eran I knew and the one Gershom knew were the same. I had to keep reminding myself the Eran I knew existed here on earth or I would never be calm enough to fall asleep.

On the way back to my room, Rufus was coming down the hall with his towel and soap in hand. He must have noticed my nervousness, because he stopped.

"Are ya doin' okay?" he asked, in his thick Irish accent.

"Yeah...have some things on my mind." I shrugged.

"Hmm. If it's 'bout classes rememba that ya won't care in ten years if ya miss a question or two; if it's 'bout friends ya got plenty of 'em in this house; and if it's 'bout a boy...give him a shot. Take pity on us wankers." He winked at me and continued his stroll to the bathroom.

Strangely, Rufus's advice made me feel a little more relaxed. When I got to my room, I closed the door, turned off the lights, and slipped into bed. It only took a few minutes before I was asleep.

I'm not sure if others enter the afterlife the same way I do. I've heard of tunnels and bright lights, an arched gate, even relatives greeting you. Any of that would be nice. I always wake up on a concrete bench in the middle of a large, stone hall lined with scrolls. Not the most welcoming way to arrive, which is why I figure it took me a while to realize I was actually visiting the afterlife in my sleep.

I picked myself up, giving a fleeting look to the clothes I had on. While most people believe everyone wears robes in heaven, I've never actually woken up in one. Oddly, I'm always wearing the same clothes in the afterlife that I'd dressed in that day. I went to school today in faded jeans, a band t-shirt, and my biker boots, so that was what I was wearing now.

A warm wind brushed past me and I glanced up in time to see someone flitting by. She was hovering a foot from the ground with her back arched and her feet dragging behind her. The purple dress she wore flew out behind her in waves as she moved through the hall, stopping only a few feet away.

Although she spoke in a different language, I understood what she meant. "Are you lost, dear?"

"No," I said, in English.

She smiled and nodded, moving on again, barely skirting the ground.

I watched her enviously. Since I was never given the ability to fly when visiting here, I enjoyed watching those who could. It was beautiful.

Snapping from my admiration, I quickly got to work.

Since I have to start my work in the Hall of Records anyway, it is efficient that I always wake up here. The hall contains the records of everyone's existence on earth, alphabetized by place of death.

I moved down the long corridor, finding the G's midway, and prepared myself for the climb.

One thing I could do in the afterlife very well was climb. For some reason, I had amazing strength and agility. I can haul myself over mountains as large as Everest, never breaking a sweat or needing to stop and catch my breath. That strength gave me some leverage. I could climb any wall in the Hall of Records in seconds whereas on earth it would have taken me hours and required cumbersome equipment. I rested my finger tips on the coarse edges that stuck out like very small shelves and slipped the toe of my boot into the lowest one, beginning my climb. It only took a few seconds to reach the place on the wall where I found Gettysburg.

Once there, I gripped the wall with one hand and pulled a scroll from its pocket with my other. I held one end and let the other end drop down.

Scrolls are made of liquid concrete. They are so light you wouldn't know it if one floated down and came to rest on you. They are flexible, moving with the fluidity of a flag dancing in the wind, while still retaining the durability concrete offers. If I could figure out how to create this material on earth, I'd be very wealthy.

A single list of names, written in cursive, stretched the length of each scroll. Some scrolls' names lasted only a few inches while others – in places where many had passed on – stretched down several feet. When this one unraveled it nearly reached the floor about five stories below.

I took a deep breath, noticing how shaky I was as I exhaled. "Gettysburg, Pennsylvania, July 3rd, 1863…Eran Talor." A lump gathered in my throat, as I spoke his name.

The scroll slipped up through my hands until Eran's name rested just above my thumb.

Eran Talor – Died Gettysburg, Pennsylvania, July 3, 1863
Previously Jacques Lafayette – Died Paris, France, July 14, 1789
Previously William Whitlock – Died London, England, April 13, 1665
Previously Thomas Jurgen – Died Muehlhausen, Germany June, 5, 1525

Three things struck me at once while reading down the list. First, Eran had gone back to earth only once each century; second, he'd lived in different places each time; and third, he'd gone back during eras of turbulence.

History was my favorite subject in school, so I read as much as I could on all cultures – far exceeding any of my teacher's requirements. If it wasn't for this, I would have missed the significance of the dates of Eran's deaths. From this list, it looked like he'd died during the Battle of Gettysburg, during the Storming of the Bastille in France, during London's Black Plague, and during the Peasant Wars in Germany.

As I surveyed the list, I knew I was delaying. What came next was the part of my delivery I could never quite get used to. I held my breath and drifted my finger over the name of his last time on earth, whispering to myself, "Eran Talor…"

A moment later, the stone wall I'd been holding dissolved from my grip, but I didn't fall. Instead, I was being carried – swiftly – as if a gust of warm wind had picked me up. Below me cities, forest, and oceans passed. Other people's heavens…There was no sound, just silence. The wind slowed, and I began to fall toward a distant territory.

This time, I was standing on the edge of a clearing, encircled by boulders. Instantly, I wondered if I'd made a mistake or something went wrong. Most people's heavens were typically constructed using simple reminders of their favorite things on earth, like spending a peaceful day at the beach or vacationing in tranquil Tuscan villas. I've even visited one designed around an amusement park with hot dogs appearing out of thin air by snapping your fingers and soda pouring from straws suspended throughout the park. But this heaven was definitely not typical.

All around me, bright, white lights flashed back and forth through the clearing, mimicking giant bolts of lightning. Some of them collided, resonating fantastic booms, but it seemed that most were evading each other.

I noticed with a slight amount of apprehension, the boulders surrounding me were too close together. A piece of paper couldn't be wedged between them.

It didn't take long to realize that despite the storm of lights swirling around me, I was going to need to climb out. I turned, gripping the jagged part of the rock, and hauled myself up. I was halfway to the top when I found myself being pulled back into the middle of the clearing. I landed nearly twenty feet away from where I'd been, hitting a hard dirt patch that would have broken bones if it had been on earth. One of the bright, white lights was hovering over me, and I realized I was in trouble. I grabbed a reed, conveniently lying at my side, bringing it up to defend myself just as the light came down on me. The entire instance – from the boulder to being attacked –

took less than a second. Whatever these things were, they moved fast.

That's when I heard a deep, rumbling laugh a few feet to my right. I had closed my eyes without knowing it, and suddenly, they snapped open. Staring up toward the sky, I found Eran standing over me, where the light had been just a second ago.

His blue-green eyes were wide and intense, focusing on me.

Something in the back of my mind registered that the light had been Eran. With all that action, I would have thought he'd be heaving for breath, but he wasn't. In fact, his mouth was pinched – again, showing disapproval.

I avoided his stare and sat up, quickly noticing I was surrounded by men, each wearing clothes from a different era and holding a staff. Eran was wearing clothes I was more familiar with…a flannel shirt, dark jeans, hiking boots, and a baseball cap. The staff he held was made of brass with a purple jewel at the top and looked out of place next to his informal attire. I'd never seen him so casual, yet despite the impracticality of it, he still managed to look like a model from a sporting goods catalogue.

"She has talent, Eran," said an Asian man with a braided white beard, hanging to his knees. A staff lay at his feet until he reached out his hand. As if he were beckoning it, the staff levitated and moved effortlessly into the man's waiting palm. "You may think about sparring with her from now on," he added, chuckling.

The men laughed and turned, as if they knew their warring session was over. Gracefully, they lifted off the ground, floating up over the trees.

Eran offered me a hand as I picked myself up, but I ignored it.

Once on my feet, he inspected me. "Are you hurt?"

I rolled my eyes. "I wish you'd stop asking that."

"And I wish you'd stop placing yourself in danger so I wouldn't need to ask."

He lightly snickered and delicately pulled a piece of straw from my hair, his hand coming so close to me that I quivered with excitement.

"Don't worry. No one will throw you to the ground again," he commented.

"Is that what happened?" I asked, brushing myself off. "It was so fast..."

This time he allowed himself a hurried laugh at my expense. "Ivan mistook you for me. I stepped in to stop him from pummeling you."

"Oh," I said, feeling ridiculous. "Thank you."

He blinked in surprise, taking a step back with mock sarcasm. "What was that? Did you actually thank me?"

"I don't mind thanking you when it's due."

"Well, like I've said, you're hard to please."

I grinned back, showing no hint of repentance.

"So," he said, leaning back against the side of a boulder. "You found me."

"I did," I said, taking a place beside him.

"I'm not surprised."

"Really? Why is that?"

"You're a smart girl. I knew you'd figure it out," he said, casually scuffing his heel in the dirt.

I thought at first that he was trying to avoid my eyes when delivering his compliment, but then he glanced up and gave me a wide grin.

"Well, I'm still a little confused. I mean...I saw you on earth. How can you be here when...when you're supposed to be on earth?" I shrugged, impulsively.

"I would have thought you'd have figured that out by now too," he replied, folding his arms across his chest, amused.

"Nope..." I replied, plainly.

"Now why would you think I could appear in both places?" he asked, teasing.

I let my gaze drop, thinking through the possibilities. "You're supernatural. That much is obvious. But…ghosts don't talk on earth, do they?"

He laughed lightly. "No, not often."

"So…you're not a ghost?" I asked, and to prove my point, I added, "Because you do talk to me."

"Correct."

"Then…are you a messenger too?"

He burst out laughing, cocking his head back so he could release it with full force. When he finished entertaining himself at my expense, he still didn't answer me.

"Are you?" I demanded.

He drew in a breath and clapped his hands in his lap, as if he were going to be here for a while. "There are various ways souls can return to earth, Magdalene. In ghostly or silhouette form – as you've seen me – is just one of them."

"So you're not a messenger…but you return to earth in ghostly form…"

"That's right." He was staring at me, waiting for me to piece it all together, which was taking an infuriatingly long time.

"And you return to earth…when?"

"Only to see you."

He admitted this so readily and without any reservation, causing me to glance up at him. His smile had faded, and he was watching me with a deep interest. Our eyes met and I felt my pulse quicken; although, I couldn't bring myself to look away.

"Really?" I whispered, incredulously.

"Really," he replied softly.

I had trouble understanding how this handsome, ethereal man would purposefully seek me out. There were plenty of other better-looking girls to watch on earth. I never saw myself as anything remotely close to beautiful. My eyes were too large.

Still, here he was, the one I daydreamed about…the one I was always thinking of, admitting he thought about me too…at least, on occasion.

Reality hit me, realizing exactly when those occasions were.

"Oh," I said, hating how my voice sounded bashful. "You come to earth to save me."

"Yes," he confirmed. "Now why would I come to earth only to find you and only to save you?"

I gasped, instantly feeling ridiculous. I closed my eyes and felt my body cave with embarrassment. Of course…the reason was so obvious I couldn't believe I hadn't thought of it sooner.

When I opened my eyes, he had lifted his eyebrows in expectation.

"So? Would you like to say it out loud?" he persisted.

"You return to earth in ghostly form when you think I need saving…because you're a guardian."

He smiled back in his breathtakingly attractive way.

"Did I figure it out?" I asked, waiting for affirmation.

It felt like a decade passed before he finally answered, though I'm sure it was only as long as it took for him to open his mouth and speak.

"No." He shook his head and then leaned toward me, so close his sweet-scented breath brushed lightly past my cheeks. "I am your guardian."

I stood there, stunned, unable to inhale for far too long.

"Breathe, Magdalene," he said with a smile. "Not that you really need to here, but familiarity with the basics is important in surprise situations."

I drew in a breath, only slightly acknowledging that it felt good. "You watch over me…and only me?"

He nodded. "And that's a very good thing. I don't believe I'd have time for anyone else. You keep me quite busy."

"I do?" I asked, still too stunned to comprehend all of this. I have my own personal guardian?

"Far more so than anyone I've ever guarded."

"A guardian..." I whispered to myself. The surreal haze I was lingering in was lifting; I jerked my head up to catch his eyes. I needed his attention, because I wanted full disclosure. "Why didn't you tell me who you were when we first met?"

"And make my job that much harder on me?" He scoffed.

"You didn't answer my question."

"You were dead set against anyone protecting you, Magdalene. What would you have done if I'd announced I was solely there to protect you? Hmmm?"

Despite myself, I had to agree. I would have done everything in my power to get rid of him.

As if he'd heard my thoughts, he added, "You would have done your best, irritating me to no end, trying to ensure I wouldn't show up when you needed me most. That would have just frustrated me and it would have been ineffective. You've perfected the art of pushing others away, and you would have used that art on me. I won't let that happen."

I believed him, and regardless of my harbored resentment at needing to be watched over, I was glad it was him doing the watching.

He unclasped his hands and moved to place them on either side of his thighs. My hands happened to be in the same position and whether by accident or by design our hands gently brushed.

"Oh, my apologies."

"It's alright," I responded, a little too quickly. "Your skin...it's not hot here," I added, attempting to divert him from thinking I enjoyed the contact with him a little too much…even though it was the truth.

That was when it dawned on me that as our skin had made contact; I would swear he felt the same surge of excitement rush through his own body. Though it was brief, he quickly returned to his typical indifference.

"Everything here is a fabrication…" he was explaining, "including our bodies. On earth, there are…limitations to how we can project ourselves."

He fell silent, scuffing the ground again with his foot. Even though he seemed calm, I still had excitement running through me. To break the silence, I asked the first question that came to mind.

"Are you always around me, with me?"

"When you need me I'm there – even if you don't see me."

"Were you there at the shanty?" I didn't bother giving him any clues or hinting to which shanty. If Battersbee had been right, Eran wouldn't need any assistance.

He didn't answer right away. Instead, he repositioned his staff against the boulder. I got the feeling his action was merely to avoid looking directly at me.

"I was," he finally admitted.

"Why? I wasn't in any danger."

"No, you weren't. But you didn't know where you were going so you could have been."

"I see." My heart sank; his reasoning was perfectly understandable and had nothing to do with wanting to be near me.

As if he sensed this reaction, he started shifting his feet again uncomfortably. The gravel beneath them made a loud scratching sound.

"Have you always been around me? I only just started to see you…"

135

"I think you saw me once when you were a baby..." His face twisted, appearing to be caused by a painful memory. "I wasn't able to save you then."

My heart stuttered. "When I died..." I whispered. He nodded in confirmation, his eyes focusing on the ground; his gestures giving me the impression he felt guilty. I didn't like seeing him in pain. It was odd, but I also felt his sensation of guilt course through me, like searing hot liquid flowing through my veins. I almost mentioned it, but held back. I didn't like that feeling, or the fact that I knew he was feeling it too. Trying to suppress these feelings, I briskly changed the subject.

"You said there are other ways you can visit earth. What are those?"

He drew in a deep breath, trying to shake free from the emotions that seemed to be overwhelming him. I felt them begin to dwindle in me like a flame being snuffed out, as he refocused his thoughts. "Umm...well there are a few ways. We can be reborn...such is the case with you. We can go as a hot, white light and that is typical when you are filled with powerful emotions. And we can also fall to earth. Although any one of us can fall, that is often times reserved for those souls who have committed a sin such as injuring those on earth. Thankfully, they are rare because those souls can be powerful – often times bringing to earth with them some ability they had here and all too often using it against others."

"Those souls end up on earth? Surrounded by people who can't protect themselves? That doesn't seem fair."

Eran looked at me with a hinting smile. "That's why guardians were created."

"Ah...have you always been a guardian? I mean...you've been to earth a few times – once every century in fact – and during unstable times."

He lifted his eyebrows in astonishment, so I freely admitted how I figured it out.

"I saw the list of your lives."

"I see," he replied, smiling to himself. It was obvious he was flattered. "Yes, I've lived a few lives, each one purposefully chosen during those time periods. I believe each soul is drawn to earth at specific times for specific reasons. Mine was to fight."

"To fight?" I repeated, shocked. "Why?"

"I was needed, Magdalene. I told you...I appear when I am needed."

I felt myself gawking at him, pondering how the word 'altruism' had taken on a completely different meaning to me now. Some people might assume my act of delivering messages was altruistic on some level, but it was laughable in comparison to Eran's actions. He risked pain and injury, even his own life, for others.

Uncomfortable with my stare, he straightened his back and drew in another long breath. Suddenly, his exasperated tone returned. "So...now that you've interrupted my skills training, what can I do for you?"

"Oh...uh," I stammered, breaking free of his striking face. "That was skills training?"

"It was. Even us heaven-bound souls need to keep up our skills, so we train regularly with each other. It keeps us sharp. But I assume you came here for a different reason...other than to discuss my training."

"Yes," I said, noticing how much more handsome he looked now that I had seen him in action. "I-I have a message to deliver."

"To me?" he asked, bewildered, catching me with his blue-green eyes again.

"Yes, it's from someone I know at my school," I said, wondering if my heart would ever stop fluttering whenever our eyes meet. "His name is Gershom. I don't think you'd know him. Born in my time. But he said to tell you that you should consider returning to earth."

Eran was clearly taken aback. "And you said his name is…Gershom?"

"Yes, he's a friend of mine." I paused, realizing how easy it was to admit, despite what I learned about him.

"Did your friend say how he knew me?"

"Just said he'd heard of you."

"Heard of me? How…?" Eran asked more to himself than me, but I answered.

"I'm not sure, but he knew your name and when you died last."

Eran sat transfixed for a moment. When it didn't look like he had any more questions to ask, I asked one of my own.

"Eran…is this…where you live?" I couldn't imagine how this boulder-lined clearing could offer a comfortable existence.

He chuckled to himself but didn't answer. Instead, he took my hand, drew me up, and led me across the clearing. Again, my heart throbbed when he touched me. Because of it, my awareness was less on where we were headed than on the feeling of his solid, protecting grasp.

I did notice though that by the time we'd taken three steps, the clearing was fading and another place was taking shape. It appeared as if someone had tossed water on a giant canvas all around us and blended the two scenes together.

It was dusk here and everything was damp. The air was chilly and smelled of freshly fallen rain. Overhead, clouds were beginning to clear and along the mountains patches of fog clung to the jagged peaks.

We stepped out onto a rutted wood dock with a small red boat tied to it. On our right, a brook bubbled down and over rocks, flowing into an enormous lake behind us. The dock was met by a muddy, dirt road that cut through a grassy hill, leading to a log cabin at the top. The cabin was cloaked in the shade of giant ponderosa pines but with the hazy yellow lights inside, and smoke drifting up from the chimney, it looked welcoming. Two dogs ran around the side of the cabin and bounded down the hill toward us.

"This is Annie and Charlie," said Eran, as the dogs happily circled us, rubbing against our legs until we reached down to pet them.

"French mastiffs," he explained, just as I was about to ask what kind they were. "Got them during my time in France. They didn't survive guarding my estate during the rebellion, but they were waiting for me when I returned here." He watched as the dogs continued jumping up to lick my face, unable to contain their excitement.

"Wow, it's almost like they know me!" I said, laughing.

Eran chuckled through his nose, as if in response to a secret joke.

"They're sweet," I said, as I stood.

Eran appeared to appreciate this, smiling to himself as we headed toward the cabin.

I immediately felt at home in Eran's heaven. In fact, it seemed oddly familiar somehow. Without having to look, I already knew there was a hammock hung between two pines and an Adirondack chair with a steaming pot of what smelled to be coffee set on the ground next to it. I also knew the layout of the cabin before I stepped foot inside. I couldn't discern if this was because it was exactly how I saw Eran, rugged but comfortable, or if there was some other reason that evaded me.

In the distance, a wolf howled, and I smiled to myself.

"What?" Eran asked, noticing.

"Oh, it's just so…perfect."

"Yes, I think so." He sighed, seeming to savor the air here.

"Is this where you've always lived in the afterlife?" I was intrigued, never having been able to ask others how they came to create their own existence here.

"I built it bit by bit. Like most others build theirs. You know…" he said, resolutely.

"Actually, I don't."

He paused on the dirt path, openly studying me. His eyes widened slightly and realization spread across his face. "Of course you don't. You couldn't, could you?" He fumbled, and I could see he understood something for the first time. "Without knowing where you died last you wouldn't be able to find your past lives or your permanent residence here. Am I right?"

I nodded. "Being able to just visit has its disadvantages…I'm here on passport."

He seemed to contemplate this as we stepped onto the porch. Stew was simmering inside, and it smelled delicious. I was slightly surprised when my stomach growled, which had never happened here. Eran had really gone to great lengths to make his piece of the afterlife as real as possible.

"I never considered that…that you would be…limited here," he said, thoughtfully.

"More than you think. I can't fly like others and how we got here just now…passing between realms by stepping through…I can't do that either."

"Huh," he muttered. "I never knew that." He said this in a way that made it sound like he'd known me as a messenger for a very long time.

"You know…that stew smells great," I said, hinting.

He took the bait and replied with a grin, "And I'd say it's just about ready." He opened the door and ushered me in.

Inside, the cabin was rustic and relaxed. It was a single room with just a table and some chairs, a worn leather couch, and a wall entirely covered with cluttered book shelves. The kitchen, with dated, worn appliances, was immediately to the right from where we walked in. A fire was burning in the hearth, where a small iron pot hung over the flames containing the bubbling stew.

Annie and Charlie leapt up on the couch, curling themselves into balls, and immediately began to snore. Eran filled two bowls with stew and placed them on the table before taking a seat.

"Oh...it's comfortable," I said, as I sat down in the only other chair.

Eran smiled to himself. "We old things are well worn."

I picked up my spoon, noticing it was already warm to the touch, so it wouldn't chill the stew. Hesitantly, I asked, "How old are you exactly?"

"Centuries," he replied simply, as if this were commonplace.

"You're kidding," I said, astounded.

"Why? Do I strike you as immature?" he teased.

"At times," I replied, flatly.

He glanced up surprised, until he saw I was grinning playfully back at him.

"Actually, you...have a certain kind of awareness about you that...sort of demonstrates your age."

"Is that so?" His eyebrows raised in interest.

"Yes. It seems like you know what is around every corner and you're not concerned, because you've handled it before. It seems as if you are...infallible."

He paused, holding his spoon, and snickered lightly. "That is certainly not the case."

"It's not? You mean, you're vulnerable? But how could that be?" I teased.

Eran's reply was more serious. "We all are, Magdalene, each of us in our own way."

I mulled this over as we ate, realizing the truth behind his statement. Less than a minute had passed when I noticed that my stew was almost gone. It was so delicious; I had almost devoured it. After finishing off the last of it, I settled back into the chair.

Glancing around and enjoying the feeling of being with Eran in this particular place, I thought to ask, "What do your guests think…of this place?"

He shook his head languidly at me. "Guests? Oh, I don't have guests here. This is my private paradise."

"But you brought me," I stated, watching him though he'd dropped his head to avoid eye contact. "Yes, yes, I did."

I couldn't ignore the butterflies that flitted in my stomach at this acknowledgement. "So why me? Why did you bring me?"

He didn't answer immediately, taking another spoonful of stew. "You…you asked about where I live," he said faintly. With a deeper, more evocative tone, he added, "And I get a sense that you miss the feeling of home sometimes."

My breath caught in my throat at the obvious sense of awareness he had about me. He knew me better than I thought.

"Home wasn't something I could comprehend for a long time. But, I'm getting a sense of it now," I replied.

"With your roommates," he added.

"Yes, definitely. They make our house a home. But, I feel at home here too."

"You do?" he asked, enthusiastically.

"Yes."

Not bothering to hide his grin, he cleared his throat and set down his spoon, clanging it loudly against the rim of his bowl. He'd finished his dinner and was now leaning back, folding his hands across his abdomen, watching me.

I felt transparent with his blatant attention and had the urge to keep the conversation going as a diversion. He'd let me see his piece of paradise and it now made me question mine.

"Eran…you were there when I died last, right? I believe that's what you said. When I was just a baby…you thought I saw you before I passed on."

He noticeably cringed at the memory and I instantly felt bad about bringing it up. I reminded myself there was an important reason behind why I was asking but it didn't help much. When he nodded, I continued even though he wouldn't look up from his empty bowl.

"Well…if you were there, when I died, you must know where I died."

He nodded again, still avoiding my eyes.

"Will you tell me where it happened? So I can find out who I was?"

His head finally rose, and a sharp pain pierced my heart when I saw his expression was blanketed with regret.

"Please don't look at me like that," I whispered.

"It's the thought that I couldn't stop it…couldn't prevent you from feeling the pain…" his voice trailed off, shaking his head, clear contempt for himself etching his beautiful face.

"It's not your fault." When it looked like he was about to refute, I didn't allow it. "You would do anything in your power to protect me. You've already proven that."

"I would," he looked up at me through his long eyelashes and lifted his head to be level with mine again. "I would," he repeated, more firmly, erasing any doubt I may have held. Though, I didn't.

"And that is why you are the only person I would want to show me who I was before…"

His breathing became labored, clearly indicating he was battling some pressing desire to not help me, though I didn't understand why.

Finally, he conceded, grudgingly. "Next time. Right now…" he tapped the skin on his wrist as if a watch were there, and said, "…you have to get back to earth."

At that moment, I awoke to my alarm clock and the smell of Felix's eggplant crepes.

I didn't sit up immediately but took a few minutes to remember Eran's face, as I was pulled far too quickly away from him. Reluctantly, I got out of bed and headed for the bathroom, regretful that time did not exist in the afterlife while it was so prevalent here on earth.

8. PAST LIVES

It felt like time stopped, teasing me each time I looked at my watch…which was often. For the first time in my life, I could relate to all those infatuated girls fawning over their love interests. Every minute was too long to wait before I could see Eran again. I sat in The Square all day, hoping to wear myself out so I would fall asleep quickly when I got back to the house.

Eran was such a strong distraction that I actually had to record people's messages on a piece of paper I'd torn from Rufus's sketch book. I just didn't trust that I would remember them correctly when half of my attention was focused on my feelings for Eran. It was driving me crazy; I could barely concentrate. It wasn't until a girl I recognized from school approached me that I was able to focus a little more.

It was Saturday and I'd set up my chairs in their usual spot, beneath one of the dappled oak trees dotting The Square. Today was a busy one with throngs of tourists buying trinkets and their caricatures from local artists. Still, despite the swarm of people, I saw her coming. She had a self-assured air that was hard to miss.

She was from my English Interpretive Literature class, and she sat several rows in front of me. I'd caught her staring at me recently when I entered or left the classroom. As she took a seat in my customer chair, I knew why.

"You're Miranda, right?" I asked.

"Yes, how did you know?" She seemed surprised.

"I pay attention."

"Ah…Did you also know I was on the school paper?" She asked, grinning broadly at me. There was a hint hidden in the tone of her voice which instantly concerned me. It meant I had guessed her reason for being here correctly.

"Yes," I said, hesitantly.

"Good. I'd like to do an article on you."

I laughed, awkwardly. "Oh, I'm sure there are more interesting topics you can write about…"

"No…there really isn't," she said decisively, making it clear she wasn't going to concede. She sensed my apprehension and quickly added, "Look, you are by far the most interesting person in school – from your bike…"

"Harley Davidson 883 Sportster," I clarified. If she was going to do a story about me, then she was going to do it accurately.

"Thank you," she replied, confirming she understood my point. "You weren't born and raised here in New Orleans. You don't work at a souvenir shop, like everyone else, or have a wealthy family paying your tuition. No…you come from the unknown…working in Jackson Square for your money doing psychic readings." She enunciated this last part for emphasis. I stopped her there.

"I don't do psychic readings, and I'm not psychic. I deliver messages to those who have passed on. At least get that right."

She didn't appear offended at my verbal jab and that made me feel a little more comfortable with her. Instead, she smiled confidently and said, "Let me interview you.

I'll write the story, you'll read it before anyone else sees it, and you can make changes if you wish."

"I don't even want the story written in the first place."

She sighed and leaned back in the chair, clearly displeased. "I can either write the story with your help, making sure it's correct, or I can write it based on my observations...which may be entirely wrong."

"What do I care?" I shrugged, trying to dissuade her.

"Do you really want people thinking you do séances? Because that's what I see here."

She was tough, but I could relate to that. I repositioned myself, glaring openly at her. "You're going to write this story with or without me, aren't you?"

"I prefer it be with you," she replied, bolting forward in her seat. The girl had a lot of energy. "People are intrigued, Maggie. They want to know you, but they're too afraid to ask. You are a...phenomenon. Explain it to them."

I rolled my eyes.

"Through me," she added. "Ah, come on. If nothing else, it'll drive The Warden batty."

I instantly perked up. "Did you...Did you just call him The Warden?"

She frowned back. "Did you think we're all a bunch of status quo, mindless followers? We know what he's like. Give us some credit, Maggie."

I laughed at her response, regardless of my frustration with her. I then decided anyone who could see the man for what he was – an overbearing dictator – couldn't be all that bad.

"Alright, what do you want to know?" I begrudgingly asked.

She beamed, swiftly retrieving her notepad like a professional, before launching into countless questions, most of which were written down in shorthand – a skill I thought died in 1969. She asked about my past; including my adoptive aunt, previous schools, where I'd lived, who I lived with now – which I elaborated on with pride, because I truly thought my roommates were wonderful people. Finally, with the preliminary details out of the way, she asked about my work.

"How exactly do you do it?" She was eagerly leaning forward in her chair, again.

I shook my head. "I don't know. I don't know why me...and not someone else. I don't know what allows me to wake up in the morning after spending the night in the afterlife. I don't even know that I could stop it if I tried."

"Have you ever tried? I mean...it must get exhausting."

"Not really. I wake up as refreshed as everyone else seems to be. And I don't want to stop trying. I think, or at least I like to believe, the service I perform helps people." She had her head down, rapidly jotting notes, but nodded once, signaling for me to go on. "Miranda, you should see the joy, the pure excitement, on their faces and sometimes the complete humbling appreciation. Imagine waiting years to tell someone that you weren't mad at them when they passed on and finally being able to release that guilt or being able to check up on a newly departed loved one ensuring their transition was smooth and they're happy. I perform that service." I paused for a moment, thinking about it. "No...I wouldn't stop even if I could."

By the end of my chatter, Miranda's face was frozen in awe, her jaw slightly dropped, her eyes glassed over. "You really don't do this for the money, do you?"

"I needed it at first, but the truth is, I can live on very little – and I have. The money now...it makes my customers feel better. I get the sense they need an insurance policy to ensure their message will be delivered."

She laughed at that, making notes on her pad, and smiled warmly at me.

"Maggie, thank you so much for the opportunity to get to know you a little better."

"Sure. Are we done?" I asked, watching a man shifting from foot to foot, eagerly waiting to be my next customer.

"Yes, we are."

She held out her hand, which I shook, and a moment later she was gone.

Although I didn't regret having taken the interview, I did start to wonder later if she'd keep her word and let me review the article before it was published – my skepticism mostly caused by having found very few heartfelt people at the Academy of the Immaculate Heart. But, what was done...was done. If she chose to run her own version that decision was now hers. I was never good at judging others and I couldn't tell if she was trustworthy, so I just had to have faith.

By the end of the day, my concerns over whether Miranda would portray me in an honest, positive light had been chased away by my eagerness to see Eran. As dusk fell across New Orleans, shadows rose up and Cajun music began filtering out from neighborhood bars, I was preparing myself for what I was about to learn – who I was before.

At the house, I rushed through dinner, polishing off Felix's Sprout and Eggplant Egg White Crepe Special which boosted his pride and surprised Rufus and Ezra. Rufus had been busy preparing hamburgers and steak fries when I refused to wait so I'm certain they thought something was up. To assuage their suspicions, I explained I had a lot of work to do...which was true. I did have quite a few messages to deliver since The Square was really busy today. I'd already determined I would tackle those first, before I could see Eran, or I was convinced I'd never get around to delivering at all.

A few minutes later, I was upstairs hastily brushing my teeth. I splashed some water on my face, in place of a good scrub, and hopped into bed, finishing my nightly routine in less than a quarter of the time it typically takes me.

Just as I had hoped, keeping busy at The Square today helped put me to sleep quickly. The next moment I was waking up on the stone bench in the middle of the Hall of Records, only this time I wasn't alone.

With my eyes closed, I didn't see him, but I felt a surge of elation run through me, reaching from the top of my head to the tips of my toes.

"Pleasant trip back?" Eran's sensual, deep accent was lined with enthusiasm and made my heart beat faster.

Sitting up, I opened my eyes and found him standing over me.

"Far too overdue," I said, taking him in while trying not to show it.

"You were counting the minutes until you saw me next, weren't you?" he asked, playfully.

I rolled my eyes at him, trying not to show how close to the truth he actually was. "No one will ever accuse you of modesty."

"Never," he grinned, brazenly.

I noted that he smelled of fresh earth, spring air, and warm sun. In fact, he looked like he'd just walked off a vineyard during harvest time. The flannel and jeans he'd worn last time I'd seen him had been replaced with khakis and a white cotton tank top, helping his dark tan skin stand out. I could see his carved muscles lining the inside of his shirt, making it very hard for me to look away.

"When you arrived, you were smiling. No, beaming is more like it," he stated.

I shrugged, intentionally not explaining. There was no reason I could give without letting him know I was thrilled to see him.

I stood giving myself something to do before my attention could be drawn back to the enticing curvature of his muscles.

"So, what are you doing here? Looking for a record?"

"No..." he replied, offhandedly. "I was waiting for you."

"Me?" I asked, stunned.

"I said I'd show you the record with your past lives on it."

"Oh, that..." So, he had only come to fulfill a promise and nothing more.

He chuckled. "For some reason, I thought you'd be more excited."

"I am! I am. I just...I need to deliver a few messages first."

"Okay," he said, turning to walk toward the wall closest to us. "I'm here. I might as well help."

I was surprised at his offer. I'd never had help before, and his enthusiasm caught me off-guard. Still, I was glad he suggested it. Company would be a welcomed benefit on this visit, especially his company.

"So, who is first," he asked, walking toward the wall, anticipating the search for our first scroll.

It struck me while watching him, either he was naturally intuitive at using the scrolls or he had done this before. I had never seen Eran in the hall, but that didn't mean he wasn't here during my off-hours.

"Tipper McNeal is first...died last in Omaha, Nebraska on December 14, 2000."

He nodded and then pointed down the wall toward the "O's".

Reaching the spot where I needed to climb the wall, I grabbed hold and began to lift myself up.

"What are you doing?" he asked, holding back laughter.

"I'm climbing," I told him, my voice tinged with defensiveness.

This time he released a hearty laugh and said, "I'm happy to carry you." He moved slightly up and down in the air, boasting his ability to float.

I scoffed at the proposal. "Show off. No thank you."

His response was a mere glimmer in his eyes, the meaning of which was unmistakable. He was going to race me.

I sprang upward, carrying myself faster than I'd ever moved to reach a record.

Less than a second later, I was several stories high when I heard him clear his throat.

"You passed it," he called out, not bothering to hold back his laughter.

I felt the flush creep over my cheeks as I turned and found him floating a few feet down from me, next to the scroll for Omaha.

I grimaced. The point I was trying to make was that I didn't need help, but it was futile.

I climbed back down and looked at him, purposely, before reaching to open the scroll.

He was smirking but gave me what I wanted...confirmation. "You're fast."

"Beat you..." I muttered, pulling out the scroll to review.

I found Tipper McNeal's information midway down the page. Reaching out my thumb to drift over the entry, it surprised me when Eran took hold of me, preparing to be guided there also. His gentle touch made me shiver in reaction.

In the afterlife, as on earth, much of the time I spent alone with only my thoughts to keep me company. On both planes, I watched people move about their business, holding conversations and interacting with others, while I handled my own duties and never really connected with them. Eran's simple touch had emphasized the void in me that I didn't know had been created.

We moved through several worlds until reaching a street on Knob Hill in San Francisco. Judging from the style of cars meandering down the hill through the fog and rain, it was sometime in the 1940s.

Tipper McNeal lived well in her chosen paradise - inside a large brownstone home decorated elaborately with artwork that rotated from one famous painting to another, disappearing instantly as another appeared in its place. She had a butler open the door for us. He disappeared after escorting us into the sitting room where we found an old woman, draped with a plush blanket, holding a cup of tea.

She motioned for us to sit and we did. Without speaking, she drew a circle on the coffee table between us and it was instantly filled with a tray holding tea cups in matching saucers and long, round cookies. Eran and I politely shook our heads as she offered them to us, so she drifted her hand over the tea set and it faded away.

"How can I help you, dear?" Her voice was soft and melodic, but jolted me. Not because I was surprised at the beauty of it but because I heard her words inside the back of my ears, like Battersbee's had been. "I'm sorry for upsetting you. I couldn't hear in my last life and when I came here I felt most comfortable using this way of speaking."

I replied but not with spoken words. "That's alright. I've done this once before." I then smiled at her to show I was no longer startled. "I have a message for you...from your daughter."

Tipper immediately sat up, eagerly asking, "How is she?"

"She seems to be doing well. In fact, she's pregnant."

Tipper drew in a breath and slowly placed a hand to her chest in surprise.

"She says she's going to name her baby after you – Tipper - and that she misses you."

Tears suddenly began to well up at the corner of her eyes but she blinked them back. "I was hoping so...I was hoping..."

I looked at Eran who was now glancing between Tipper and me, curiously. From his expression I judged that he knew something was going on but didn't know exactly what. I'd fill him in later.

"Will you tell her that..." she placed a hand to her chest and breathed in deeply, closing her eyes, as emotion overwhelmed her. "Please tell her that nothing could have made me happier."

"I will. And just so that she knows...believes that the message was delivered...could you provide some proof? Some piece of information that only she would know?"

Tipper thought for a moment, a smile stretching across her face. "Tell her that I hope she kept those stories she wrote as a child...the ones she secretly hid behind her bed."

I made a mental note and said, "That's perfect. Thank you."

Her eyes widened. "I should be thanking you, dear. It was truly a wonderful surprise...and to be told by someone so important," she said. Although I didn't hear it, I saw her shoulders rise and fall with a sigh.

The last part of her sentence left me slightly confused and I didn't want to leave her misguided, so I explained, "I think you have me confused with someone else."

Tipper tilted her head to the side, puzzled. "Aren't you the messenger?"

"I'm the one who delivers messages to those who have passed on..." I said slowly enunciating each word in my mind, wondering how she could mistake me for someone important.

"I thought so. I've heard about you before."

"You've heard about me?" I asked, stunned.

"Of course."

"From who?"

"Oh, well, several others. You seem surprised," she noted.

"I am." I had no idea.

"You have a special gift, even when compared to what we can do here," she replied, moving her hand over her blanket and watching it change to a quilt.

"I guess everyone has special abilities," I said, noticing that even the lint left by her previous blanket vanished from the couch.

"Some more special than others," she replied, looking pensively at me.

A moment passed when neither of us spoke but simply stared at each other, she in a motherly way and me in uncomfortable shock.

Finally able to think straight again, I said, "I appreciate you telling me. No one ever has."

"It was only a matter of time before someone did," Tipper replied, smiling warmly.

When I stood, Eran followed.

"It was a pleasure to meet you both," Tipper said, though this time she spoke out loud for Eran's benefit. "You and your gentleman friend are welcome back any time."

We thanked her and stepped outside the door, finding the rain had stopped. The sky was clear blue and the trees lining the street, which had been bare before, were now blossoming into thick bouquets of color.

"I'm not sure what was said in there," Eran mentioned, confirming that the conversation had been a private one by Tipper's choice, "but whatever it was, I think you made her more content." He motioned to the now bloom-filled trees.

Pausing to watch them, I noted their beauty and glanced up to find Eran staring down at me in awe. I swelled with pride at that moment, knowing that I had impressed him – finally.

Basking in his admiration but not wanting to be obvious, I stated, "We should deliver the rest."

He softly but firmly took hold of my elbow and escorted me a few steps. The city around us disappeared and was replaced with the Hall of Records.

"That was far faster than usual," I muttered, already looking for the next scroll.

"What's the usual?"

"Running…" I said, moving along the wall to the Q's. "I can't float but I have incredible strength so running is how I travel here."

"It's settled then," he firmly stated. "I'll stick around and help you with the rest of your deliveries."

I was facing away from him so I allowed myself the freedom to smile at his decision. He cleared his throat awkwardly, as if he knew he'd made me happy, and launched into his new chore, asking for details about the next delivery.

We repeated the same process until all the messages were delivered: the two of us racing each other to the next scroll; Eran following me and helping to deliver the message; and Eran escorting me back to retrieve the next scroll. I had never had so much fun.

After delivering the last message, we stood anxiously in the middle of the hall, both knowing it was time for the last scroll…mine.

It was quiet as usual but this time I actually felt the breeze, flowing constantly through the hall, as the temperature dropped. As it continued to cool some, I wondered if Eran had done this purposely. If so, I was thankful, because it helped me overcome a sudden bout of nausea. How could anyone feel faint in the afterlife? I wondered. But there I stood, holding on to Eran's stable, solid arm, not allowing myself to let go because I didn't trust myself not to collapse.

"Are you ready for this?" he asked, watching me with a concerned expression.

"I-I think so."

I drew in a deep breath and turned toward the wall. This time, there was no racing up it. I moved slowly, deliberately, as he floated beside me, still watching, still looking concerned.

And then he stopped.

We were in the B section, I noticed. He reached out and pulled a scroll from its pocket.

Billings, Montana.

"You're a long way from home," he stated, insinuating the distance from Louisiana to Montana.

"I never even knew I'd been there."

He noticed I was trembling and asked dubiously, "Would you like me to do the honors?"

I stared at the scroll for a moment but reached out to take it.

Then my hand slipped, and suddenly, I was falling.

The cool wind raced by me, the shelves becoming a blur.

All of a sudden, I felt Eran's arms wrapping tightly around me, holding me securely to him. I felt our bodies intrinsically intertwining; my legs seemed to fuse with his and my chest pressed comfortably up against him. I enjoyed the warmth and safety his firm body offered.

A moment later – far too soon – he was whispering in my ear.

"We're on the ground now." He smirked down at me, knowing I had been focused on…other things.

"Thanks," I said, stepping back away. "I've fallen before. It doesn't hurt."

"I see. I'm still learning your limitations here."

We stood in uncomfortable silence until I realized I still held the scroll. I loosened my grip on it, allowing it to unravel, coming to rest some ten feet away.

I drew in a shaky breath, closing my eyes for a moment, and said, "Magdalene Tanner." I instantly glanced up at Eran to make sure this was correct – after all, my name could have changed between this life and the last. But the scroll began to move.

It ended up toward the bottom of the list. My eyes traced the names down until they landed on my past lives.

Previously Magdalene Tanner – Died Billings, Montana, October 12, 1990

Previously Margaret Talor – Died Gettysburg, Pennsylvania, July 3, 1863

Previously Marie Lafayette – Died Paris, France, July 14, 1789

Previously Anna Willowsby – Died London, England, April 13, 1665

Previously Friedricha Schaffhausen – Died Muehlhausen, Germany, June, 5, 1525

I felt my eyebrows raise together as a sense of confusion came over me. The dates and places looked so familiar, but I couldn't figure out why.

"Notice anything?" Eran asked.

"The dates…and the…" I replied, shaking my head.

And then it hit me.

"The dates and places are the same as yours…" I looked up at him. "Is that odd?"

He laughed to himself, taking a seat on the stone bench. "I was hoping you wouldn't notice. Then I wouldn't need to explain. But I should have known you'd see it. You're too observant for your own good, Magdalene."

"I have no idea what you're talking about," I said, still standing where he'd left me, too frightened to move.

Why was he so reticent?

He put his face in his hands, rubbing exasperatedly, and then sat up quickly, as if he'd made a firm decision to be straight forward with me. This was good. I needed to fully understand what was going on because that woozy feeling was coming back again. Advisedly, he began to speak.

"It's not that you went to earth at the same time I did. It's the opposite. I followed you. I followed you because you're a messenger and I am a guardian – your guardian. It wasn't me who chose to return to earth during volatile times, Magdalene. You chose it. You understand that people need your service most during turbulence, chaos, and so you go. I follow to protect you. It was only this last time that I didn't trail you, thinking I'd be more capable of keeping you safe in this form than in any other."

"I chose?"

He nodded. "It's always been your choice."

And then he snickered to himself. "I couldn't understand why you didn't recognize me that first time I saved you in the street...when the Ford Mustang was chasing you down. To be honest, I was hurt about it until I realized the reason. You had returned to earth as a reborn. Reborn's don't begin again with a memory. Doing so only impedes their progress in the next life."

"We've known each other before?" I asked, barely above a whisper because that was all the energy I could muster, the rest of it was focusing on my shock.

"Oh, yes."

"For how long?"

"Lifetimes, Magdalene."

I moved to the bench, uncertain my legs would endure much more of this news before collapsing. "Lifetimes..." I whispered, indulging in the impossibility of it. "You've followed me for lifetimes..."

"I have," he admitted, though he didn't seem as inhibited about it as I would have thought.

I stopped in front of him. "Were we friends?" I inquired, knowing the opposite could have been true too.

He confirmed my fear. "Not always." But then he chuckled and I felt slightly placated. "Would you like to hear our story?"

I had a difficult time suppressing the exhilaration rushing through me, as I noted the last two words he'd used. We had a story together. It seems implausible that this man, the embodiment of perfection, and I have been so connected throughout time.

"Undeniably...yes!"

"Sit, and I'll tell you," he said, patting the seat beside him.

As I did, our legs touched, creating a warm, firm pressure, from hip to knee. He drew in a quick breath, responding to our contact, and I glanced at him, wondering if he did have some hidden attraction toward me. The thought of it made me dizzy, even though he quickly recovered.

Eran drew in a breath and began then. "The very first time I set eyes on you was almost five hundred years ago. Our families shared a property line and despite the Germanic Wars taking place around us and the feud between our two families...well, it certainly took precedence."

"Our families were fighting?"

"Every chance we got. But the women were kept well away from the conflict. We lived less than a mile away from each other, never knowing the other existed until one night. I caught you walking through our property, cloaked because it had been raining. I thought that you were a boy up to no good. When I stopped and demanded that you show yourself, you..." He paused, laughing at the image playing in his mind.

"What? I what?" I persisted.

"You fought me." Despite his words, he was smiling in amusement. "Very well, too. You are excellent with the sword."

"I am?" I asked. Surrounded by disbelief, I thought back to fencing class and my pathetic attempts at wielding the weapon.

"When you're reborn, it takes time to remember these things. It'll come back to you," he assured me.

"So..." I said hesitant of what his answer might be to my next question. "Did I hurt you?"

This time he rolled his head back and roared with laughter. After recovering, he continued, "Nothing that left me debilitated."

I sighed with relief. "Good."

"But you wanted to...and fought hard at it. Eventually, you ended up pinned to a tree where I was able to get a good look at you and found that you were a girl."

"Were you surprised?" I asked, intrigued.

"Very much."

"So, were we friends after that?" I ventured, hopeful.

"Not friends, business partners. You were on your way to deliver messages for the rich and I came along...as your guard."

My mouth fell open. "Is that how we started? How you became my guardian?"

He nodded slowly, thoughtfully. "If we aren't putting too fine a point on the moment in time...yes. I met you every fortnight from then on to walk with you, protecting you against whatever miserable characters you might come across."

"What did our families think of it? Our partnership?"

"They never learned of us. I made certain of it."

"So, is that how we've been every lifetime? Partners?"

A nostalgic smile moved across his face before answering cautiously, "In one form or another."

I decided against pressing him for a clearer answer, feeling that my effort would be in vain. Instead, I opted to ask another question, one that piqued my curiosity. "What were we like back then?"

"Well…" He shrugged. "Very much the way we are now. You were stubborn…" He paused to grin at me. "Courageous. Caring. You have an instinct to help others so you've followed that path throughout your lives."

Our eyes locked and I couldn't explain it but I suddenly felt an intense urge to reach out and wrap my arms around him. It took every bit of my effort to resist that urge. I literally had to fold my hands into fists and refocus my attention. A moment later, we both looked away, heaving a sigh. Right then I realized he had to fight off the same urge I had. Disappointment overwhelmed me. We hadn't acted on it, and I was uncertain now of how to behave. So I asked the first question that came to mind.

"Was I-Was I always like you describe me? In every life?"

"Yes…You are who you are and that is carried with you…regardless."

"So if you knew me for so long, why didn't you want to tell me who I was? You seemed so hesitant."

He opened his mouth to speak and then clamped it shut.

"What? What is it? What are you not telling me?"

His eyes dropped and he shook his head. "Nothing…there's nothing more."

I knew there was more. I felt it, and I felt him fighting to hold it back. "Okay, if you won't tell me now just promise that you will eventually tell me?" I placed my hand on his, which I noticed was gripping his thigh tightly, evidence of his struggle. "Eventually…not now but sometime in the future?"

He sighed, but conceded. "I will," he promised.

"Thank you…" I whispered, and then said more clearly, "What would you like to talk about instead?"

A gleam came to his eyes. "You."

"Me?" I said, taken aback.

"Definitely you."

"I have no idea why," I told him, rolling my eyes.

"No? Then I'll explain. But first, do you mind if we go some place more comfortable?"

"I don't mind at all." Anywhere with Eran would be just fine with me, though I was going to miss his leg pressing against mine.

He thought for a moment and then took my hand, standing to guide us a few steps. We drifted back to his private paradise.

The cabin was just as I'd seen it last, cozy and welcoming, though this time it was summer and fireflies flickered throughout the warm air. I heard Annie and Charlie barking in the distance as we stepped firmly onto the dry dirt path leading to the cabin.

"Better," he said decisively as we approached the front porch.

He gestured for me to take a seat in one of the rocking chairs, as he sat down in the one beside it. I was still perplexed but genuinely happy he wanted to get to know me better.

"Alright, now are you going to explain?"

He stared back at me, content. "Yes..." His tone was teasingly sarcastic but grew more serious. "You see I've never gone this long without being with you. There is a void during the time you were born until I met you again in which I have no idea what you've experienced."

"You want to know about how I grew up?" I asked, unable to see how that could be interesting.

He nodded, firmly. "Absolutely."

"Okay, but if you get bored it'll be your own fault."

"I have complete confidence that won't happen."

He then eagerly launched into questions about my past, delving for details on Aunt Teresa and my life with her, what schools I attended, and the cities I lived in.

His attention was undivided and earnestly interested, asking questions attentively. At some point though, I grew tired of talking, and during that break, rested my head back against the chair.

When I opened my eyes I was back in my bedroom with the alarm beeping painfully in my ear. I'd forgotten to turn it off before going to sleep last night. Fighting the urge to throw it across the room, I settled for yanking the cord out of the wall.

Rolling back over, I pulled the pillow down over my face. If I tried, maybe I could still get back…

"Maggie!" Rufus called through the door, pounding on it. I'm sure it seemed like just a tap to him. "You up? Could I get a ride ta The Square? Felix left in a huff without me, the wanka'. Afta' I joked about his olive pancakes. He he he…"

I groaned, shoving the pillow off my face.

Whatever divine intervention was keeping me from getting back to Eran, it was powerful. I gave in, telling Rufus to be ready in fifteen minutes, and started to prepare myself for the day.

9. LEGENDARY STORIES

All day at The Square I only offered proof and took payment from those customers I'd delivered messages for the night prior. I refused to take on any new messages for delivery, because I'd be in school tomorrow and unable to deliver them. This was my routine. Saturday: take messages. Sunday: deliver them.

It was a good thing I had a routine because half my mind was focused elsewhere, recounting my conversation with Eran. Even Rufus acknowledged it on the ride there.

He tapped my shoulder and shouted over the engine's rumble. "Somethin' on yer mind?"

"Yes," I called back to him, not bothering to explain further.

When I parked at my spot, he removed his helmet and faced me. "Well? Ya gonna fill me in?"

I sighed, dropping my shoulders in response. I wasn't ready. I needed time to understand it myself.

"Back in me home country, I was the one everyone told their problems to," he began to explain, propping his helmet on the handlebar. "Hated it really, 'cause I neva asked fer it. Turned out, they came ta me 'cause I had a

165

knack. Found I neva gave lousy advice. So, even if I neva got any bloody sleep n' was always helpin' others with their problems, at least they walked 'way with some peace."

I turned to pull my chairs from their hiding place and set them up, noticing Rufus didn't move until the customer chair was set down. Then he took a seat and waited.

He wasn't going to let me off without some feeling of having helped me. Realizing this, I sat too.

"What would you do if someone withheld information…details about your own life?"

"That it?" Rufus asked.

"Yes, that's what is bothering me."

Rufus threw his hands up. "Well, that's easy enough."

I felt instantly relieved. Rufus was going to give me insight, worldly wisdom on how to get the information I desperately wanted.

He leaned forward in his seat and said, "Mags, there ain't a thing you kin do 'bout it."

I remained silent, not at all satisfied with his response.

"Yer at their mercy," he added plainly, as he stood. I kept my focus on the cracks in the cement, internally debating Rufus's outlook, until he spoke again.

"Ever think they're holdin' back on ya ta keep ya safe?"

"Huh?"

"That's the main reason people keep things to themselves – at least when it involves someone else. Could be they're refusin' ta disclose anything to keep from gettin' ya hurt."

Rufus feebly shrugged his shoulders at me and left to start setting up his own spot. I spent the better part of the day trying to figure out what could possibly hurt me and returned repeatedly to one final answer: there were too many unknowns. Whatever Eran was holding back, I was at his mercy to tell me.

That night, I went to bed as quickly as I could – even skipping Ezra's delicious coffee ice cream pie. Once asleep, I looked at the cabin but only found Annie and Charlie lounging on the porch. I also checked the clearing where I'd found him doing his training drills, but it was vacant. I even went back to the Hall of Records in hopes of finding him there but it, too, was empty. I also tried drifting my finger over his scroll in hopes it would send me directly to him, but for the first time since I'd learned that technique, it didn't work. Everything I tried was fruitless.

If he was avoiding me – and I had the distinct feeling he was – I couldn't figure out what I had done to deserve it. He hadn't appeared particularly offended by anything I said the night before. In fact, the last thing I remember before waking up in my bed were his eyes, shining blissfully back at me. This was what hurt the most. I had gotten the impression – once again – that he had some interest in me other than his self-proclaimed responsibility to guard over me. He might have feelings he refused to acknowledge. Again, all evidence pointed to the fact that I was nothing more than an unpredictable part of his duties.

Eventually, my alarm clock went off again and I woke up in my bed back on Magazine Street in New Orleans.

I inhaled a bowl of cereal, without paying much attention to the taste, and got on my motorcycle, heading to school, before anyone else was even awake.

I needed something to keep my mind off Eran. Since I arrived before the rest of the student body, well before classes started for the day, I parked myself at a large table in the library. I had fencing class to study up on. We were having a test and sparing today for the first time. When called on, I need to know what an Attaque au Fer and Prise de Fer meant. I hadn't picked up my foil once to practice my footwork so I needed to ace the written part. By the end of my studying, I was desperately hoping that Eran would be right – that the skill would come back to me – and that it would return some time before last period. Feeling little difference in my physical aptitude, I knew this was a slim possibility.

When classes started, I resorted to hiding my fencing instruction manual behind other textbooks in each of my classes, doing my best to memorize all the terms. In fact, I was going to ask Gershom to test me at lunch, but he was interested in talking about something else far more intriguing.

He arrived early to our spot beneath the tree and immediately launched into his interrogation.

"Did you deliver the message to Eran?" he asked, before sitting down.

I cringed. The sound of his name left an ache in my chest.

"I did," I replied, pulling out my muffuletta and a bag of chips even though I had no appetite.

"Did he say anything in return?"

"Mmhmmm…" I replied. Lots of things.

"Well? What was it?"

Gershom looked impatient. He clearly wanted an answer. Idle conversation would not suffice today.

"Sorry," I said, between chews. "I feel a little scattered today. Nothing really. Um, Eran was surprised you'd sent him a message and asked who you were." I said this rapidly, trying to get the conversation over with quickly. The thought of Eran was leaving a void in my chest where my heart had once been, and discussing him was only amplifying it.

Gershom leaned back, looking like I'd just pulled a black widow from my bag.

"What? What did I say?" I asked, confused.

"He asked about me? What did you tell him?" Gershom's voice was strained, bordering on nervous.

"Nothing really. Just that you were a friend of mine at school."

He watched me in silence for a moment and then an uneasy smile rose up. "You used the word...friend?"

"Yes. I consider you a friend." I was surprised once again at how easy it was to say the word. I'd never really been comfortable using it, much less referring to anyone in my life with it. Then, to use it in front of the very person I was referring to was a very big step. This, I decided, was directly influenced by Ezra, Felix, and Rufus.

"Did he take the message seriously?"

"He seemed to," I replied.

Only then did Gershom relax and pick up his sandwich. "We both wondered though...how you knew of him."

Those words made Gershom choke.

After I was done whacking his back and he was breathing freely again, I explained. "I mean...Eran died so long ago. How could you possibly know him?"

"Yes, that's...that's an understandable question," he said, even though he looked like he was at a loss for words. He cleared his throat, giving me the impression it was to drag out the answer. When he did explain though, it made sense to me. "I'd heard stories about Eran from my family before...before we were separated."

"Really?" I was instantly far more curious than I had been a moment ago. "What stories?"

"Well..." he said, relaxing and stretching his legs out in front of him before continuing. "As you know, he died at Gettysburg. But, before that he lived a wild life...and I mean that literally. He'd grown up on a Native American reservation with his parents – even though they were white - and as a test of courage he'd provoke mountain lions, bears, and other animals most people did their best to avoid. Eran did it simply to fight them."

"No kidding?" I was impressed and didn't bother hiding it. Apparently Gershom had just as much respect for Eran as I did because he spoke with wide eyes and exclamations as he recounted the story of Eran's last life on earth. It was a side of Gershom I'd never seen before.

"Eran rejected his heritage and lived out his life in the backwoods. Most said he slept in caves or makeshift tents but others believed that he built a remote cabin far from any commonly used trails."

"A cabin?" I asked, dazed and wondering whether I'd been to the recreated version of it.

"Right, somewhere near a lake."

Yes...yes, I believe I had.

"He stayed mostly to himself, only going into town for supplies. Then the Civil War broke out and he volunteered. From what I heard, that was unexpected...because he was so reclusive. But, it turned out he was a good fighter. There was this one time during the war he told his commanders that their defense strategy was flawed. They refused to believe him. So, later that night, he gathered a group of men and went out to dig holes in the area where they were most exposed. Then they covered the holes with fallen leaves and branches. At morning light, just as they were heading back to their tents, they felt the ground begin to shake and when they turned they found a group of eighty men charging their camp. Eran and his five men – just five men – turned to face the challenge head on. But the traps worked. They captured every one of their attackers. Their camp was saved and no one died...that day, anyways."

Eran had mentioned he was a fighter. This story alone proved it to me.

"I can see that in him...him doing that," I said, trying not to show how seriously I had become attracted to Eran.

Gershom didn't seem to notice. He simply nodded fervently and went on. "There is story after story of how he could never be beat in a fist fight, without ever striking his opponent."

"Without making contact? How did he…win then?" I asked in earnest, reminding myself to contain my enthusiasm.

"He had some fancy way of fighting were he'd avoid punches, wearing down his attacker until they gave in. Leaning back just before the fist would land and jumping up on tables and chairs…to get out of the way…that sort of thing. They said it looked like he was fencing - but without a foil."

So Eran was good at fencing, too. Figures…

"And he was liked by the woman too…" Gershom smiled slyly. While the words left his mouth my stomach writhed in knots.

"Oh?" I muttered, far less enthusiastic.

"They fawned over him," said Gershom, taking a bite of his sandwich and nodding. "But he didn't pay any attention to them. There was only one true love for him. They grew up together – on the reservation – went to school together, and eventually married. They were inseparable."

Slowly, as Gershom's words settled, an enormous lump rose up in my throat.

Eran had loved someone before, truly loved her so much that no other woman could pry his attention away. Inseparable was what Gershom had just said. Inseparable on earth so much that they went through life together and he never appeared to even glance at another woman. Instantly, I felt a wave of jealousy rush over me, which I subconsciously acknowledged was ridiculous. There was no way I had any chance with someone like him. I shouldn't have been so upset to learn he found someone to partner with in a way that was more than business.

So where was she now? Not at the cabin, his private residence where he never brought anyone. And he'd never mentioned her. Not once! You'd think if she had that much importance in one of his past lives that he'd bring her up at least once!

Then it struck me. Maybe this was the secret Eran didn't want to disclose. Maybe this was what Eran refused to tell me during that last night with him. He probably saw the unmistakable longing in me, which would make perfect sense as to why he was now avoiding me. He had his one true love, and he didn't want to lead me on any further.

Jealousy was swiftly replaced with acute humiliation.

Gershom was still talking though I wasn't paying any attention. I was trying to keep from blacking out.

"They said her name was M-something. Margo…Madeline…Margaret! Yes, that's it! Margaret! Margaret Talor."

My breathing stopped completely. I recognized that name. "Are you sure?"

Gershom stared at me innocently. "Yeah."

Margaret Talor…Margaret Talor…Margaret Talor…calm down, I told myself. Could it be? Was that the name I saw on my list of past lives? The one from Gettysburg, Pennsylvania? The one that died the same day Eran had died? Instantly, I thought back to the scroll, my scroll…but I already knew the answer. At the time, I hadn't paid attention so much to the names as I did to the coincidence of the dates and places of death, yet some narrow part of my consciousness had caught it.

I had been Margaret Talor.

That was Eran's secret.

It felt as if the world around me stopped. Nothing moved. There was no sound.

I had been Eran's wife.

Gershom's quiet, patient voice found its way into my numb world.

"Um…are you okay?" he asked, tipping his head toward my sandwich which was now nothing more than a blob of colors squished inside my fist.

At this realization I released my breath to laugh at myself. "I think so. At least I think I will be."

"Wow…" Gershom muttered, watching me dubiously.

"It's okay…I'm okay…"

He nodded though it didn't look like he believed me.

"Here." He passed me a napkin to wipe what used to be my sandwich off the palm of my hand. "Better get a grip. We have visitors."

Just then a shy, high-pitched voice said, "Hello."

I hadn't even noticed the two girls approaching.

I glanced up to find them sheepishly staring at me.

It was Jenny McKintridge from my European History class. She had a friend with her who I'd only seen around but didn't know. But it was the piece of paper in her hand that actually drew my attention. It looked like our school newspaper.

"Hi," she said again, having stopped in front of us and was now shifting stances uncomfortably. "Is this you?"

She held out the newspaper, and I took it. Across the top of the page in all caps read:

MAGDALENE TANNER: THE REAL DEAL

I skimmed the article and found that most of it was true. Miranda had gotten a few facts wrong but nothing of consequence, just some dates and locations.

"Yes, that would be me," I told Jenny, handing the newspaper back to her.

"So you're the one who sits in Jackson's Square? The one who speaks to the dead?"

"Yes…"

She stepped forward again, still dragging her friend. "I'm Jenny. This is Sheila. She just lost her aunt."

"I'm sorry to hear that," I said sincerely. "Did you want to tell her something?"

That question, so simple and so innocent, was the catalyst to the unimaginable journey I was embarking on. This moment marked the beginning of me delivering messages for fellow students…again.

Sheila's eyes lit up as she inched forward with another small step.

"Yes, could you…could you tell her that I've saved all her paintings? They won't be auctioned off. That was very important to her. It was her last request to me."

"Sure, I can tell her tonight."

"Tonight? So soon?" she asked, astounded.

"Unless you prefer I wait…"

"No," she replied abruptly. "Tonight would be great. I…I just didn't know you could do it so fast."

"Yes, this is the express service."

"Oh, does that cost more?" she asked.

"No." I laughed. "No…I was joking."

She still seemed unable to comprehend the humor in it. "Okay, I'd pay for it, if it were," she said sheepishly, as she opened her purse and started digging for money.

Instantly, the regret creeping just inside my consciousness, for violating Ezra's terms, vanished. I realized that if someone were going to pay more for her message to be delivered, it was obviously important to her – so much so that any trouble I may get into, with Ezra or The Warden, for delivering the message would be a worthy tradeoff. "You know, don't worry about the money," I said.

"Well, I need to pay you…" she stated, as if it weren't up for debate.

Recognizing that it made her feel more comfortable if she paid, I agreed to accept the money. "Sure, but you can pay me tomorrow when I confirm with you that your aunt got her message."

Sheila smiled, the pain in her eyes lifting visibly. "Thanks. That sounds great."

By that point, I had two more students forming a line to talk with me.

"Uh-oh. Here we go…" Gershom muttered and immediately began packing up his lunch.

It seemed what had become an innocent byline in our school newspaper had turned into a massive advertisement.

By the time I got to fencing class, I had a total of ten deliveries to make and another two customers caught up to me right before fencing started. I already had my protective gear on by the time the thirteenth, and final, customer of the day approached me.

Sitting and waiting for class to begin, I heard the auditorium door open. Without having to look, I knew who it was because the hair on the back of my neck stood at attention.

Sarai took a gym bag into the locker room and returned a few minutes later, her street clothes having been replaced with her uniform. Without speaking a word to anyone, she sat down on the opposite side of the circle, facing me.

She hadn't put on her mask yet, so I could see her face clearly. It was glowering, eyes incensed. I envisioned her grabbing hold of her sword and screaming, as she sprinted across the gym floor, refusing to stop until her sword had decapitated me. Thankfully, she hadn't moved. I had to give her credit. The fact that she didn't even flinch as her nemesis sat directly in front of her, exposed and unprotected, spoke volumes about her self-control.

Ms. Valentine walked around the inside of the circle, checking everyone's gear aloud. "Jacket…Plastron…Breeches…Mask…Gloves…Foil…Ex cellent. Now, I told you we would be having a quiz today both written and sparing but a student – especially a fencing student – must always be prepared for the unexpected. So, there will be no written part of the quiz."

Whispers, happy ones, swirled around the class.

To my dread, Ms. Valentine went on to say, "That will give us more than enough time to test everyone's skills on the pad."

It seemed I was the only one who wasn't ecstatic about this change of plans. With everyone else so eager to jump in the circle and be pocked and jabbed, I figured the best thing I could do was scoot to the very outer edge of the circle. Maybe Ms. Valentine wouldn't have time to get to me before class ended, and I wouldn't have to spar. I knew this was wishful thinking. She had been a sergeant in the Army before coming to the Academy of the Immaculate Heart. Promptness was a necessity, and the stop watch around her neck was not a fashion statement. She would stay on time.

"Now," said Ms. Valentine turning in my direction. "Who's ready for the first assaut?" Her eyes scanned the room. I dropped my head silently, hoping she wouldn't select me. Yet it was almost as if I could feel the weight of her stare when she stopped at me. I was on the verge of desperation when she called out, "Maggie Tanner...I haven't seen you spar all semester."

It was almost as if I had a flashing beacon on my head.

"It's only been a few days into the semester," I commented. "There will be plenty of time later."

I knew my response fell on deaf ears when her mouth pursed out of aggravation and she placed her meaty fists on her hips, protesting my obvious disinterest in participating. She had singled me out already. There was no possibility of me avoiding the inevitable sparring match.

"The time is now," she stated staunchly.

I groaned, unashamedly showing my disappointment in being called first, and I displayed my reservation by getting up slowly – very slowly.

"And who for a partner?" She spun in the opposite direction, searching for an appropriate candidate with the same height and build. I was making my way onto the mat when I heard her say, "How about...Sarai?"

My head snapped up just as her name was called. Sure enough, Sarai was in the motion of standing, all too eagerly. She still hadn't put on her mask so when she shot me a glare, oozing with anticipation, it was clear that she expected to enjoy this sparring match.

Reluctantly, I slipped my mask over my head and met Sarai in the middle of the mat. As Ms. Valentine stood between us and reviewed the rules of engagement, I didn't bother listening. I already knew this was going to be a blowout. The foil I held in my hand - the one assigned to me - still had dust on it.

"En garde!" Ms. Valentine screamed with her usual voracity.

Sarai's mask had a see-through visor and when our eyes met the side of her mouth turned up in an evil grin.

In the next moment, Ms. Valentine was at the edge of the mat and Sarai was parrying, moving around with fancy footwork that I hadn't practiced once.

She was so fluid that it only took a few steps before she made it clear that she knew what she was doing.

I felt like a lamb at the slaughterhouse.

After a few more steps and a little more dancing, without any warning, she came at me, lunging deep.

Oddly, if it wasn't for me moving into her blade by accident, she would have missed her mark, slicing down across the left side of my waistline. Apparently, footwork aside, Sarai could use a little practice, too. This gave me some relief.

Because of my clumsy maneuvering, the point of her blade hit me squarely in the chest. Ms. Valentine enthusiastically called out the points. I ignored her.

Shockingly, the impact didn't hurt, it felt more like someone had poked me rather than stabbed me. The rubber tip on the end actually worked. I only had time to realize this when Sarai burst toward me again.

This one made contact too, on the same side and in the same area as her first strike, just below my ribs. Ms. Valentine screamed out another point.

Another lunge landed in the same spot.

"Recovery! Retreat!" Ms. Valentine commanded.

I ignored her again. What good was it?

More fancy footwork and parrying by Sarai.

Another lunge…same side…same area.

Another point.

I felt something rip. It was at my waist, on the left side. I looked down, my mask blocking my view.

Realization swept over me as I figured out what Sarai had been doing. She hadn't been aiming poorly. She knew exactly what she was doing, hitting the same spot repeatedly until it weakened and tore my uniform.

I was now exposed, defenseless.

Another lunge came, this one aimed directly at the tear.

I brought my foil up to recovery stance and suddenly Sarai was moving lightning fast, advancing aggressively, as if she were an animal and smelled blood.

Unexpectedly, coming from some faint memory, I began parrying left, right, semi-circle. It was more reaction than anything, but I was good at it. I knew this because I heard gasps from the class and even applause a few times. I felt just as fluid as Sarai looked.

To my satisfaction, I was wearing her down. I could hear her through our masks, heaving for breath.

Our blades met, bringing our faces close enough that I was looking directly into her eyes.

The opportunity was too good to pass up, I grinned at her, taunting her.

Sarai released a guttural scream and shoved me to the side. That is when I felt the blade slice into my skin.

As if a trigger had been set, the hair on the back of my neck responded wildly.

I didn't retreat, though. I advanced.

Out of the corner of my eye, I saw a flash of light move from the rafters above. It swooped down, cutting a path between Sarai and me, so forceful it took my breath with it.

Sarai screamed, this one in agony, and fell backwards landing with a loud thud on the mat in front of me, her expression was just as confused as I felt.

Suddenly, the class was still.

Only Sarai's heaving from her sprawled position on the mat could be heard.

In the quiet, someone to my right said, "You're bleeding."

Ms. Valentine rushed toward me and bent down at my waist. "Okay…okay…to the nurse's office. Sarai, are you hurt?"

Sarai didn't respond, she didn't move. She remained on her back, trying to catch her breath, glaring up at me.

"Sarai," said Ms. Valentine, more insistently. "Are you hurt?"

Her response was a low growl, sounding more animal than human. She shook her head.

"Maggie, will you make it to the nurse's office?"

I nodded, and she ordered me to go straight there…immediately.

I did but not before checking the rafters again for any sign of the bright, white light. It was gone, but it didn't matter. I already knew it had been Eran who had shoved Sarai to the ground, once again, protecting me.

By the time I walked through Nurse McKintrich's door, the white fencer's uniform was drenched in blood. She gasped and immediately went to work preparing her tools to suture me.

In truth, the anesthesia needle hurt worse than the cut. The wound just happened to look awful. So when Nurse McKintrich left the room, allowing time for the numbness to take effect, I had to mindfully stop myself from pressing on the open wound.

It was during that brief time I sensed I was not alone. A few quick glances around made me question it. Without anyone visible it was hard to be convinced. But whether by a subliminal need to be with him again or as a result of the onset of shock, I felt him near.

"I know you're here," I whispered, so that my voice didn't carry into the other room. The door was slightly ajar and if they heard me talking to myself they might consider calling a different type of doctor.

"I can feel you."

There was no voice, no bright, white light as there had been in the gym. Regardless, I seized the opportunity to talk to Eran. Even if he wasn't there listening, and I was only imagining him, at least I was getting it off my chest.

"I-I don't understand why you are avoiding me. If I've done something wrong…something that offended you, I'm sorry." My voice trembled in reaction to the emotions running through me. I had to stop and draw in a few deep breaths. I was compelled to do something only made possible after quickly surveying the empty room again. He could be here, watching me and listening. Or, I could be speaking to no one at all. Somehow, my convincing myself that I was alone made it easier to make my confession.

"I am in love with you." I stopped, absorbing the unavoidable nervousness that had taken over every muscle in my body. "And I miss you," I whispered, noticing that my body began to shake uncontrollably.

Nurse McKintrich pushed the door open, noticing I was in the midst of a trembling fit. Rushing to my side in a panic, she was about to call an ambulance when I stopped her.

"I'm f-fine." I had to say it three times before I could get her attention. "Just cold…"

She mumbled something, a curse word I thought, and yanked open a drawer at the bottom of the bed. Withdrawing a blanket and wrapping it around my shoulders, she admitted, "I thought you were going into shock…"

"It's definitely not that," I told her, knowing too well that it was the overpowering intensity of my emotions. "I'm fine, really."

As I spoke those words, I felt it. A feeling of something being drawn away from the room, one that I could only assume was the effect of Eran's departure.

Afterwards, I quietly watched Nurse McKintrich stitch and dress my wound feeling very much alone despite her presence. I felt isolated even with her right beside me, because she wasn't the one who I wished was here with me now.

No, he had gone somewhere else.

10. SUBSTITUTE

Weeks passed, Eran didn't reappear after the incident in fencing class. I still wasn't sure whether he'd been in the nurse's office or not when I declared my love for him, and this helped a bit. The awkwardness I would feel if I knew he was there to hear it and then vanished again would have been unrecoverable.

Business picked up at school, which I was thankful for because it helped keep my mind off Eran. Students approached me more and more in class, in the restroom, and at lunch. It was as if a floodgate had been released, and I had to struggle to keep afloat.

After delivering messages, I'd always end up on the porch at Eran's cabin, petting Annie and Charlie and waiting for any glimpse of Eran.

He never came.

What hurt the most was that I missed him, being around him. I felt as if my best friend simply vanished and I had no way of seeing him again. The pain of loneliness persisted inside me, resonating through every pore in my body, its presence permeating my thoughts relentlessly. My concentration in classes, never having been very good to begin with, was awful. I was certain my teachers were giving The Warden a full write-up on apparent disregard of their class work. Gershom noticed too but mercifully avoided acknowledging it. He did his best to keep our lunchtime conversations lapse-free. At home, my roommates did everything they could think of to get me to discuss my sudden depression, but I flatly refused, not wanting to relive the pain.

One day in the middle of the week, my depression changed to alarm. Gershom didn't show up for class. At lunch, I found the plot beneath our tree vacant. I waited all lunch hour, keeping an eye out for him, but he never came.

By the third day, I skipped lunch, heading instead for the main office to ask about his absence.

The Warden's door was closed but Ms. Saggy-Arm, his secretary whose name happened to be Ms. Olsonite, was propped behind her desk, clicking away on her keyboard.

When the door opened, she glanced up, immediately frowning.

I knew instantly this was going to be harder than I imagined.

"Ms. Olsonite," I said to the top of her head, as she was purposely ignoring me. "I wanted to ask about a student."

"We don't give out personal information," she replied curtly, not bothering to look up.

"I understand, but he hasn't been to class recently…"

"We don't give out personal information." This time, her voice wielded a sharper edge.

"He's a friend of mine, and I'm worried about him." As I explained this, I noticed a report on her desk with the title clear and easy to read upside down, Absence List. I had to hold back a smile when I saw it.

Her head snapped up, drawing my attention back to her. The loathing in her expression was clear. She made no attempt to hide her dislike for me in her tone, either. "We. Don't. Give. Out. Personal. Information."

I stared at her a moment, trying to control the anger welling up in me. Unfortunately, it won. "Can you say it one more time? I didn't hear you the first three."

Her face instantly contorted in blind fury. She stood up, knocking down her thick, wooden chair, causing a resounding clatter, and stomped toward The Warden's door.

By her first knock on his door, I was already out in the hallway, tucking the Absence List under my arm.

I nearly skipped my way down the hall to the girl's bathroom. Inside, the stalls were empty, but I still moved to the last one, closing the door behind me. If anyone came in and saw me reading the Absence List, I'm fairly certain The Warden would find it reason enough to send me to detention for the rest of the semester.

I opened the report and scanned it for Gershom's name. There weren't many students out of class so he wasn't hard to find. I saw the message next to it and my shoulder's dropped. Gershom wouldn't be coming back any time soon. He had moved again, this time to Georgia.

I stared blindly at the graffiti on the stall door without reading any of it.

He hadn't even left me a note.

Gershom had no email and no cell phone, preferring to stay on the fringe of society rather than in it. That quality had been fascinating to me before but suddenly turned into a great point of annoyance.

Slowly, I comprehended what was happening. First, Eran and, now, Gershom had disappeared from my life. I had never felt more alone.

I deposited the Absence List in the trash and left the girl's restroom wondering if my day could get any worse. The halls were busy with the rest of the student body trying to get to their next class. I stopped by my locker, turned my combination to open it, and pulled out my books with no hint of enthusiasm.

It was the middle of December and finals were a week away, yet I still considered simply walking off campus and heading for The Square. Despite the overcast sky, I would welcome the opportunity to ignore my troubles and concentrate on my work. In fact, if there had been an exit door on my way to Biochemistry, I believe I would never have made it to class.

Still distraught when I walked in, I found that, Mr. Sparks, the school's most notable chemistry teacher hailing from M.I.T., was not at his desk.

The class had tables lining both sides of the classroom with an aisle in the middle. I happen to sit at the desk to the far left and was lucky enough to have the normally two-seater table to myself. I preferred it this way because despite the enormous amount of money being poured into the other students' education, they truly struggled with their class exercises. I always finished at least fifteen minutes before anyone else.

As I took my seat, I heard Ashley whispering across the aisle to a friend of hers. Though I tried to ignore her, the topic of conversation drew me in.

"He has several doctorates…and he's taught at Harvard and Yale. Must have cost the school their savings to bring him onboard…" Ashley remarked, leaning halfway across the aisle. "And, Liz, he's not even close to looking like a nerd."

Liz was leaning across the aisle too, fixated on what Ashley was saying. "What's he look like?" she asked in a whisper, glancing back to check the door. "Shouldn't he be here already?"

"I saw him in the main office, probably getting the assignment list or something. Anyways…he's absolutely stunning. Like…like a model. Tall, long legs, trim, dark hair, tanned skin, but his face…" She paused to draw in an exaggerated breath. "He clearly missed his calling for the runway."

"Oh, I can't wait to see him," Liz said, eagerly looking again toward the door.

"And get this…" Bridgette went on, her voice low but excited. "He insists on being called Elam. Not by his last name but by his first. Isn't that so…normal? He doesn't have this stuffy, I'm-so-important demeanor that all the other teachers have."

"Wow…" Liz replied, shaking her head as her eyes glazed over. "How old is he?"

"You know that's the only odd thing about him." Bridgette shook her head in astonishment. "He looks like he's thirty-something but with those credentials he's got to be older than that. And there's also…"

"What?" Liz pressed.

"Well…I just get the impression that he's a lot older than he looks. He has a young face, no wrinkles, but he comes across as old, like centuries old."

Liz leaned back, perplexed, as if Bridgette had just spoken in gibberish. "How can that be?"

Bridgette appeared to think better about explaining further and retracted what she'd said. "You know, I'm sure I've just had too much sugar today."

"Yeah," Liz emphasized. "You've probably had fifteen licorice sticks by now."

"Twenty," clarified Bridgette, and they both laughed.

I wasn't laughing, however.

I knew without a doubt, without anyone needing to tell me, that another one of the Fallen Ones had arrived.

The thought crossed my mind that Eran would appear if anything should happen, and considering my eagerness to see him, I almost wished something would. As ridiculous as I knew that to be, I couldn't help missing him terribly.

As I waited for Elam to walk through the door, I was balancing several emotions at once. A small part of me – very small – tried to convince myself to leave the class. That was unacceptable. I had a strong aversion to running

186

away, even if staying meant the threat of bodily harm. A larger part of me was curious about this newest Fallen One and how he would behave. Gershom had been a good friend during the time he'd been here so maybe I shouldn't judge this one so harshly.

Just as the bell rang, my built-in radar went off, signaling the substitute teacher had arrived.

He was just as Bridgette had described, but I would add a few more descriptions, including dark and ominous. As he made his way to Mr. Sparks' desk, his eyes scanned the classroom, finally landing on me.

I didn't do it intentionally – and I was even surprised by it – but I ended up smiling at him.

He hid it well, but I still saw his reaction. Just as he dropped his gaze to Mr. Sparks' chair his recoil of surprise turned immediately to a deep, furious frown.

No, this one was not like Gershom.

"Good morning, students…" he said in a gruff, yet youthful, voice. "It must still be morning since I see some of you with eye crust."

Giggles flittered throughout the classroom and it was easy to see the students instantly warming up to him.

"As you may know, Mr. Sparks has taken to an unfortunate illness. I am your substitute. You may call me Elam. Not Mister or Sir, I'm far too young for that."

Another eruption of giggles broke out.

"Elam will be just fine. Now, I understand you are currently in the middle of a lesson, and this is lab day. So please take out your supplies and get to work. I am here to supervise and answer any questions you may have."

I rose with most of the other students and headed for the cabinets that contained our lab sets, feeling Elam's focus on me. Once I'd collected my equipment and turned around, sure enough, I found Elam still watching me. He was no longer frowning but staring intently at me, analyzing, like a mountain lion watches its prey. I ignored him, returning to my desk to prepare for the lab.

As I got to work, I heard students chatting and laughing as they progressed with their experiments. I pulled out my textbook and turned to the lab instructions, reading them through once. I could still feel Elam watching but looked up only once to confirm it.

I was happy with myself, able to focus my attention away from the hairs parading on my neck and away from the unrelenting, intense stare of an attacker. It felt like I had done this for centuries. I maintained my comfort level, and I was able to remain calm and unruffled until close to the end of class when I heard Liz whispering to me from across the aisle.

"Maggie..."

I glanced up noticing quickly that while I was nearly finished with my lab work, her lab partner was gone today and she was only midway through her procedure.

"Yes?" I asked, curiously. She never talked to me before and, although I was glad she acknowledged me, I couldn't immediately see any reason for it.

She was looking at me expectantly.

"Can I borrow your beaker?"

"Sure, let me wash it," I said, already moving toward the sink. "I just used it."

I reached the basin and turned on the cold tap water, avoiding the faucet's spurt that sprayed back at me. After it was cleaned and dried, I brought it back to Liz and handed it to her.

"Thanks," she whispered, appreciatively.

A movement caught my attention out of the corner of my eye and I glanced toward the sink to find Elam standing in front of it. He was there less than a few seconds and then returned back to the front of the room. He took a seat just as my eyes darted back to Liz.

"Do you need help?" I asked her.

"No," she shook her head, still concentrating on her experiment. "I need more time…"

I looked up at the clock and saw the bell was going to ring soon.

All at once, an explosion rocked the room.

The floor shook beneath my feet and Liz's sturdy, wood desk, where my hand had been resting, rattled violently.

I only felt a sudden cloak of heat engulf me. It was so brief, lasting only as long as the immediate danger was present, that I almost doubted that I'd felt it at all.

The next second, I was surrounded by broken glass, billowing smoke, and screaming students.

I spun around realizing that everyone was bent over, choking on smoke, bleeding – everyone but me – and I knew undoubtedly then that Eran had been here.

Several guys moved around the room, asking if anyone was injured. Others were staring, vacantly, at the destruction around them.

Dazed, I watched Elam walk through the classroom door just as the students began to stand up and filter out into the hallway. My peers were gravely pressing their hands against their cheeks as blood streamed down their foreheads and stained their clothing.

"This way! Out of the classroom, this way!" Elam was yelling over the commotion and weeping.

Students began filtering out the door and passed me, coughing, trying to expel the smoke and chemicals from their lungs.

I was the last to leave, just as The Warden arrived.

"What's this?" he franticly demanded. "What's happened here?"

Elam put his arm around The Warden's shoulders and directed him to a distance where no one could overhear them.

I tried but with all the coughing it was impossible.

Instead, I moved through the throng of students, some of which were from other classes now gawking in the hallway, having come out after hearing the explosion. A few paces down the hallway I found what I was looking for – a first aid kit.

I opened it and grabbed bandages, ointments, and anything I could carry back.

As I reached the spot where the majority of my class was standing, I looked for those with the most blood streaming down their faces. I heard someone mumble, "The sink...It came from the sink." He was one of the guys from the back of the class so he would have had a better vantage point than others.

"Who was at the sink before it blew?" asked someone standing beside him. He was clean and uninjured, clearly from another classroom.

Their eyes searched the crowd until another guy called out, coughing through his words, "That girl...who talks to the dead..."

I halted with the first aid items still stacked in my arms.

Almost in unison the crowd turned to me.

"That's true, isn't it?" Bridgette asked Liz, both of them had singed hair and black streaks marring their faces.

Liz nodded, expressionless. "She...she washed out her beaker."

"What was in that beaker?" A guy stepped through the crowd, demanding. I recognized him as someone who sat near the sink.

"It was the same thing you put in your beaker," I said, indignant. "Didn't any of you notice Elam at the sink after me?"

I watched as some of their expressions faltered. "You did, didn't you?" I said, quietly, my voice seeming to roar in the now silent hallway.

The Warden, who had been talking with Elam during this time, glanced in my direction and then stood to his full height, stomping down the hall toward me.

"Ms. Tanner, in my office. Now!"

That was all the confirmation the other students needed. Hearing my name, furiously screamed by the principal, right after they had been severely injured, gave them the scapegoat they were looking for. I dared a look in their direction and found those not coughing or choking staring at me with unwavering contempt. Yet, it was Elam's face that lingered in my memory as The Warden marched me back to his office, because his was the only one in a sea of repugnance that stood out in contrast.

He was sneering.

Following The Warden, who was obviously upset, I remained a good three paces behind him and struggled to keep up. Thankfully, this gave me few minutes to think about what had just happened. I thought back, step-by-step, on what had happened just prior to the explosion and I could have sworn I saw Elam pouring something down the drain just before leaving the classroom.

The Warden screamed at Ms. Olsonite to call for an ambulance – several of them – before slamming the door to his office behind me.

"Sit!" he demanded, and I did.

The Warden leaned against his desk, too furious to sit. His arms were crossed in front of him and he was now breathing through his cheeks like a bull.

"Can you explain, Ms. Tanner," he said my name with revulsion, "how everyone was injured in that blast but you?"

I stared back, unable to answer.

"Can you?" he shrieked.

I slowly shook my head and innocently replied, without thinking, "Right place, right time?"

The Warden's face went beet red and started to pulse in places I didn't think could pulse.

I held up my hands in defense. "Look, I don't know. One minute I was asking Liz if she needed help and the next minute the lab exploded."

"Elam mentioned you were at the sink prior to the explosion," he seethed.

"Did he mention that he was, too?"

The Warden's eyes shot wide open in disbelief. "You aren't accusing a notable professor of a criminal act, are you?"

"I'm telling you the facts."

"Well then, let's start with what you put down the drain to ignite the explosion."

Shocked from being accused of something I didn't do, I reacted by standing up, which put The Warden on edge. "I used the same liquids that everyone else in the class used, Mr. Warden. Despite what Elam told you, you're going to be hard pressed to find evidence proving otherwise."

I realized I was challenging him, meeting his argument and insinuated threats head on, but I didn't care.

I would not be accused of harming others.

"How do you explain…" he said, visibly shaking with fury. "How do you explain that you were the only one left untouched in that classroom?"

The fact was I could explain it, but he would never believe me. His mind wouldn't have been able to comprehend that my guardian, my husband from my past life, had swooped in to protect me like an ethereal blast blanket.

"I was lucky enough to avoid flying shards of glass, Mr. Warden. That doesn't make me the cause of it." I stared at him, daring him to continue.

The Warden seemed to rationally think through what I'd said because he took a moment before speaking again.

"You have been a pain in my side since you started here. Now, you have put these students at risk – even if I can't prove it – yet." He paused, taking in a deep, shaky breath. "Do not think for one second you are off the hook. The moment I find proof that you caused that damage, you will be expelled."

Oddly, a few weeks ago that would have been welcomed news. I may even have considered fabricating evidence just to expedite the process. But now...I had truly started to enjoy it here. It took only a second to decide I was going to fight to stay.

I opened my mouth and began to speak, but The Warden cut me off.

"Leave...now!" he seethed through his teeth, never taking his eyes off me.

I exited his office and headed for my next class. At lunch, I avoided the cafeteria entirely, finding a small alcove in the library. My sandwich was left untouched in the bag as I sat, staring out the window going over what had happened. Elam had poured something down that drain. I was sure of it, and it angered me even further knowing he managed to put everyone else at risk just to get to me.

At the end of lunch, I headed for European History, not averting but also not meeting the watchful stares of the rest of the student body. Judging from the number of eyes on me, everyone had heard, and they had heard I caused it.

Achan was already in the room, sitting in his usual seat. I only had to sneak a quick glance to know that he'd been told, too. His sneer was unmistakably visible and clearly unreserved. The rest of the students were talking about the explosion until Mr. Morow entered and went straight into his lecture. At the end of class, I moved swiftly through the crowded room and headed for the gym, holding my head high while avoiding direct eye contact with everyone.

Once there, I readily changed clothes and took a seat on the mat nearest the dressing room door, waiting for class to begin. As the other students began to sit on the open floor, the wide berth everyone gave me wasn't easily ignored.

Sarai chose a spot in front of me, her typical routine. She was the only one who kept her eyes locked on me when I looked up, not bothering to hide her scorn.

It didn't take long for me to realize it was expected of me to leave school grounds after being blamed for something of this magnitude. I flatly refused to meet that expectation. For one, I wanted to make sure the students injured were recovering well and the only way I could learn this was by staying at school and listening to the passing conversations. Another reason was because running only makes you look guilty – which I was not. I had just as much right to be here as any of the other students. And then there was the fact that the last two times Eran had shown up was on school grounds. I knew he wouldn't reappear again – unless my life was at risk – but school was the closest I could be to him right now. I missed him, and as irrational as it was, I felt closer to him at school than any other place. And right now, I really needed him.

11. ADMISSION

When I got home, Ezra was sitting in the kitchen with a cup of coffee. The moment she saw me, she stood, urgently moved toward me, and took my face in her hands, inspecting it.

"You're not hurt," she stated, though I knew this was a question.

"No."

She let out a deep sigh of relief and wrapped her arms around my shoulders. I had never seen her so shaken before.

"Really, Ezra. I'm fine." I pulled away from her so she could see my sincerity.

She released me and went back to her chair, shaking her head. "When Mr. Warden called-"

"He called you?" I asked, allowing my alarm to be shown. "He didn't call when I was cut in fencing class so that must mean he still thinks I'm responsible for what happened today."

Ezra stared at me, confused. "You were cut in fencing?" I had never told her, not wanting her to worry.

"Yeah, a while ago…" I replied, pulling out a chair at the table and avoiding her eyes, because I didn't want to see the concern.

"Were you hurt?" Her voice was thick and filled with emotion.

"I was fine. It was no big deal," I said and to avoid talking about it – because in reality the wound had left a small, thin scar along my torso - I stood back up to grab a cola from the refrigerator. Felix would be home soon to harangue me for it, but I didn't care. "So what did The Warden say?"

"He told me what happened. And I told him that I would wait to hear your side of the story before making any judgments."

"Thanks for that," I told her with a smile. I continued, recounting my perspective but keeping out the part about Eran's involvement. No need to go into explaining that whole thing. I did, however, tell her that I thought I saw Elam, the new professor, pour liquid down the drain just before the explosion.

"Did you mention Elam's actions to Mr. Warden?" Her concern was clearly turning into agitation now.

"I didn't bother. The Warden believes what he wants."

She released an aggravated sigh, turning her head slightly away from me to shoot a dark look out the kitchen window.

"The fool," she muttered. I was shocked. I had never heard Ezra utter a single negative word against another person.

Rufus and Felix came through the kitchen door and Ezra had me fill them in while she fixed dinner.

Rufus cursed The Warden in Gaelic while Felix paced the kitchen anxiously only stopping when Rufus snapped at him.

I didn't want a fight breaking out on my behalf, so I said, "I'm more concerned about the others in my class.

Some of them looked like they had been seriously injured."

Felix was now sitting at the kitchen table, his right knee twitched at an incredible speed. He was staring at me, attentively. "So you believe this Elam fellow did it on purpose?"

Not wanting them to get any more involved than they were, I replied, "I can't be sure."

Rufus slammed his hand down on the table, startling everyone. "Stop shakin' the bloody table," he screamed at Felix. Turning to me, he growled, "I wanna pull his guts out through his nose..."

Though I appreciated the support, I immediately shook my head. "That's not necessary."

Ezra must have had the same sense I did, that Rufus wasn't making a casual comment, because she said, "He'll get what's coming to him." I noticed the look she gave me and the meaning behind it: move on from the conversation. I agreed, so I stood and pulled a wooden stirring spoon from the drawer. Rufus and Felix took the bait without hesitation, both jumping up and vehemently disagreeing with my participation in preparing dinner. It was now a standard joke in the household that I couldn't cook and their expressions reflected the panic I hoped my insinuated actions would inspire.

Felix, instead, led me by my shoulders to the china pantry, opened the door for me, and motioned for me to do as I typically did. My boundaries in cooking were still limited to table setting and clean up.

Dinner was quicker than usual, and I was glad that we avoided dragging out the conversation on what happened at school, instead opting for making a decision on how to handle Christmas presents – the holiday being just two weeks away now. Instead of presents, we decided we'd celebrate with a reveillon menu, an old French holiday dining tradition. Given my inability to cook much of anything, I offered to buy and decorate a holiday tree which all of them happily agreed to.

This put me in a good mood, something I thought impossible after today at school. I even hummed a carol while I brushed my teeth, and I didn't even think I knew any carols.

I was incredibly thankful for my three housemates, who were always there when I needed them and who allowed me to be there for them when they needed it. With Eran's disappearance still leaving a hole in my heart, I couldn't have asked for better people to be surrounded by.

Then I closed my door and turned off the lights and everything changed.

The quiet rekindled the emptiness I felt at losing Eran, and my heart ached because of it. I rolled over and watched the French doors from my pillow, remembering back to when Eran had come through them once before.

An idea occurred to me.

Eran had known back then, had sensed, that I needed to talk with him. If I tried just as hard now…maybe he would hear me again.

I concentrated on sending him an unspoken message, focusing on this effort for over an hour. I thought back, remembering the striking curves of his face, how he stood so confident, and the smirk he commonly displayed whenever he thought I was hopelessly irrational. The entire time I was using my emotions to call out to him and bring him back to me. In the end, the balcony door didn't move once, not even an inch, and Eran never appeared.

I drifted to sleep, barely noticing the tears that rolled down and dampened my pillow.

A few moments later I woke up as I usually did, in the Hall of Records.

Though, I was immediately aware that the cold stone bench was not beneath me. I was being held.

Warm, firm arms were wrapped around me, comforting me.

"I heard you...I heard you..." Eran whispered in my ear, his voice trembling.

I moaned and sunk into his solid chest, sobs releasing from me and my body shaking against his.

"I needed you," I mumbled against his chest, my breath uneven in my throat.

When he didn't respond I lifted my head. His expression – so immersed in pain and guilt – did something I thought impossible. It cut an even deeper swath through the void in my chest, left in the aftermath of his disappearance.

"I was here for you, even when you couldn't see me." He leaned in, speaking against my forehead. "I was always here."

I let my head drop, drawing in a shuddering gasp, unable to comprehend his words.

We sat there for an indescribable length of time, neither of us wanting to move apart. I could feel in him the need to hold me, to touch me, and I was too happy to move. His arms stayed wrapped around me; his soft, sweet breath brushing my neck.

"How is your hip healing?" he whispered into my hair, tickling the back of my neck in a pleasant way.

"I don't even know it's there," I said, trembling.

I could feel his body relax and loosen upon hearing the news. "Good. I was concerned with all the blood you lost."

My head snapped up. I could feel my eyes glowing at this partial confession. "You were there, weren't you? In the nurse's office..."

He smiled wistfully at me. "I was."

"I knew it," I muttered, pleased. "I could feel you with me." I paused, watching him. A wave of apprehension swept over me as I recalled my declaration to him. "Did you hear everything I said?"

"I did," he replied, simply.

"Then why are you still avoiding me?" I asked noticing that my tone was just a level below pleading. "Is it because…" I swallowed before continuing because my throat seemed to be holding back the words I needed to say. "Is it because you don't feel the same?"

He looked away, staring at nothing in particular, and I grew nervous. In reaction, I slid away from him, away from the warmth and protection of his arms and shifted to the hard, cold bench. I thought, though I couldn't be certain, that his arms tightened for just an instance, refusing to let me go, but then released their hold entirely.

"I can take the truth," I said, staring at him, willing him to answer me honestly.

"My feelings for you are not the issue." His voice was strained. Something was still holding him back.

"I'm confused. What does that mean?"

"There is a lot you don't understand. You don't remember it all…but I do. You'll need to trust me when I say that what I do, I do for your own good."

"That is not an answer."

"Until the time comes when I explain it all to you, that answer will need to suffice," he replied, continuing to avoid my eyes.

I sighed in frustration, but it did no good. Judging from his restraint, I was not going to win this argument.

I recognized in myself something I didn't think was possible. I submitted to him, entirely. I gave him the uninhibited ability to make decisions that would include my welfare, knowing I only allowed this because I trusted him completely, without any reservation.

"I know you are holding back, not telling me everything, but I also know that you're doing it for my well-being. So, despite my frustration in that, I want to thank you for saving me from the Fallen One."

He suddenly pulled back, attempting to get a better look at me. "What did you say?"

"I'm being serious. I actually felt genuine fear this time-"

"No, about the Fallen One," he corrected. Only then did I realize he wasn't teasing. He was frighteningly serious.

"Elam…" I clarified.

"Elam?" he said, alarmed.

"Yeah, he came in as a substitute teacher and tried to…well, he tried to blow me up." I realized how ridiculous that sounded and I almost laughed at myself but Eran didn't seem to find anything about what I said to be funny. He was now absorbed in thought – a thought that distressed him, judging by his expression.

"How did you know? That he was a Fallen One?" Eran asked, slowly and deliberately, his eyes still focused downward.

"My built in radar," I said with a smile, which faded when Eran remained head down, mouth set in a firm line. "The hair…on the back of my neck. It stands up. I met a guy named Battersbee who helped me understand it. Eran…" I waited for him to finally look up. "You're scaring me."

"I'm sorry. This is serious."

"I can see that."

Eran stared into the distance, deep in thought. "But we had killed them," he muttered, confused. "Every last one of them."

"Killed them?" I said, alarmed.

"There's no time to discuss the past. I have to get you to safety."

I was nervous to admit it, not knowing if Eran might think of me as a fool from this point forward, but I went ahead and mentioned it anyways. "I would have told you sooner but I didn't think you knew anything about them."

"Sooner?" he asked, his eyes lifting to meet mine, drilling into me. An unsettling pang coursed through me and I shoved back the feeling of incompetency. Yet Eran's next words made it clear that he didn't consider me a fool. He was worried about something else entirely. "You said this Fallen One had just arrived."

"Yes, but there are more." I began to get nervous at this point, realizing I'd made a mistake in not bringing this up sooner.

He stared pointedly at me. "More? How many more?"

"Well, there's Achan and Sarai. Sharar only showed up once."

"So four…" Eran said to himself.

"Achan and Sarai are the only ones who've been around for a while though."

"Doesn't matter." He shook his head. "Even if you don't see them yourself, they're there. They wait for the right time to attack."

"Oh…" I muttered, again feeling foolish.

Eran released his breath in a rush.

"Of course," he muttered as he came to understand something that I hadn't yet. He shifted to stand up. I stayed seated on the bench as he floated a few paces away, his hand to his mouth, deep in thought. He dropped it just before explaining. "I couldn't understand why you get into trouble so often. It's not common. I see now…"

"What do you mean?"

He turned to me, his expression tense, and began to explain. "Didn't you find it odd that the moment you grew roots and stayed longer than a few months in any one place that your life was suddenly and consistently in danger?"

I thought about this for a moment. "Well, I've always been in trouble, causing trouble for the most part as I deliver messages, but my life was never actually at risk until…" my voice fell away.

"Until just a few months ago," Eran finished my thought aloud.

Eran was right. I mean nearly being run over, being impaled, narrowly escaping being bitten by a venomous snake, and having the room you are in be blown up were not run of the mill – at least not all happening to the same person within a matter of months.

Eran came to squat in front of me so our eyes were level. His face was drawn in and strained. "Remember how I told you that Fallen Ones take with them to earth different abilities? They don't know that when they took your life before – as an infant – that you came back reborn. They think you chose to fall and they had no idea what kind of ability you brought with you."

"Okay, what does that mean?" I asked, thoroughly confused on his point.

"Magdalene, they were testing different ways to kill you."

Eran waited for me to make a move, to speak, to…at the very least…flinch. I couldn't. The awareness of their intentions and their coordinated strategy caused the memories of each attempt to flood back to me, feeling as if I were suddenly locked in a concrete block.

After some time, I drew in a shaky breath. "I didn't know…" I mumbled.

"I'm sure you didn't." He placed his finger beneath my chin and gently lifted it. When we were staring at each other, he added, "But you do now. How quickly can you leave the city?"

Before I even realized it, I was shaking my head, adamantly refusing.

"Magdalene, listen to me very closely. These Fallen Ones…they wait for your return and when they learn you have…they come after you. They will stop at nothing to get to you."

"Isn't that-isn't that why I have a guardian?"

203

"There are limits to what I can do, Magdalene," he said, restlessly. "There's a reason I didn't know they were here at all. Only you can sense them."

"But Eran...I've waited so long for a home. And New Orleans is my home."

He paused and I could see him working through his thoughts. In the end, he demonstrated just how well he knew me by choosing the one reason above all others that would make me see the sense in leaving.

"When I say they will stop at nothing to get to you that includes hurting others around you...including your roommates."

I stopped shaking my head and focused on him and the pain he held in his expression.

I realized that I had done it again...bring trouble to others. Then I felt my chest cave in as a direct result of my disgruntled compliance.

"Is this the only way to keep everyone safe? To run?" I had a challenge saying that last word. I hated it and the entire cowardliness wrapped up in it.

I could see the sadness in him as he nodded confirmation.

I took a deep breath and ignored the sinking feeling in my stomach as I gave him my answer. "Then I understand what I need to do," I said, very careful on how I phrased my words.

He breathed a deep sigh of relief and gave me an indecisive smile, held only until I spoke again.

"Was this part of the secret you were keeping from me? The one you wouldn't tell me the last time I saw you here? Because I already know the other piece – I know we were in love in our past life together."

The shock that ran across his face told me that he had no idea I'd figured it out. He stood and walked a few feet away and stopped.

"How did you know?"

"Does it matter?"

He thought for a moment before replying. "No, it doesn't. It doesn't change anything. Magdalene, you need to understand something…despite what happened in our past life together…" as he said this, he drew his shoulders in as if someone had just stabbed him, caused by some memory that clearly left an indelible mark. He recovered with a shiver and went on. "I am a guardian. With this post comes responsibilities and boundaries that must be followed. And regardless of your feelings for me, regardless of your love…"

We both froze at those words. It was the first time he'd acknowledged them and the nakedness of their meaning settled over us equally as awkward.

"You do, don't you?" he stared at me, waiting for an answer which I didn't freely offer. "I can feel it, Magdalene. How do you think I know when you're fearful? How do you think I know when to show up just as you need help? I feel you. I feel your fear, your anger, and your apprehension for falling in love with me." He turned to me with stark conviction. "And you should be apprehensive, Magdalene. We can't be together. Not in this lifetime or the next."

"But why not?" I refused to believe it.

He closed his eyes and a shudder ran through him. By the end, his fists were tightened and his teeth were grinding. He was struggling with something intense and painful. I almost stood to go to him but he began to speak. "I told you that I would help you understand why I was avoiding you when the time came." His jaw clenched for a brief moment as if he were sensing physical pain. In turn, I felt his ache course through me, a feeling of being torn between remaining carefully silent and telling the agonizing truth. "The time has come, though it's far sooner than I thought it would be." He sighed, profoundly troubled, and then opened his eyes to bore his focus into me. "The secret I kept wasn't that we were husband and wife. What I held back..." another shudder ran through him... "was what they did to you on earth when they learned who we were. The Fallen Ones will never allow us to be together."

"I don't care. I'm not scared of them. All I want is to be with you," I pleaded, something else I'd never done before in my life.

"Enough, Magdalene," he said softly but firmly. "I won't let it happen again. You don't remember what they can do, what their abilities are, but I can't forget...Damn it!" He raged, though I understood that it was not directed at me but at the unfairness of our circumstances. "Why do you think I only appear when you absolutely need me and only then? We...cannot...be...together."

"But why not?" I said carefully, keeping my voice balanced and calm. "You haven't given me a good enough reason."

He remained silent, unmoving. He looked up at me with fierce, dark eyes and I was momentarily stunned. "If preserving your life isn't good enough, you'll need to understand this...I am a guardian, Magdalene. Guardians were made to fight. That's all we do. That's all we are. The Fallen Ones know this and if they were to ever realize your feelings for me..." his words fell away as he stifled another tremor in response to a dark thought invading his mind. "I will protect you...even if it means protecting you from yourself."

"So you're warning me away from you?" I was appalled. "Then why are you doing this...guarding me at all? Why the torment? Why watch over me when you know that...that we should be more?" I felt on the verge of tears, which amazed me. How could pain be so sharp in the afterlife? "Answer me, Eran. Why?"

He sighed. "Because it is my job."

I gasped, more offended than I'd ever been. "I'm a job to you?" I stared at him and waited for his head to rise but he refused to look at me.

"Yes," he said weakly, defeated. His beautiful, rugged voice released as a whimper and the pain inside me grew. "You are just a job."

I didn't think it was possible but the emptiness I'd felt with Eran being gone those many weeks held no comparison to the magnitude of what I was experiencing right now.

I felt as if I had been gutted.

"No…" I shook my head. "I don't believe you because you see, Eran, I can feel your emotions run through me. Whether you want to admit them or not, I know how you feel about me."

Stunned, his head jerked up, his brilliant blue-green eyes drilling into mine. "You feel me too? How can that be?"

"I don't know. But I do know that I feel in you the same emotions I have."

He groaned and turned away. "That's not possible…" he muttered, pausing. When he spoke again his voice was strained, determined. I drew in a breath as the intensity of these emotions ran through me. "It doesn't matter. I won't let this happen. This will not happen…I will not let us be together."

"Because you are my guardian? Then let me make it easy on us…You're fired."

"It doesn't work that way, Magdalene," he said, quieter but still resolute.

"I didn't want you to watch over me, Eran. I never asked for it."

As if he'd become an entirely new person, his reply was flat and detached. "You're a messenger. You require a guardian. It's as simple as that."

"Then we've just solved the issue, didn't we?" I said causing him to finally look up. "This will be my last message. It's from me to you…goodbye Eran."

Turning swiftly, I walked away just before the tears came.

12. SECRET

When I woke up that morning, I was crying.

The fact that the alarm was still going didn't register with me – not even when Rufus came through the door and yanked the cord out of the wall.

"What the…" he started to say, but stopped abruptly.

He must have noticed my face, swollen, red, and wet with tears, because he pulled the chair in from the balcony and took a seat in front of me.

He didn't say a word, just waited patiently until I was ready to explain.

"How…how can love hurt so much?" I mumbled, slipping my hands up from beneath the blankets to cover my face.

My body was shaking uncontrollably as I sobbed. I had gone weak as I lay there, involuntary muscle spasms being the only movements my body made.

Rufus did his best to comfort me, clumsily patting my head, sitting back so far his entire arm needed to be extended fully to reach me. I appreciated it nonetheless, knowing it was uncommon for him to delve into his sensitive side.

Finally, after I had cried until no more tears would come, I sat up.

His face was apologetic, harboring some level of guilt. "Maybe I shouldn't have told ya ta go easy on the wanka'..."

On any other day, his statement would have made me laugh. Today, there was nothing. "It's not your fault, Rufus," I said, my voice sounding odd. "You were just trying to make me happy." I sniffed long and loud at the end.

Rufus stood and hurried to the bathroom where he brought back an entire roll of toilet paper. "Here, think ya need this."

I smiled gratefully at him and unwound a few squares to blow my nose.

Again, I realized how lucky I was to know Rufus...and Ezra...and Felix. That realization started another bout of tears, knowing today would be the last day I would see them. It took every bit of energy to close the floodgates.

When my sobs quieted he patted me once more and stood, saying, "Dry up. Felix's makin' ya chocolate chip crepes special fer yer finals this week...but don't ya get too excited. They're made from coconut milk and will likely give ya the runs."

He disappeared down the stairs to tell Felix what he was doing wrong in the kitchen. I waited at the top of the stairs, listening to them bicker and to Ezra's intermittent "Now boys..." realizing just how much I would miss them.

I had never dared to allow anyone into my life, to get as close as they had become. Then I found loving them came easy and that I needed it, going so far as feeling like I deserved to be loved and to love them in turn.

It was this love that I had for them that told me what I was going to do today was not insane but an act of love – the most indisputable action love can inspire.

I went back to my room and unzipped my backpack. Removing a piece of paper and a pen, I sat down on my bed and prepared to write. But I couldn't summon the words that would make them truly understand how much I cared for them. Minutes passed as I felt consumed by emptiness. I felt like a shell, hard on the outside and hollow within.

Finally, I scribbled in uneasy lines four simple, straightforward words: I will miss you.

I pulled out a second piece of paper and wrote: Aunt Teresa, take care of yourself.

I turned to make my bed for the first time, straightening the sheets and comforter and taking extra care to pile the pillows just perfectly. Lastly, I leaned in and placed the notes so that they rested against the pillows. My roommates would have no trouble finding them.

When I went downstairs to the kitchen, a cup of coffee was waiting for me, my textbooks were piled up in case I wanted to do any last minute studying, and a surprisingly delicious plate of crepes was placed at my seat.

No one said a word to me. Whether they saw my red eyes or Rufus had told them about my weeping attack, I couldn't tell. But, they each showed in their own way that they cared. Ezra came up behind me and placed a comforting hand on my shoulder and Felix set a small vase of flowers cut from the backyard beside my plate.

I ate slowly, cherishing my time with them. I had so much to ask them, so much I wanted to learn about them. Despite the void of emotion I suffered as a result of last night's argument with Eran, I felt a longing to stay here and be a part of this family.

When I left for school, the three of them each gave their own encouragements: Rufus...a hearty pat to my back which almost sent me sprawling, Ezra...with a pencil and pen set engraved with the profoundly appropriate words "choose wisely," and Felix…who stood at the steps as I started my bike, beaming like a proud father.

I would have said my goodbyes but that would have opened a whole slew of questions that would not benefit them or me by answering. I hesitantly decided a clean break would be best.

As I headed in the direction of school, I knew I should have taken the streets that led me to the Interstate. I watched the green sign, signaling the onramp, as I passed by. I needed to make one stop before I left…I needed to find Gershom.

He was the only one I knew who could explain to me how the Fallen Ones worked, how they found me, and how I could draw them to me and distract them from my roommates.

As I entered the school parking lot, it was evident that news of yesterday's explosion was still spreading. Students and teachers alike avoided me when walking toward the main entrance. I didn't see a single friendly face in the crowd. As I entered the building, even a few of my customers who I was supposed to deliver messages back to avoided me by slipping into the bathroom or nearby classrooms. In all honesty, I didn't care. My heart had already been broken the night before.

I had no emotion left.

I entered the main office to find Ms. Olsonite standing inside The Warden's office, his door slightly ajar.

"I'll be with you in a moment," she called out sweetly. She obviously had no idea it was me.

I moved quickly, unsure when she would return to her desk, choosing the tallest filing cabinet first. It had the most drawers and, I thought, might be where the student's files were kept. As I moved around her desk, I caught a glimpse of The Warden through the door, his head bowed, shaking it back and forth.

"That can't be," The Warden stated, incensed.

Ms. Olsonite refuted him in a weak, unsure tone. "It's what the report says. I couldn't believe it myself."

I reached the file cabinet and gently pulled it open, holding my breath that it wouldn't squeak against its hinges. To my relief, it came open easily.

"She was at the sink moments before it happened," The Warden said, exasperated. "It had to be her."

My hands, already skimming through the files for Gershom's name, froze. My attention was now on the conversation in the next room.

Ms. Olsonite replied encouragingly, "Mr. Warden, you'll really need to read the police report yourself. All I can tell you is that they said there was no sign of the chemicals used in the blast anywhere on her desk or in her locker but that trace amounts were found on the professor's desk."

The Warden sighed, flustered and exasperated.

"Apparently," said Ms. Olsonite, continuing, "They've already tried to contact Professor Elam and have been unable to bring him in for questioning. The phone numbers he gave us have been disconnected and his home address was fictitious."

"But it makes no sense. He was a highly esteemed professor," The Warden refuted.

"Yes, well." Ms. Olsonite cleared her throat uneasily. "The police have learned that the documents he provided were all fabricated."

There was a few seconds of silence before The Warden asked, drowning in disbelief, "He was a fraud?"

"It seems so," said Ms. Olsonite, gently, trying to console The Warden while still delivering the undeniable truth.

"The students all seem to be doing well," Ms. Olsonite added, cheerfully, obviously trying to change the mood of the conversation.

The Warden replied meekly, "That...that is good news."

Finally, something The Warden and I agreed on. The fact that no students had been seriously injured gave me a sense of relief, which I didn't think would be possible for a very long time. It was the kind of news I had hoped to hear and it left me with some sense of optimism.

I realized that their conversation appeared to be coming to an end and returned to the files. A few more tabs and I found Gershom's.

Pulling it from cabinet and not bothering to close the drawer, I ducked around the desk, heading for the door.

The last thing I heard before I slipped through, into the hallway, was The Warden falling back into his leather office chair, humbled and distraught.

I knew I should have been elated that the facts were proving Elam to have been the culprit and that my name would be cleared, but there wasn't even a remote part of me that cared. I would be gone, permanently, from this school in a few minutes.

I went around the corner and found a quiet nook where I opened the file.

Many of the fields traditionally filled out on school documents were blank on Gershom's. Not even his birth date was listed, which seemed odd to me. That was a standard detail and easily recorded, or so I thought. So it wasn't surprising when I found the lines where his home address was supposed to be and saw that over it, written in all red, capital letters, was the word "NONEXISTENT."

I stood there, realizing how disappointed I was to not be able to say goodbye to Gershom. Of anyone, he could tell me what to expect from my enemies on my next encounter – one that I knew was not going to be far off. But also, he was the only true friend – Fallen One or not – that I'd made in any school I'd ever attended. I desperately wanted to say goodbye to him.

The first class bell rang and I was left standing alone in the hallway. I could hear a teacher's muted voice through the doorway next to me, lecturing on some indistinct topic. I exhaled slowly and then willed myself to move.

The time had come to leave.

This was when I heard my name whispered.

"Maggie…"

I turned then to find Gershom racing down the hall toward me. As I stood there, stunned, wondering if I was seeing clearly, he soared down the hallway. Yes, it was Gershom. Still, something about him didn't look quite right and it took me a moment to figure out what it was. Something was flapping just behind him. Grey wings twenty feet across and thick with feathers were carrying him…and fast. Before I could even tense up, he'd swooped by me, picking me up and carrying me through the double doors leading to the front quad.

I twisted to look over my shoulder and saw the wings entering and disappearing from my view as they flapped. With each motion, they made a high-pitched whizzing sound that reminded me of wind blowing through the crack in a window.

Only a few seconds passed and we had already turned right, gone around the back of the building, and cut across the lawn in front of the cafeteria.

In the woods, he came to a halt, his head swiveling back and forth looking for anyone who might be nearby. There was no one.

"Are you okay?" he asked, setting me on the ground.

"Yeah…" I replied, though I was still stunned. "I didn't know you could do that."

"Yes, well…" he replied bashfully, as his gaze fell.

I cocked my head to the side and asked, "Where have you been, Gershom? It's been weeks…and you left no note, nothing."

He looked at me, perplexed. "I just picked you up off your feet and carried you across school grounds in seconds and that's the first question that comes to mind?"

I thought about this for a moment and replied, "Yes."

He laughed through his nose in amusement and then lowered himself so that his feet touched the layer of fall leaves carpeting the woodland floor. His wings folded together and slipped down to the center of his body, disappearing altogether in just a few seconds.

"Nice wings, by the way."

He gave me a cocked grin and said, "Nothing fazes you, does it?"

"No," I replied flatly. "So are you going to answer me? Where have you been?" I demanded, suddenly far more upset with his absence than I had realized.

"Yes, I will answer you. But first, I have to tell you something just as important. It'll help you understand..." he paused, seeming to struggle with his words. "It'll help you understand where I've been."

"Okay..." I folded my arms and waited, watching him closely.

"Maggie, I'm not sure how you're going to take this but..." He drew in a deep breath. "I wish there was some place for you to sit down. I don't want you fainting." He glanced around us and, finding nothing, turned his concentration back to me.

I was sure my expression was sour. "Please...give me more credit than that, Gershom."

"Okay, sorry. It's just that I've never actually admitted this to anyone before. And to admit it to you of all people...well that just makes it...far more difficult."

"Then the best thing to do is just spit it out. Why enter the water slowly and freeze, right?"

Gershom nodded. He flashed an insecure smile at me and said in a rapid rush of words, "I'm a fallen soul." Immediately after the words were spoken he released a sigh and clapped his hands loudly once. "I can't believe how good that felt! Like a dirty little secret disclosed!" He chuckled, tilting his head back and letting out a whoop before refocusing on me again. "You're smiling. Why are you smiling?"

I shrugged. "Thank you for admitting it."

He took a stumbling step back, shocked. "You-you knew?"

"All along."

"How?" He was astounded.

"I have built-in radar. At least that's the best way I can describe it," I explained, still pleased with his confession and the way it made him feel.

"Right..." he whispered, thoughtfully.

"As a messenger, I come prepared...And should I assume you knew I was the messenger all along?"

"I did," he confirmed, his guilty expression returning. "When I told you the first day we met that I was looking for someone and that I'd found her here. That someone was you."

Now it was me who was astonished. "Because I'm the messenger..." I couldn't believe how ignorant I'd been. "Obviously...you showed up at the same time as all the rest of the Fallen Ones."

"Right. I wasn't the first. Achan discovered you before me."

"That's something I wanted to ask you actually..." I ventured. "How exactly did you find me?"

He stared at me awkwardly, debating on how best to answer, and replied hesitantly, "We, uh, we feel you."

"Really?"

"Yes, um, the best way to describe it is feeling like you are in a constant state of electrocution."

"So it's painful?" I clarified.

"Yes, very much at first but you get used to it."

"It's no wonder you're all glaring at me all the time," I pondered.

He gave me an odd expression. "So you know I'm not the only one?"

"For a while now."

"Can you sense any Fallen One?"

"I think so. I sensed Achan, Sarai, Sharar...You."

He stared at me, dumbfounded. "And you still befriended me?"

"I didn't know who you were until it was too late. By then, your soft side had already been revealed." Though I intended to tease him, my voice sounded bland, unrecognizable to me.

"This isn't funny," he chastised and the seriousness of his tone chilled me a bit. "That radar is there for a reason, Maggie."

"I know...I know." I looked away not wanting to hear it.

"You're lucky...that I'm different than the others," he said, clearly perturbed.

"Yes, I realize that..." I was tired of hearing others tell me that my life was constantly in danger. That fact was clear to me. "There's something that I don't understand. Why are you different? You're the only one who hasn't tried to kill me yet."

His jaw immediately clamped shut and he looked away, his face etched with remorse.

"Or do you plan to?" I asked, hesitantly, hoping I was misreading his expression.

He shook his head, still looking away. "No, I'm not like the others." He sighed, discouraged. "That's not true. I am like them in the way that...that I have taken lives before."

He waited to see how I would react but I concentrated on keeping my face still. I didn't want my actions to keep him from telling me what he evidently needed to confess.

Seeing nothing, he continued, struggling through his declaration of guilt. "But I will not take yours. Your life is safe with me." He stopped to stare intently at me and what he said next seemed more like an apology to me than a statement. "I will forever be repaying that debt. I openly accept it, whether I'm forgiven or not."

When he fell quiet, I reached out to place a comforting hand on his shoulder but he shied away.

"It should be me who is comforting you," he mumbled. He gave me a grave expression and said, "The least I can do is attempt to save you. That is why I'm here. I came back for you. I-I move around Fallen Ones and there's talk that Abaddon will appear. I'm not sure, but I think other Fallen Ones will be there too, to assist. If not assist, then simply to watch."

"Abaddon? Who's Abaddon?"

"He's the most feared of our kind. He's imperious, Maggie…indestructible…tenacious. Once he has decided to take a life – human or otherwise – he never fails."

"Great…" I muttered. "And am I to assume he's appearing again in order to come after me?"

"There's no assuming, Maggie. It's been confirmed."

I allowed that news to sink in, waiting for the feeling of fear to surface, but nothing came. The emptiness permeating me after Eran's admission the night before left me inescapably repressed.

I shoved aside that line of thought to find Gershom shaking his head at me. "You have some powerful enemies, Maggie. It takes a lot to protect you. Time and energy."

I almost laughed, but couldn't muster the emotional energy it required. "I've heard that before."

He didn't find the humor in my reply. "You and your roommates need to leave town…now."

"I was just on my way," I commented as my heart skipped a beat. It took a minute for his entire message to register with me. "What did you just say? About my roommates?"

He gave me a bleak look. "Abaddon doesn't leave any loose ends."

"They aren't loose ends, Gershom. They have nothing to do with this."

Gershom shook his head and dropped his shoulders reluctantly. "It doesn't matter. Abaddon will use them to get to you. They're in danger, Maggie. They need to leave town with you."

Anger welled up in me, surprising me with its intensity. When I spoke, it was through clenched teeth. "I was told once that the Fallen Ones will never stop chasing me. Does that now include my roommates?"

Our eyes met and I noticed his were filled with sadness. "He leaves no loose ends, Maggie."

It took what seemed like a long time before I could quell my fury. I was only slightly aware of my fists opening and closing and my pursed lips quivering. Gershom gave me time, though I could see the nervous hurry in his expression.

Once again, I was putting others at risk. This was not acceptable.

"What will you do, Gershom? Are you in danger also?"

"I've walked with Abaddon for a moment in time. I know him better than anyone, what he's capable of. I'm your best chance at getting you all out of here alive."

"I'll ask it again. Are you in danger?" I demanded.

He was reluctant to answer, his mouth pinching together in protest.

"I won't leave without knowing you'll be alright," I stated, unwavering.

"I don't deserve your sympathy, Maggie."

"Gershom," I urged.

"I will do my best to stay out of harm's way, all right?" he finally conceded, though it was clear he only did it for my benefit. Still, I'd gotten his word for it and that appeased me more than if he hadn't said anything at all.

"Good. What do we do now?"

"Now…" He drew in a quick breath. "Now we run."

13. FALLEN ONES

I'd never experienced the same level of urgency before as I did now. I even considered asking Gershom to pick me up and carry me to Jackson Square the way he carried me across school grounds but realized that would cause a stir and make it easier for the Fallen Ones to find us. Instead, I raced my bike through the city faster than I'd ever gone before. Gershom held on to the back and took the turns well. I was thankful he wasn't entirely human because if we were to collide with anything I wasn't sure either of us would survive at these speeds.

When we reached Jackson Square I didn't bother to stop on the street like I usually did when the area was crowded – as it was now. I pulled right up to Felix who was in the middle of a palm reading. The loud roar of my bike caused them to postpone the reading until I'd turned off my engine.

"Sorry," I said to both of them to which the woman in his customer chair scoffed. "Felix, there's an emergency. I need you to get home…right now."

"Is Ezra all right?" He was suddenly wide-eyed and standing.

"So far…" I replied and he let out a whimper. "I need you to get Rufus into the car and meet me back at the house."

Noticing a security guard furiously marching through the crowd toward us, I started my bike and yelled to Felix, "Hurry!"

He listened, briskly handing the woman's money back, and started in the direction of Rufus's table. I turned my bike and began to head out of The Square, narrowly avoiding a young couple walking hand in hand.

With Felix and Rufus on their way home, I was now focused on getting us back to the house safely. I had just reached the street when, without any warning, it felt as if someone was ripping out the hair on the back of my neck. The feeling was so intense it made my head jerk – causing my helmet to knock against Gershom's. My stomach was now churning, my hands were sweating, and my eyes were burning. I felt as if someone had shot mace at me. It was the most extreme reaction I'd had yet to any Fallen One.

Instantly, I knew what this meant.

Gershom made two fast, light taps to my shoulder, an action that would not have been detected by anyone unless they had been standing right beside us. It confirmed my assumption.

Across The Square, in the shadows beneath a wrought-iron balcony, stood a group of ten men and women. They were of all different heights, sizes, and ethnicities. Only one distinct similarity stood out. Despite their superficial characteristics, you could detect their age was far older than any of them appeared.

Each focused on us, all with the same furious glare. I was surprised I missed them before. They weren't exactly dressed to fit in with the crowd – each wearing a grey trench coat and black gloves despite the humidity. I immediately recognized Achan, Elam, Sarai, and Sharar.

223

The rest I didn't recall but I wondered if they knew me from past lives.

The one in front, the one that towered over the others, drew my attention the strongest.

His hair was long and black, hanging knotted and straggling down his shoulders. His arms dangled at their sides appearing long enough to reach across The Square and take hold of us. His elongated, narrow nose had the curvature of a beak. His skin was just as smooth as I'd noted the other Fallen Ones had, not a single wrinkle but unable to hide the years aging beneath it.

"Abaddon..." Gershom said, just loud enough for me to hear over my engine's roar.

I spun my bike around and headed back into The Square.

"Where are you going? We've got to get out of here," Gershom clamored in my ear.

"Felix and Rufus! I need to make sure they're safe!"

I headed to the side street where I knew Felix regularly parked and found the two of them already in Felix's car. Behind the wheel, I saw Felix's face and it stunned me. His carefree, flighty countenance was gone, replaced with stone cold determination. He almost looked like an entirely different person. That was comforting, knowing he took my urgency serious. The moment the car started, he raced through the lot, out on to the city street, and headed for home.

I followed them, keeping an eye out for Abaddon and any other Fallen Ones. It appeared that we lost them and I was relieved – but only slightly because I still remembered Eran saying that Fallen Ones stay hidden and wait for the right time and place to attack.

Eran...the thought of his name made my stomach churn from the pain. I was certain he'd felt that – my longing for him – so I instantly pushed it away, not wanting him to know I was thinking about him. Despite realizing I needed him now more than ever, my pride kept me from allowing my emotions to run free and send him a signal. I was on my own now and I had to remember that.

I told myself to focus. This was not the time to dwell on a broken heart. I needed to concentrate, to remain alert. There were things far more important at risk than my pain: My roommates' lives. My job now was to get my roommates and Gershom out of harm's way.

Once at the house, the four of us charged through the door so quickly that Ezra was on her feet before we got to her office.

"What's happened?" she asked, instantly apprehensive.

A moment later, I realized they were all looking at me, waiting for the reason why I collected everyone to the same spot.

"Sit and I'll explain," I said, which they did, each stiffly on the edge of their chairs.

I inhaled deeply, preparing myself for what I was about to admit, the guilt welling up in me before I even spoke. "I have put you in danger. There is someone after me – more like a group after me - and now they've found me. I had planned to leave this morning to keep you all safe. Rufus, that's part of the reason you found me crying."

They turned to Rufus for answers but he simply shrugged in confusion.

Ezra cleared her throat. "When you say 'leave' do you mean you were planning on leaving the city – for good?"

Her question, it being the first one of all the ones she could ask, made me pause. "Ezra, you're in danger," I stated.

"I understand that. Please answer me," she said insistently.

Certain my face was fully expressing the guilt I felt, I gave in. "Yes."

Ezra let her head drop as if my confirmation was the worst of her fears. When she raised her head again, and

225

focused on me, she didn't bother hiding her disappointment. "Maggie, you are in greater danger alone than with us."

"No – I'm not explaining this clearly." I groaned, much to my chagrin. "I am putting you in danger just by being near you. They are after me! Not you!"

"And who ya talkin' 'bout anyways?" asked Rufus, again with a shrug. "Who're 'they'?"

I was speechless. They didn't care that these Fallen Ones could walk through the door at any moment, each with their own ability to inflict harm. They were more insistent on asking questions than protecting themselves. It was incredibly antagonizing. I knew the only way I could help them understand the risk they were in was to help them understand who the Fallen Ones were, so I looked to Gershom for assistance.

Gershom raised his hand meekly and said, "Hi, I'm Gershom." He then laughed uncomfortably.

No one laughed with him. They simply stared, waiting for an explanation.

"Gershom is a friend of mine from school. He knows these…people."

"Are 'these people' from your school?" asked Ezra.

"Yes…and no. I-I think they came to school to find me," I said.

Ezra was now standing. "You mean you've been going to school with these people?"

Finally, at least Ezra was alarmed.

"Not all of them. Listen…Gershom knows them better than I do."

Ezra didn't bother to sit back down. Instead, she turned to face Gershom, not intending to but very much looking like a mother who'd just found out her son was ditching school.

"Um…yes, I can explain." He leaned forward in his chair propping his elbows on his knees. "I…uh…I'll start with Abaddon…"

At the sound of that name, I noticed out of the corner of my eye that Ezra, Felix, and Rufus each turned to look at one other but by the time I'd glanced in their direction they were back to staring at Gershom.

"Abaddon, well, he's…he's…"

Rufus growled and said, "Wouldya just spit it out already?"

Gershom shook at Rufus's ferocity and replied, streaming his words together. "He's seen what Maggie is capable of. He knows that she can destroy him…and all others like him. Her very existence threatens him."

He paused and glanced around the room, waiting for acknowledgement that everyone understood him and grasped the severity of his message.

"I see," said Ezra, unshaken. "Go on."

Gershom's face conveyed no affect to Ezra's nonchalance as he began to speak again. "Abaddon has been sending his followers to find and to…to kill Maggie before she can do the same to them. And he's here now…looking for her."

"Does he feel this way because of her ability to speak with the dead?" Ezra asked, sounding as if she were a detective interviewing a witness.

Gershom's eyebrows rose. "That…that's very insightful." Gershom paused and turned to me. "Maggie, you returned to earth fully human." He glanced around the room uncertain. When no one bristled at this statement, he continued. "So what you don't know is that you're involved in a war that has been in existence for centuries. Many lifetimes ago, you came here to exterminate Fallen Ones. Since then you and Abaddon have hunted each other, battled each other, during every incarnation on earth. It was only the last time you incarnated that a battle between all Fallen Ones and your...well, your kind...raged for days, and it was thought that we were eradicated. But the Fallen Ones did survive, staying hidden...until your return. There is bad blood between you and Abaddon, centuries of it, and nothing will stop him in finding you and killing you."

"If he can find her," Rufus suggested, determined.

"That won't be a problem," Gershom said wistfully. "He senses her."

"Senses? What does that mean?" asked Felix, speaking up for the first time. His stoic expression hadn't budged since I spoke with him in The Square and I was amazed at how well he could hold himself together during times of emergency. "How does one sense another person?"

Gershom was incredibly shaken up being in the same room as my family and it occurred to me that it may be because he didn't have any family of his own. That thought filled me with sadness and I answered the question to help him shake the feeling. "We sense each other when we're near without even trying. My main sensor is the hair on the back of my neck. It goes crazy, standing on end...among other reactions."

I was thankful when I looked around the room and didn't find them staring back as if I was crazy.

"Well..." said Rufus, calmly. "That must come in handy."

"You have no idea..."

"And we..." Gershom paused uncomfortably. "They, I mean, feel electricity run through their bodies when she is near."

"Okay, so this Abaddon character...What can you tell us about him, Gershom?" asked Ezra, taking a seat again, coolly watching him.

"The most important thing you need to know is...well, he has this ability to control your movement. A form of telekinesis but far stronger."

Gershom and I waited for them to respond. What he was explaining was commonplace for him and for me but to them it would sound strange, impossible even.

Instead, Ezra nodded serenely.

Again, my roommates weren't taken aback. It took me a moment to figure out the reason and when I came to it I instantly relaxed a little. They were shock-proof. After years on the psychic circuit, dealing with all types of individuals, certainly ones with questionable sanity, they were more prepared than most to hear this news.

As if Gershom read my mind, he threw up his hands lightly and asked, "How-how is it that none of you are surprised by any of this?"

The three of them chuckled together but it was Ezra who answered.

"Gershom, having traveled around the world, you wouldn't believe what we've seen on the road."

"Ay, this is nothin'," added Rufus.

Felix shrugged one shoulder and nodded in agreement.

When Ezra spoke again, I quickly found the nearest vacant chair before my legs collapsed under me.

"I'd have to say Abaddon may have been the cause of a few of our friends disappearing along the way."

Felix and Rufus nodded in agreement.

"Do you think you know him?" I asked, leaning forward, reminding myself to breath, unable to contain my anxiety.

"Actually…I think we've been introduced."

Gershom and I glanced at each other, completely shocked.

"If I recall, he didn't travel alone, though."

"That's right," said Gershom, more relaxed now. Apparently his angst was partly the challenge of explaining something to others assumedly unable to comprehend it. Thankfully, this issue had been resolved.

Gershom spoke freely from that point on.

"Maggie, that's why I left, as more of his group appeared at school. I figured he would follow shortly. Unfortunately, that was indeed the plan." He gave me an overwhelmed grin and continued. "So, to give you all an understanding of what we're up against...Abaddon started collecting his followers one by one. The first was Sarai. She is his daughter who followed him here and she's just as deadly. She has the unique ability to make any man, who she speaks directly to, fall in love with her. Not a balanced, well-meaning, healthy kind of love but a sad, painful one that leaves the man tearful and desperate. I've been conscientious and thankfully have never felt the affect but it does not look pleasant. Although she seems to have control over the level of lust and obsession she can create in her victims, she typically doesn't hold any of it back. So..." Gershom addressed Rufus and Felix. "...if she attempts to speak to you, if you see the smallest hint that she is addressing you, try to get out of earshot. This will be challenging because...well, I've actually never seen anyone successfully evade it. Just do your best to avoid her at all costs. The good news is that this affect, this power, lasts only until she leaves. Unfortunately, she uses her ability merely to debilitate, so most men don't survive that long."

"Wonderful..." Rufus muttered sarcastically.

Felix didn't appear concerned, which didn't surprise me.

"Then there's Elam. When Abaddon isn't around, Elam acts as the paternal overseer. They picked him up in the Tower of London while he was working as an executioner. He's said to have been the one to execute Anne Boleyn and he enjoyed doing it. The makeup of the human body has intrigued him ever since."

"Anne Boleyn? The Queen of England, Anne Boleyn?" asked Ezra, showing surprise for the first time.

"That's correct."

"But she was executed in 1536..." Ezra stated under her breath.

"Most of those I am talking about have been alive for hundreds of years, Elam included."

To this, my roommates raised their eyebrows.

Gershom, if he noticed, ignored it. "Elam has one weakness. Although his skin cannot be punctured – evidence from the explosion in Mr. Sparks' Biochemistry class – any part of his body not covered in skin can be harmed. This includes his eyes and the inside of his mouth. I know of one attempt on his life in which he was given poison. It nearly killed him but with his love of chemistry he was able to narrowly escape death by concocting an antidote serum. His attacker later became the victim and was found gutted from the inside out, hanging from a spike on the grounds of the Tower of London."

"Ugh..." Felix dipped his head and shuttered.

"The next most powerful one is Achan. Abaddon discovered him sometime during the French Revolution, picking off rebels from high positions with his choice of weapon – the bow and arrow. Something Maggie knows, unfortunately, all too well. But what you don't know is his strength. I've never seen anyone with the magnitude of his ability. No one has ever been able to match him. And lastly, there's Sharar. He came to Abaddon not long ago and asked to be a follower. I don't know his history but what I can tell you is that he's unpredictable. He strikes without thought or strategy...it seems...whenever the urge appeals to him. His only weakness that I'm aware of is his ego. He thinks very highly of himself. No one is above him. "

"Not even Abaddon?" I asked.

"That remains to be seen."

"Alright," said Ezra, thoughtfully. "So we know that Elam must be attacked through the eyes or the mouth, Achan's strength can possibly be used against the others if we position ourselves tactically, the women would need to handle Sarai for obvious reasons, and we can possibly use Sharar's ego against Abaddon."

Ezra – always the supportive, selfless caregiver – left me unnerved hearing her talk with such strategic derision. It even took Gershom by surprise.

"Y-Yes," he stammered. "That's well thought out, Ezra. But let's hope it doesn't come to that. What you should be focusing on is leaving the city. We've wasted too much time already."

"Agreed," she said, glancing at each one of us. "So…what do you think about Key West this time of year?" She asked this languidly, as if she were offering up the location as a vacation spot.

Felix clapped his hands in excitement. "Yessss!"

Rufus lifted his shoulders, displaying indifference.

Within minutes, our bags were being haphazardly stuffed with clothing and toiletries before leaving the house. As I followed Rufus out the front door, I paused and turned one last time. I could see down the hallway to the kitchen where I'd first met these people I was now leaving with; where I'd eaten meals and held soulful conversations with them; where I felt that my life had finally begun. Now, here I was a few short months later running from the first place I could call home.

The sad, stark reality of our situation hit me as I passed the parlor and caught sight of the polished gold rod next to the fireplace screen. It had been covered in cobwebs the first time I'd seen it but had remained polished and ready since my roommates had moved in. So long as Abaddon and the Fallen Ones were after us, we would never be able to stay in one place for too long again. We'd always be glancing over our shoulders, waiting for one of them to walk through the door when we least expected it, and keeping our toothbrushes and clothes in bags for a quick getaway. None of this seemed fair – least of all to Ezra,

Felix, and Rufus. They hadn't asked for this type of life. I had drawn them into it. These thoughts more than any other reason were what resolved me to do what I had planned to do this morning. I only needed to get everyone else safely out of town before I could act out the decision I'd secretly made.

With Felix, Rufus, Ezra, and Gershom in the car and me on my motorcycle, we headed east on I-10. I followed, patiently, for over an hour until I was certain they were no longer looking back to make sure I was still there. When I was completely sure, I exited onto an inconspicuous off-ramp and I parked there, under the overpass, to wait. I allowed enough time so they wouldn't see me, and then I started my engine, drove up the onramp for I-10 West, and headed back to New Orleans.

14. OUT OF HIDING

It didn't feel like I was driving my bike toward to the jaws of death, like I was delivering myself to evil. In fact, I felt nothing at all. This consciousness – or more accurately my lack of emotion, thought, or free will - only slightly registered with me. I was on autopilot. The bike moved itself through the cars back toward the city, back to the Fallen Ones.

I did, however, understand that without any feelings, it would be far more difficult for Eran to find me. Knowing this calmed me even further. By the time he learned what I was doing, I'd be dead. I would be dead and, more importantly, my roommates would be safe. Abaddon and his followers wanted me and that was exactly what I was planning to give them. I was their beacon, their honing light, used by the Fallen Ones to track down my roommates wherever they may be. Gershom had made that clear when explaining how I gave them the sensation of being electrocuted. Being removed from the equation, my roommates would be undetectable and free to live out their lives in peace.

I wasn't certain that what I was about to do would be 'acceptable' or that I would end up in Eran's world, but if it didn't happen, if I went somewhere else, at least my efforts here on earth would not be in vain. Ezra, Rufus, Felix, and Gershom would be safe and that mattered more.

Of course, they'd wonder what happened to me, why I suddenly disappeared while following them on our escape. They'd turn around and come looking, first at the house where they'd go through every room, calling my name, and in the end they would only find my letter...the letter I had left on my bed.

I never had any intention of running. It's not in my nature, as much as Eran, Gershom, and the others wished it to be. I said I would leave and that was what I planned to do. So when I went in search of Gershom this morning, it was to say goodbye but it was also to understand the Fallen Ones – what I should expect. He'd given me a pretty clear picture while describing them to us in Ezra's office. The prospect of pity was laughable. I had a solid understanding that my death would be drawn out and painful, even entertaining for them.

By the time I reached the city limits, the sun had just touched the horizon. It would be dark soon enough. With it being close to Christmas, colorful strings of lights were already lit on the houses as I rode by them, their cheerfulness not being lost on my decidedly darker situation. As I exited the interstate, and headed down Canal Street, I noticed that tourists and locals alike moved in and out of stores for last minute shopping and the street cars and horse-drawn carriages were blazing with lit decorations.

I appreciated the city's mood, feeling a pang of disappointment that I would never be able to experience it all again, and then I immediately brushed the thought away.

No feeling, I reminded myself. I wasn't certain I could keep that promise, in light of what I was expecting to encounter shortly. I would sure try. The last thing I'd want is for Eran to stop this from happening. He'd proven more times than I cared to count that he'd do his best to save me from death. If he was successful at it this time, it would only cause me to find another time to confront the Fallen Ones, delaying the inevitable. I much preferred to get this over with quickly.

So I turned my thoughts to finding them.

Knowing who they were, that they were visitors to the city, and that they indulged in vices – countless ones I imagined – there was really only one place I could think to find them.

Bourbon Street.

So I pulled onto the thin, cobblestone lane, infamous for its brazen entertainment, and inched my way through the gathering of partiers milling around. They heard my engine's rumble and parted the way, making it easy to move freely down the street without worries of running into anyone. It also allowed me to scan the open doors of bars, clubs, and restaurants. Although they were packed with people, I kept my sight focused on looking across the top of the crowds' heads, in search of just one who stood out, towering over the rest.

Abaddon.

I was midway down the street when I felt him. The same intense reaction I'd encountered earlier in The Square came over me and I nearly swerved into a group of college students before regaining control of myself. Through it all, I realized that I didn't feel a moment of fear, anxiety, or any other emotion – just the odd symptoms of a Fallen One's presence. I realized this was the result of my still being in a daze, reacting more than thinking.

That moment of lost control over my bike drew enough attention that I was sure Abaddon, or one of the others, had seen me. Still, I wasn't able to see them. They were somewhere in the crowd, somewhere nearby, but as I looked from side to side the only ones in sight were tourists – none of whom looked familiar.

I decided to park my bike on one of the side streets, before heading back to the place where I'd felt the Fallen Ones. This bike had been my first venture into independence and freedom, carrying me toward it wherever I went. It was a part of me. It defined me. As I stepped away from it, I was aware that it now carried me to my death.

I didn't allow myself to look back as I left it, for fear of another pang of disappointment, but instead, I focused on Bourbon Street and the packs of people moving along it. I still didn't see Abaddon or any of his followers as I stopped at the street corner. Variations of music pumped from the establishments lining the broken sidewalk. Meagerly clad woman gestured to men walking the street and beckoned them into dark doorways with strobe lights and dancing girls beyond. Tourists stood on balconies lit with strands of holiday lights, slopping beer from enormous plastic cups. There was too much going on. If I was going to coerce them out of their hiding, I would need to draw attention to myself.

On Bourbon Street, there was really only one way to do it. It was not what I preferred but it would be effective.

I entered the nearest bar with access to a balcony and climbed the stairs. Even in the dark staircase I felt the Fallen Ones so strongly that I expected to run into them as I reached the top. There were only college girls hanging over the side of the balcony. I joined them, squeezing myself in between the crowd until I too was overlooking the street below.

From above, it looked less crowded. This was good. Easier to identify them.

"You...you..." a deep voice from below called up a few moments later.

I looked down to find a guy in his early twenties pointing at the balcony where I stood.

"Me?" called a blonde girl standing to my right. She didn't bother to hide the thrill in her voice.

"No," the guy shook his head and pointed again.

By then, I was certain his finger was focused on me.

"Oh..." said the girl bitterly, turning to me with narrowed eyes. "He means you."

"Come on!" The guy from below called, dangling a cheap plastic necklace, as if that would entice me.

He had no idea he was simply a means to an end. Still, I knew I needed to play the part. I smiled seductively at him, hoping it looked that way at least. I'd never attempted that expression before. Then, I slipped my fingers up underneath the hem of my shirt – like I'd seen other girls do before when I was forced to venture onto this street.

"Don't you have anything better?" I called down to him, my eyes disregarding him and scanning the street for any sign of a Fallen One.

"Oh, he's got something better," his friend called out lewdly.

As much as this attention made my skin crawl, it was effective. The crowd of onlookers was growing.

"Well don't make me wait," he called out, still dangling the plastic bead necklace.

I stalled as long as I could, throwing back a flirtatious laugh, and lifting my shirt a little higher, careful not to go any farther than my belly button.

Hoots and howls rose up from the crowd below.

"Just do it," the blonde girl next to me insisted, her voice tainted with jealousy.

I ignored her.

Just as the girl nudged me with her elbow to get on with it and the crowd started to get antsy, Abaddon appeared from around the street corner, his followers directly behind.

I froze, watching them as they stopped across the street, folding their arms and staring up at me, like a small army waiting to advance.

They wouldn't have to wait long.

I dropped my shirt and turned away from the balcony, boo's and jeers erupting and filtering up from the street. I disregarded them. Let them call me a prude. I was dealing with an issue far more important than baring my chest.

I made it down the staircase without falling, despite the innate hesitancy I felt in moving closer to my end. Out on the street, I found the Fallen Ones where they'd been before. Abaddon's eyes met mine, and I turned to head down the dark street toward a quieter spot, a less public place. I wasn't sure what Abaddon had in mind, but I knew it wasn't going to be pleasant. I didn't want anyone to accidentally find us or to valiantly step in, trying to be a hero.

As I headed farther away from the commotion of Bourbon Street, into the darkness, I didn't need to turn to make sure they were following me.

I could feel them.

As we got farther from safety, my radar grew more and more intense, as if it was sensing their anticipation of what was to come.

I approached a dark alleyway and figured this would be as good a place as any to do it. Only the hazy illumination of a streetlight reached here, and no doors or windows could be seen, just the back sides of two buildings.

An efficient place to die.

It was here and now. I turned to face Abaddon, startled to find him leaning down, merely an inch away.

One moment I was staring into the cold, black eyes of a killer and the next I was flying backwards at lightning speed, inches off the ground.

I braced myself, ready for the sure collision between the brick wall at the end of the alley and my spine.

It never came.

My body stopped a foot away, still inches off the ground, hovering.

I could feel my heart racing, trying to overcome the impact of what had just happened as Abaddon and his followers stalked down the alley toward me, their shadows stretching long across the building's walls.

They halted their march just a few paces from me. Only Abaddon continued his approach until he was barely out of arms reach. He smiled, and again, I was struck by how he appeared so young on the outside while I could see the wrinkles of age moving just beneath his skin, as if the top layer was translucent.

"You'll forgive me if I keep you at a distance, won't you?" he said in a deep, raspy voice.

I shrugged. "It's not as if I have a choice." I moved my legs to prove my point, and they flailed uselessly beneath me.

His raspy voice released a laugh, sounding oddly like two pieces of metal grating together. "It's for our protection...you understand." He said this flippantly, as if he truly thought I did.

I was certain my expression reflected my confusion when Abaddon blinked in surprise, a very human reaction I noticed.

"Don't tell me you've forgotten."

"Forgotten what, Abaddon?"

He sighed, a half-cocked smile lifting his face. "I've missed the way you speak to me," he whispered, contentedly. "Such fury...but I don't recall you being one for games, Magdalene."

"I'm not…"

He opened his mouth to speak, pausing and starting again, ultimately releasing another deep chuckle. "Am I to understand that you have no recollection of me?" He seemed incredulous.

I kept silent. There was no sense in dragging this out with frivolous conversation.

Abaddon glanced over his shoulders, sending a dubious grin toward his followers and then back at me.

"You always keep me guessing, Magdalene," he said, wistfully. I got the distinct feeling that I had known Abaddon for a very long time, for lifetimes possibly. He drew a finger up to his lips, grinning behind it, and then dropped it to his chest, acting playfully glib. "So how is it that you have no remembrance of me and…" he motioned behind him, "…my cohorts?"

"Don't you have something more important to do than ask questions, Abaddon?" I said, reminding him of why we were here.

Just as important, I wanted to avoid admitting I had been reborn which would also inform them that I had no abilities, no defenses as they had assumed I did. If they did learn this, I had no doubt they would drag out my death.

It was Achan who figured it out.

He moved toward us with a curious grin. "She didn't fall, Abaddon," he said in a low voice, never breaking his glare from me. "I think she chose to be reborn. She hasn't had a clue who I was all along nor Sarai or Elam…"

Abaddon drew in an eager, shuttering breath and his eyes widened with excitement. His elation with hearing that news was unmistakable.

"Reborn…" he sighed. "Right you are Achan…"

For the first time, Abaddon stepped forward breaching the space where I could reach for him.

"You know what this means, Magdalene…" he stepped even closer, drawn to me without hesitation. "You gave up

241

the last defense you have…the secret that you have no defenses at all." He stared at me, inquisitively. "You realize now this won't be sudden." His tone desperate, containing pity.

He was referring to my impending death.

"Yes," I seethed.

"Ah, careful." He held up a finger as one does for the benefit of an overanxious child.

"We wouldn't want Eran coming and spoiling our fun now would we? At least not until the end…" He grinned mockingly. "It'll be so similar to last time. A grand trip down memory lane."

"Last time?" I whispered, immediately shoving aside all feelings, surprising myself at how capable I was at relaxing, especially during a time like this. Whatever Abaddon was referring to involved Eran, and I wanted to avoid the potential of causing him any pain.

"I know you won't remember, you being newly reborn," said Abaddon, conversationally. "That's much too bad." He raised his finger to wag it at me. "I'll tell you what I'll do. I'll remind you. That way, you can relive it just as we will."

He was playing with me, teasing me, and if I let myself go I would have been infuriated by this point. I refused to allow I, though.

"Why don't you just get on with it?" I asked, carefully keeping my emotions in check.

He pondered this, tilting his head to the side. "No, I think telling you will be far more enjoyable."

I heard laughter behind him, the other Fallen Ones clearly enjoying the direction Abaddon had decided on.

"It was a work of genius, Maggie." He inhaled dramatically at this memory. "Making you first think that he was going to die at our hands and then making him think the same. And before we knew it, there you both were, surrounded by us – your nemeses - ready to die to save each other. Oh, and you did die, Maggie. So dramatically." He said these last words passionately, savoring the memory. "Poor Eran, he had to experience it all…"

"Stop," I whispered, closing my eyes as if that would erase the sound of his voice.

"Careful now, Maggie. Careful with your emotions," Abaddon warned.

I had been cognizant of them all along, not needing any reminder.

"You see, what I don't understand is why you would ever decide to return. You know we're here. You know what we are capable of doing. You know our history together; well, at least you do when you're memory returns. Why it's…it's just illogical."

He drew in another scornful breath, playing with me. Very slowly, he removed one glove, never taking his eyes off me.

"Oh, but I'm so glad you did." His hand rose and reached for my face, I turned away but he caught my chin and held it.

His eyes widened even more.

His followers behind him gasped the moment our skins touched, shifting their positions for a better view.

"I've always wondered what your skin would feel like. Warm like a human's or hot like the others?"

It finally occurred to me why Gershom never touched me. He avoided shaking my hand on the first day of school and was always conscious of avoiding skin contact whenever there was a potential for it. Now I understood why. My skin harmed them somehow.

"The others'?" I asked without realizing I had spoken at all. My attention was drawn to the fact that he still had his cold fingers gripping my face.

He balked at me and finally released my chin. "The other messengers, of course. You really have no memory, do you?"

My breath caught in my throat. Other messengers? My head went dizzy. What other messengers?

Abaddon released my chin and tilted his head back for another raspy laugh. "She has no idea…" he called back to the others.

"There are other messengers?" I demanded.

His face dipped down like a shy boy and he grinned up at me through his lashes. "Were…there were other messengers. We got to them before they got to us."

"That's enough, Abaddon," someone called out from the opening of the alleyway. I instantly recognized the voice, the same one who I'd listened to each lunch break for the past several months, who I'd held deep conversations with, who had warned me against this very situation I was now in.

Gershom stepped through the shadows and into the filtered light of the street lamp. The glow from above distorted his face, but I could see the determination even from my place several feet away.

Abaddon didn't bother to turn around. He knew the voice too. "Still have your old traits, do you?" he asked, frowning.

"Yes, Abaddon, I can still feel fallen souls no matter where they are…most of all yours."

Abaddon's face twisted into annoyed determination.

"You should be proud, Gershom," he said, still facing me, still focusing his eyes downward. "You put forth a good effort…attempting to redeem yourself, protecting her. But you've lost. We have her now."

"Let her go," Gershom spouted furiously.

Abaddon ignored his demand. "Be mindful, Gershom. Have your efforts worked? No…you still exist on this plane. You always will. You will live out your punishment among us, Gershom. You have no choice. Come back to us, boy. You have so much to learn."

"Leave him alone," I said, unable to bear the pain on Gershom's face. "He's done nothing to you."

Abaddon glanced up, his expression softening. "Oh, but he's done quite enough to you," he replied, teasingly.

"Just leave him alone, Abaddon," I repeated, cringing at how my voice came out as a helpless whimper.

"No, my dear Magdalene," he replied, the mock sympathy in his voice making my skin crawl. "I don't think you quite understand. Allow me to explain..." He paused and a flicker of pleasure passed across his hideous face as if he were about to enjoy something. He spoke slowly, allowing the words to fully sink in. "On that dark, vacant road so long ago, it was Gershom who took your parent's lives. It was Gershom who drove the truck into the side of your parent's vehicle, projecting it across the frozen fields."

I didn't comprehend him at first, but for some reason I was slightly conscious of my insides knotting up. My parents, I thought. How could Gershom even know my parents?

"You look confused," said Abaddon, clearly enjoying himself. "Shall I continue?"

"No," I told him firmly and he laughed. I froze against the repugnant breath, as it brushed by my face.

Gershom stepped forward, the timid boy I knew from school now replaced with a virulent man resigned to admit his actions. "This is my burden to bear...I will tell her," said Gershom and turned to focus on me. "Your parents were the last messengers, Maggie. Abaddon sent me to take them...to take their lives...to erase their existence...and I did, destroying everything. Including the documents, Maggie." These last words made his voice collapse, the weight of guilt too much for him to carry.

I instantly recalled our conversation the first week of school, when he had seemed so innocent asking about my parents.

"You?" I said my chest heavy, as if someone were pressing on it.

"I was young, I was new to this, I had no idea what..." he paused, straining. "If I could just take it back..." His words fell away as his head sank to his chest in shame. "I'm so sorry."

It was Abaddon who was happy to fill in. "Why do you think he's been here all along? Guiding you, watching over you. He's been protecting you, trying to repay you for taking the lives of your parents here on earth so many years ago...True too, he's going to do his best to keep your new earthly family from being killed. Sent them off in the wrong direction, did you?" Abaddon called back to Gershom and turned to me, again with mock pity. "Fortunate for us, he's going to fail in this endeavor, too."

Understanding his insinuated threat at my roommate's lives, rage unlike anything I'd ever felt before surged within me. I was blinded by it. Instantly, I was reaching for him, clawing for him, hitting at him, desperate to make contact. When I realized he was laughing and standing a few feet back, watching, I paused. A scream boiled up from the depths inside me. "You stay away from my family!"

His eyebrows creased in confusion but it wasn't until he spoke again did I understand why. "Well, that won't be necessary. They're already here."

It was Ezra's voice that boomed down the alleyway, confirming Abaddon's announcement. "Let. Her. Go."

Abaddon smiled gingerly and slowly turned around, reminding me of a hunter who just heard its prey caught in a trap.

From where I am standing, I could see Ezra in the middle of the alley with Rufus and Felix on both sides of her. Gershom stood a few feet away, closer to me and much closer to the Fallen Ones now.

A moment of silence, an impasse, followed.

"Go away," I called out, but my voice cracked. I cleared my throat and repeated it with more force. "This isn't your fight."

"Ta hell it ain't," Rufus roared, offended.

His intensity made me shake.

Abaddon chuckled to himself, overtly confident with his abilities. He had no fear.

But it was Sarai's reaction that alarmed me.

She was so sly about it that no one but me seemed to notice as she sauntered around the group, moving closer to Rufus.

"Rufus!" I called out, but he cut me off.

"We ain't leavin'!" he charged back.

And then came Sarai's soft, sweet voice. "Now, now…"

That was all that was needed to bring Rufus to his knees, like a mountain crumbling to the valley below. He ended up with his hands on the ground, heaving and weeping.

The Fallen Ones watched in anticipation, the rest of us in horror, as Rufus reached a hand up, grasping for the hem of Sarai's trench coat. When she casually stepped away, he collapsed to the ground, sobbing.

In the blink of an eye, the Fallen Ones moved in unison, each one coming to stand beside or in front of the rest of us, as if they already knew exactly where we would be positioned and planned who each of them would guard.

Achan ended up in front of Ezra with Sharar to his left, guarding Felix, and Sarai to his right guarding Rufus. Elam didn't need to go far because Gershom had been standing next to Elam the entire time, already guarding him in return.

Abaddon still stood in front of me. He'd left me hovering though I was trying with every inch of my body to fight against it, reaching for anything that might pull me to the ground.

"Stop struggling," Abaddon said, drawing out his voice with a yawn. "This will all be over soon enough."

I did stop, just long enough to think through our options.

My plan at self-sacrifice had failed. Now my friends, my loved ones had been pulled into a fight that's lasted centuries, one in which our opponents greatly outnumbered us and were far more powerful.

My greatest fear had become reality. Those who I loved had been drawn into my troubles and were now going to pay the ultimate price. The Fallen Ones had no soul, no empathy. They understood destruction, contention, and enemies. There would be no negotiating and no bartering, only bloodshed. Our blood.

Only a few seconds passed since the Fallen Ones had taken their attack positions, but it seemed much longer. Everything was moving in slow motion now. I watched, unable to help as Achan's hand closed around Ezra's head, grabbing the back of it and pulling her to him. Her hand came out from behind her back and a blade glinted in the streetlight as she was swept forward, against Achan. She tried to bring the blade up in defense but Achan's strength was too much for her, catching her hand and twisting it until the blade dropped. His movement appeared effortless, as if he were simply reaching to take a treat from a child.

At the same time, Sharar bent down and swept Felix's legs out from beneath him, a blade slipping from Felix's hand and sliding across the pavement. Felix landed sprawled on the ground with Sharar on top of him, pinning him down.

With Rufus still cowering at Sarai's feet, there was only Gershom left to defend us. He and Elam circled each other, hands up and bodies crouched, as if each were ready to spring toward one another. As Elam passed by the blade Felix had dropped, he stooped to pick it up, smirking as Gershom's shoulders rose with heightened tension.

"Please, let them go," I heard myself pleading with Abaddon, who only turned and grinned.

"Don't cry, Magdalene." He clucked his tongue at me. "You'll get your turn, too. Oh, yes, you'll get your turn."

Abaddon winked at me, feeling very confident and it dawned on me, he had ever reason to be. He'd gotten the best deal of the century. Four for one, a Fallen One included.

Then Abaddon's face fell. In an instant, I watched as it turned from arrogant pleasure to shocked fury.

I didn't see why at first, my attention concentrated on the assault happening behind him.

All of sudden, there they were; countless bright, white lights swooping down into the alley like falling stars. They stopped in pairs, flanking the Fallen Ones.

The Fallen Ones noticed, just as Abaddon had, sensing their arrival and releasing their holds on Ezra and Felix. Rufus remained curled into a ball at Sarai's feet.

The white lights illuminated the Fallen Ones, and I recognized fear in each of them as they faced their new attackers with uncertainty.

Ezra and Felix, now free, attempted to pull Rufus to the edge of the alley but he fought them, making his best effort to stay beside Sarai, who only watched them with mild amusement.

A voice spoke then, echoing down the alleyway, its tone calm and confident. I instantly recognized the voice, and my heart stopped briefly.

"I apologize for the delay, Abaddon."

I turned my head to find Eran standing beside me, no more than a few inches away.

Excitement swelled inside me, so powerful I couldn't have contained it if I'd wanted to. The nervousness now displayed on Abaddon's face gave me even stronger encouragement.

I wanted so desperately to reach out and wrap my arms around Eran, wanted it more than anything in the world. My desperate yearning was only being held back because I still couldn't move.

I'm not sure Eran would have allowed it anyways. He was a warrior, and he was now engaged in battle. Besides, I was nothing more to him than someone to save.

Eran didn't look my way but kept his focus on Abaddon, who stepped back a few paces, his confidence faltering.

It was Sarai who strolled forward, self-assured, placing herself in the middle.

As she strolled by Abaddon, she mused, "Don't worry, I believe I can handle this one." Her face curled up into a hideous grin as she continued her approach.

I knew then what she planned...but it was too late.

"Eran, so good to see you again..." she whispered in a low drawl.

"No!" I screamed enraged, waiting for Eran to fall to the ground, whimpering with desperation as Rufus had done.

Eran remained standing.

A moment passed and Sarai's face contorted, confusion setting in. Her state of shock became more defined, deepening further when he finally replied.

"You don't work on me, Sarai..." I watched in disbelief as his gorgeous smirk, the one I missed so deeply, rose up. Eran turned and his stunning eyes settled on me, concentrating so intently I could not have mistaken his message. "I'm already in love."

The world changed for me at that moment. As Eran's confession hung in the air, I felt the passion and the power in me swell. Nothing was impossible now.

Sarai's mouth fell open, a shaken sigh escaping. She then looked at me, her eyes narrowing in fury as Eran's words sunk in.

Eran flippantly disregarded her, turning to address Abaddon. "You are outnumbered. You are overpowered. You have allowed yourself to be cornered. Shoddy work, Abaddon."

As I watched their interaction, it dawned on me that Eran was enjoying this moment and that it appeared to have been long overdue. I felt a smile on my lips, nearly causing me to giggle.

It was then Abaddon released me. I fell to the ground, hitting it hard but overwhelmed with relief. I glanced up, wondering what power Eran had over Abaddon to give up his hold on me.

In an instant, I realized what had happened.

Abaddon had let me go willingly. He needed his energy – all of it – for another reason…

Leaning forward, Abaddon's arms extended, his feet sweeping up from the ground, as he lunged for Eran.

The two of them met, twisting, spinning, and flipping over and under one another.

I had never felt horror before, but it now washed over me like a tidal wave. Desperately, I watched, feeble and unable to help Eran.

As if a trigger had been snared, the alley became a battleground. White lights darted from building to building, swooping down, picking up Fallen Ones, limbs and white lights weaving between one another. Grunts and shrieks filled the air.

Suddenly Sarai was standing in front of me. Her lips pursed out of fury as she took hold of my shoulders, digging her fingers into my flesh.

I brought my arms up, trying to force her away from me but Sarai was too quick. She lifted me as if I were nothing more than a pillow and threw me toward the concrete wall.

Something soft, yet burning hot, stopped me from colliding with the concrete; and I knew that Eran had somehow intervened. My feet landed safely on the ground a moment later. I instantly swiveled my head from side to side, looking for him, but found only a dizzying array of bright lights darting around the alley.

An infuriated screech resonated around me, one that I remembered clearly from fencing class.

It was Sarai and she was charging toward me, crouched, with her fingers reaching out like claws.

I didn't move, knowing already what I would do. Just before her hands were about to touch me, I sidestepped away from her, watching as she slammed into the wall where I'd been standing.

A muffled grunt could be heard as she slumped slightly against it, her knees nearly collapsing below her. She recovered, drew in a breath, and brought her head up to meet my gaze.

"You know…I guess I did learn a thing or two about footwork in fencing," I said, grinning.

Then I noticed the blood.

A drop of it hung at the edge of her mouth.

Stunned, I said, "Do you feel pain too?"

As I moved toward her, I pulled back my arm and squeezed my hand into a fist, leaning my weight into the force behind my punch. As she had thrown her entire body at me, I was now throwing my entire body at her.

I made contact just where I'd hoped, in the center of her face.

I felt our skins meet; hers solid but flexible, mine taut and unforgiving. Her head snapped back, smashing against the wall and making a sickening thud.

She released a low grunt.

Then, to my alarm, she brought her head back, steadying it. Her shoulder's lowered, relaxing.

And then she smiled.

"I'd almost forgotten how you hit," she stated casually.

Confused, I gazed back at her. Sarai and I had met before? I had no memory of it.

Her comment did the job she'd intended. It caught me off guard long enough to draw my attention away from her. She didn't waste any time.

I felt her fist hit me like an explosion had ignited my cheek. My body fell back, crashing to the ground, spots from the force of her strike obscuring my vision.

I felt her weight on top of me then. Her gloved hands clenched around my neck, squeezing and closing off my airway.

From above, she smiled, and her hands tightened.

My arms flailed, beating her sides, limp strands that barely made a dent. It was no good.

I saw my vision narrowing…blackening, and I knew I was losing consciousness.

Then something remote, deep inside me, clawed its way out. A faint memory that steadily grew more detailed. With it, I knew one thing with absolute certainty.

I had been in this very position before. And I had escaped it.

My body moved based on instinct; the muscles recognizing what they needed to do before I could even command them. My hips rose and twisted. Sarai's weight shifted off-center. She fell slightly, releasing her grip just enough. The heel of my hand came up and made contact. Her nose bent disturbingly to the side.

She groaned and released her hold on me.

I shifted again. Her weight rolled off.

I was on my feet. She stood too, blood trickling from her nose to her lips.

With my back arched and my hands rising, balled into fists, I darted forward, bringing the force of my weight toward her.

Though, we never made contact.

As she stood slouched, her head bowed, something curled out from behind her, steadily and methodically. There were two of them, one on each side. They unfurled and in the end their span reached beyond twenty feet. They were grey and each one was thickly covered in feathers.

With a single, smooth swipe, the wings lifted Sarai off the ground. Another flap and the inky night sky swallowed her whole.

I didn't move, too stunned to think straight. I heard the commotion again behind me and turned to find the alley still in chaos. There were more bright lights attacking each of the Fallen Ones, I noticed. At least four lights were on each of them now. It took only a second for me to realize that it wasn't that more of Eran's friends had arrived. There were less of the Fallen Ones. Eran was winning.

Then, I saw Gershom. He lay sprawled against the side of a building, his head hanging, his eyes closed, and his chest not moving.

I ran for him, dodging lights as I made my way down the alley toward him. When I reached him, I slipped my hand underneath his back and lifted him to a sitting position. Then I drew back my hand and a scream escaped my throat.

It was covered in blood.

"Gershom! Gershom!" I yelled at him, my voice choppy and broken.

His eyes fluttered, focusing and landing on me. "I'm sor…sorry…" he panted.

I shook my head, tears welling up and streaming freely down my face.

"Your parents," he reached for me and I took hold of his hands, clasping them between mine. My insides felt as if they were being ripped apart – one side with anger and one with regret – but I held on, unable to bear the fear of letting Gershom suffer in such pain alone. He gasped and I realized it was too late for him. "Harry and Alisa Tanner died... Helena...Montana..."

I struggled to breathe, understanding instantly what he was telling me. He used his last moments, his last breath on earth, to arm me with the knowledge I needed to find my parents.

And then he was gone.

I felt a deep pain at the base of my skull and a burning sensation spreading up, covering the back of my head and then my face. I slumped forward, unable to empower my body to respond. The last thing I saw before everything went black was my face slamming into Gershom's still chest.

15. FALLEN

When I woke up, the alleyway had disappeared. The bright lights were gone, too.

There was, however, Gershom kneeling over me, his eyes lit with anticipation.

"I didn't believe it was possible...even when others told me. I didn't believe you could do it..."

I sat up, wondering what had happened to Eran. "Gershom, where are we? Where's Eran?"

With my new position, I could see that we were on the top of a mountain range, overlooking a winding river that cut a path through the green valley below. The sky was lit orange in the distance with wispy clouds dotting the horizon.

"We're in my private paradise, my heaven. Just the way I left it." He laughed to himself, turning to appreciate the view. "You carried me here."

"Did I carry Eran too? And Ezra and Felix and Rufus? Where are they?" I asked, anxiously.

"Don't worry." He was blissful, content in a way I'd never seen him before. "They're safe."

He then turned and faced me, imploringly. "How could I ever repay you for this?"

"Gershom, I still don't know what I did."

"I can see that," Gershom replied, staring at me with unreserved gratitude. "Maggie, you have the ability to carry not just messages but souls back with you." He paused and drew in a shuttering breath. "I didn't think it was possible. Not after what I've done. I'm not sure it would have been possible without you...you carrying me here."

I glanced around again, realizing I hadn't woken up in the Hall of Records.

"Am I...dead?" I asked.

Gershom shook his head and smiled. "Listen..."

I did, and from a distance, I heard voices so familiar and so missed that I spun around, looking for them.

"Eran? Ezra?" I called out.

Suddenly, I was no longer standing beside Gershom. I was laying down again, this time on something bumpy and protruding, far less comfortable than when I'd first woken up. My eyes were closed and they struggled to open, as if someone had weighted them down with heavy blocks.

"Will she be okay?" I heard Felix ask, his voice filled with anxiety.

"She got a good whack but I think so," Ezra replied, a little closer. I thought I felt her hand brush by my cheek.

I heard a shuffling noise like a skirt's fabric moving against its own folds and then a grunt – Ezra's – as she stood up.

"Magdalene..."

At the sound of this voice I struggled much harder to lift my eyelids.

"Magdalene," said Eran again, coaxing me, guiding me. "I feel you trying. You can do it."

I used every bit of power to open my eyes, concentrating so hard I forgot to inhale.

Light…I could see light. Then blurred colors. Finally, the hazy outline of Eran's face came into view.

I sighed. He was more handsome than I remembered.

He reached out and touched his palm to my cheek, tenderly, its warmth giving me renewed strength.

"Eran…" I gasped.

He smiled.

"I was hoping to hear that beautiful voice of yours again."

"Hoping?" I asked. My voice sounded unfamiliar to me as I pushed myself up. Eran helped me and then kept his arms around me, securing me. Sensing a nervous longing from him, I realized he probably couldn't have let go if he tried.

"We were unsure for a moment…" he said, brushing my cheek with the back of his finger and sending chills through me.

I sat up, moving closer to his hand as if I was being drawn by a magnet. "What happened?"

When I looked around, the alley was empty. The bright lights were gone, the Fallen Ones, too. Ezra, Rufus, and Felix stood encircling us.

"Sarai…while the rest of us were engaged in combat, she attacked you."

"Oh…" I said, unable to think clearly still. I rubbed the back of my head, which pulsed lightly but without as much pain as I would have expected. "How did I ever survive that?"

Eran smiled amusingly at me, lifting his eyebrows.

"Oh…" I said again, understanding. "You…"

"At least you have your cognizance back."

"It's good to see you awake," Ezra said softly, smiling down at me in her maternal way.

I smiled awkwardly back. "Barely…"

Eran's hand came over mine, gently drawing his thumb along my pulse there. "You're going to be fine, actually.

I've been checking you regularly. Most of the swelling has already dissipated."

"You...checked me?"

Eran nodded and smiled at me reassuringly. "One of the many abilities I've brought with me..."

"That's good to know," I said and he chuckled.

I froze, realizing that I was talking to Eran with Ezra, Felix, and Rufus standing over me watching. I glanced up at them, figuring they must think I had really damaged my head good if I were holding a conversation with an invisible person.

Rufus must have understood what I was thinking because he said, "This the wanka' you were tellin' me 'bout?"

"You...you can see him?" I asked hesitant but amazed.

"We can," Ezra smiled lightheartedly down at me. "Good thing, too. We needed someone to explain all that just happened."

"Ay, ya been keepin' quite a bit to yerself, Ms. Sneak..." said Rufus, shaking his head, admonishing me.

"And if we ever learn of this happening again..." Felix reprimanded me but didn't bother to follow up with a threat of punishment.

"Let's just make certain it doesn't happen again," said Eran, giving me a sharp nod of conviction. "You knew I couldn't find you if you didn't have any emotion and you weren't fearful at all. Were you, Magdalene? You knew exactly what you were doing."

I grinned, sheepishly.

"I thought so. That's why it took me so long to find you. It wasn't until you were fearful for your friends' lives that I could signal in on you. That was a brave...and very foolish...thing you did. But you've learned now, haven't you?" he asked, clearly worried. "We're not going to give you up that easily."

I smiled, meekly, up at him. "I have learned my lesson."

"That's good to hear," Felix said, "because if that Sarai or that Achan come back..." He allowed his voice to fall away. His concern was evident.

"What do you mean? What happened with Sarai and Achan?"

It was Eran who filled me in on how the fight had ended. Apparently, the only ones to escape were the ones who I had attended school with the longest, the ones who knew me the best. Sarai and Achan.

The news was unsettling but I knew there was nothing we could do about it at the moment.

"Abaddon?" I asked, tentatively.

Eran drew in a breath and released it slowly. "Abaddon...He will no longer bother you. My friends have made sure of it." Eran tightened his grip on my hand that he'd been holding in a comforting way. "I will protect you. At all costs."

I smiled up at him. "I know, Eran. I know you will."

"But that jab of yours..." he said playfully. "I think Sarai was as surprised as I was."

"You saw that?" I asked, coyly.

"I did. Very impressive." Eran's grin faded and was replaced with impassioned eyes. I felt the distinct emitting of pride from him.

Ezra, sensing I wanted a moment alone with Eran, pulled Rufus and Felix aside and asked them to bring the car around for us.

We watched until they disappeared around the corner and Ezra stopped to wait for them at the end of the alleyway.

I looked to Eran and asked the question I'd wanted to ask since I regained consciousness.

"Eran, I can't feel your intense heat any longer. And my roommates can see you now…Does this mean what I think it means?"

"Which is what exactly?" he asked, toying with me, a smile playing across his lips.

"Did you-did you fall? Are you here on earth for good? Or will you leave soon?"

The features of his handsome face tensed, overcome with emotion. "I have been battling this decision for some time now. If I'd fallen earlier I could have protected you far better. I understand that now. So I will do my best to protect you, to guard you, to balance that responsibility with loving you. Because I do love you, Magdalene. Far more than you know."

His entire being stiffened then, frozen in agonizing wait for my answer.

I swung my arms around him, pulling him closer. Then my body started shaking, wracked with emotion.

"Love can't begin to describe how I feel about you," I said into his shoulder.

I felt him press his lips to my head and my heart skipped a beat. "It is the same for me," he whispered softly.

"Then will you stay?" I pulled back, staring at him firmly. "Don't tease me, Eran. That wouldn't be fair."

"Tease you?" he asked, incredulously. "You apparently have no idea what you do to me."

"Eran," I said, demanding an answer.

His signature smirk rose up before he replied. "Someone does need to keep you out of trouble…"

I gasped, opening my mouth to protest his joke, but he pulled me close and for the first time – that I could remember – his lips touched mine. This part of him was so familiar to me that even a lifetime apart couldn't prevent my recognition, and with it, came an impassioned response that left us clinging to each other, breathless.

"I am here now," he said, quietly against my lips.

I sighed. "It's how long you'll stay that worries me. You have a habit of disappearing."

He leaned back and caressed my face. "And that's one habit I intend to break."

I smiled, reaching my hand around his neck and pulling him closer to me, trying to persuade him to keep his resolution.

"Promise?" I whispered.

"I do, my love," he asserted as his arms tightened around me, broad and secure. "I absolutely do."

for more seduction and suspense
read the entire
Guardian Trilogy

fallen
eternity
reckoning

"4.5 Stars! While I really enjoyed the first book, Fallen, in the Guardian Trilogy, the second installment was even better. If you love angels and are looking for an intense read I highly rec this series! I'm starting the 3rd and final book tonight, Reckoning." – The Book Hookup review

""A very good read with interesting characters and a quick pace." – Life Is Better With Books review

"Great flow of interest and most unusual characters (that you will love as I have). I have laughed out loud at some of them. Good, simple, fast read that has a great hook, line and sinker." – Great Minds Think Aloud review

ABOUT THE AUTHOR

∞

Laury Falter graduated with a Bachelor's degree from Pepperdine University and a Master's degree from Michigan State University. She lives with her husband and two stray dogs in Las Vegas. She has been secretly writing for most of her life and only released her first novel, Fallen, after the insistence of her sister, Babs. She has since gone on to release the completed bestselling Guardian Trilogy and work on her next series, the Residue Series. Her website is www.lauryfalter.com

Made in the USA
Lexington, KY
19 December 2013